Music in Lubavitcher Life

Music in American Life

A list of books in the series appears at the end of this book.

Music in Lubavitcher Life

Ellen Koskoff

UNIVERSITY OF ILLINOIS PRESS

URBANA AND CHICAGO

Publication of this book was supported by a
grant from the Society for American Music.

Library of Congress Cataloging-in-Publication Data
Koskoff, Ellen, 1943–
Music in Lubavitcher life / Ellen Koskoff.
p.   cm. — (Music in American life)
Includes bibliographical references and index.
ISBN 0-252-02591-1
1. Hasidim—New York (State)—New York—Music—History and criticism.
2. Hasidim—New York (State)—New York—Social life and customs.
3. Crown Heights (New York, N.Y.)—Religious life and customs.
I. Title.
II. Series.
ML3195.K65   2001
781.62'924074723—dc21   99-051007

C 5 4 3 2 1

To Bob and David,
who can always make me laugh

Contents

Acknowledgments

The writing of a book, especially one that takes many years to materialize, cannot be done alone. Along the way, many people and institutions help in this process, giving financial, informational, and emotional support. I am truly grateful for this support and would here like to acknowledge and thank those who have helped me.

First, and foremost, I thank the many Lubavitcher men and women who sat with me for countless hours listening patiently to my questions and lovingly watching over me, as they would a child, while I learned about Hasidic life and music—and who never laughed at me or my attempts to get it right. I am especially grateful to Rabbi Ephraim Rosenblum and his wife, Miriam, who took me into their home and first awakened me to the beauty of Hasidism and Lubavitcher *nigunim*. Special thanks also go to Eli Lipsker and Rus Dvorah Shatkin, two outstanding Lubavitcher musicians, who helped me in innumerable ways to understand both the past and the present in nigun performance. I also thank Rabbi Hirshel Gansbourg and his wife Henches Gansbourg for their gracious hospitality and for the wealth of information they shared regarding the history of Lubavitcher nigunim and of the Nichoach Society. Finally, I would like to thank Rabbi Nechemia Vogel, the Rochester, New York, *shaliach,* and his wife, Masha, who trusted me and my knowledge of nigunim.

I am also grateful for the institutional support of the University of Rochester's Eastman School of Music, which provided two sabbatical leaves, one in 1991 and another in 1997, so that I could work full-time on this manuscript. I also pass along special thank-yous to the many supportive colleagues who read all (or portions of) this work during its many incarnations, especially Ralph P. Locke and Charlotte Frisbie, whose friendly editorial eyes saved me from countless embarrassments, and Ernestine McHugh, Bob Morris, Bruno Nettl, and Gretchen Wheelock, who offered intelligent and gratefully accepted editorial suggestions. Thanks also to Karen Ages, Geoff Friedley, Susan Q. Chodorow, and Leanne Rabesa, who acted as my legs and fingers when I could not do it all myself; to Theresa L. Sears and August Gering at the University of Illinois Press; and a big hug to my Brooklyn cousins, Sharon Kosakoff McQuillen and her husband, Mike, for their hospitality, lots of laughs, and good food.

Finally, I would like to thank three very special women who have each, in their own way, contributed to this book: Judith McCulloh, of the University of Illinois Press, who always supported this project, even in the days when I could not see its ending; Sheila Cummings, who helped me find the true path and enabled me to stay there; and Catherine Tait, my lovely friend, who always wanted to hear more about my book but did not live long enough to read it.

Introduction

Music in Lubavitcher Life concerns the music and musical practices of a contemporary community of Lubavitcher Hasidim centered in Crown Heights, Brooklyn, New York. This work focuses on Lubavitcher music, its creation, and performance not only as sound and structure but also as sounded materializations of core values and beliefs that are performed by Lubavitchers as they confront issues of identity in the context of late-twentieth-century American life. The study examines a body of paraliturgical, folk, and popular melodies (*nigunim*) whose performance Lubavitchers regard as a primary form of spiritual communication with the divine. Further, it demonstrates how ideas about nigunim and resulting Lubavitcher musical practices are embedded within a wide-ranging network of beliefs surrounding the nature of spirituality, of history and lineage, of gender difference, and of modernity. These beliefs, at the core of Lubavitcher life, have always been, and continue to be, reevaluated and negotiated by members of this community through interaction with mainstream Jewish and non-Jewish cultures.

On Fieldwork at Home

The book is based on fieldwork conducted on and off over a twenty-two-year period (1973–95) within three Lubavitcher communities: the center of Lubavitcher Hasidism in Crown Heights, Brooklyn, New York; and two smaller communities in Pittsburgh, Pennsylvania, and St. Paul, Minnesota. It documents Lubavitcher historical musical practices as well as social and musical changes that have occurred within the last two decades, showing how the

Lubavitcher community in the United States has creatively dealt with changes—such as the "return to roots" movement, the women's movement, and the development and increased use of technology—through new, yet also old, musics and musical practices that have helped to reformulate and revitalize Lubavitcher beliefs within postmodern times.

Some of the data presented here were collected during the period of my dissertation research in the mid-1970s through the methods of participant observation, interviewing, and recording music. The term "participant observation" is used somewhat guardedly here: in standard anthropological texts and fieldwork manuals, participant observation is usually defined as an extended period of time (one to two years) where one lives with informants, learning their language and other aspects of culture more or less in an ongoing, daily basis, usually away from one's home. My situation was somewhat different in that I worked within communities located in the United States, where most people spoke English and where it was relatively easy for me to leave for an afternoon and assume my "normal" identity.

Thus, during the data collection phase of my dissertation (1973–76), as well as during subsequent trips to the Crown Heights community and to other Lubavitcher satellite communities (Pittsburgh, Pennsylvania; St. Paul, Minnesota) to work on more specific topics, such as nigun composition and borrowing (1979, 1980), gender issues in performance (1989, 1990, 1991), and newly recorded Hasidic rock music (1991), I frequently straddled both the Lubavitcher world and my own, living sometimes for months in Brooklyn and, at other times, appearing for a weekend or an afternoon. All of the people I spoke with gave me permission to use their words and their music; in most cases, they also allowed the use of their real names. Chapter 1, "Opening Scene," was constructed from many such gatherings I attended, and proper names of the participants have been altered here as well as in some of the other scenes throughout the book. I, alone, take full responsibility for the accuracy of these words.

On Self-Reflexive Ethnography

In addition to being about Lubavitcher musical culture, this book is also about me, my changing attitudes toward Orthodox Judaism, and the process of fieldwork as a context for both other- and self-understanding. In a sense, there are two narratives here: one that explores Lubavitcher notions of identity, spirituality, and music; and the other, parallel narrative that documents my moments of growth and of the discovery of both the Lubavitcher world and my own.

I grew up in Pittsburgh, Pennsylvania, in the 1940s and 1950s; I came from an upwardly mobile, politically left-wing Jewish family that, like many others in midcentury, was for the most part ignorant of the Hasidic world and saw Hasidim as either irrelevant or embarrassing throwbacks to a long-forgotten, Eastern European, peasant past. Being raised in a completely secular home, without any firsthand knowledge of Judaism, its beliefs, or practices, I grew up more or less accepting these stereotypes.

What, then, initially attracted me to the Lubavitcher community? Lubavitcher *shelichim* (emissaries) from the Brooklyn, New York, community began arriving in my Squirrel Hill neighborhood in the late 1940s, quickly establishing schools and other social/religious institutions there (much to the dismay of families like mine). As I walked up the street to school or to the local drugstore, I often saw and heard the loud, boisterous, even raucous, singing inside the yeshivah (religious school) on my corner. Although my parents tended to dismiss the Hasidim as "childlike" or "too obviously Jewish," I was drawn to the intensity and freedom of their musical performances. There seemed to be a simple, straightforward, and joyous connection to music in these uninhibited expressions—and it sparked my curiosity.

After college in Boston and graduate school in New York, I returned to Pittsburgh in the early 1970s and began doctoral work at the University of Pittsburgh in the field of Western historical musicology. During this time, I often visited my parents on weekends and would drive or walk past the Lubavitcher yeshivah as I had in my youth, drawn again to that joyful and intense singing. What was it about these people and their music that was so compelling? It was at this time that I discovered Alan Merriam's *Anthropology of Music* (1964); also, the ethnomusicologist Theodore Grame arrived in Pittsburgh. I quickly realized that ethnomusicology could offer me an opportunity to better understand this pull toward Lubavitcher music, so I changed my dissertation topic from the study of the choral works of the fifteenth-century composer Giles Binchois to the study of the Lubavitcher musical culture, ultimately resulting in my dissertation, "The Concept of *Nigun* among Lubavitcher Hasidim in the United States" (1976).

At the beginning of my fieldwork in 1973, however, I was unsure if I had chosen my dissertation topic well, for early on I began to experience a sort of disorientation (known now as culture shock) that I had only read about in ethnographies depicting faraway cultural settings. I had never expected to confront culture shock within my own neighborhood community. I soon realized, as most ethnographers do when first entering the field, that I had unintentionally brought many of the assumptions I had grown up with into this work. But unlike the fieldworker, who travels far away from his or her own context and more or less expects to confront this issue, I was stepping into a world with which I assumed I was already somewhat familiar, a world that had been both negatively constructed by my family and positively idealized by my early self. To proceed neutrally and objectively, I had to question my own social, musical, and religious understandings in light of the new and often confusing information I was gathering within the Lubavitcher community.

In more recent ethnographic work, especially that dealing with the processes of fieldwork, analysis, and interpretation, we have all had to give up the twin ideals of objectivity and neutrality in the portraits we paint of ourselves and others. The "crisis of representation" so eloquently discussed in the works of Jay Ruby (1982), Hortense Powdermaker (1966), and James Clifford and George E. Marcus (1986), in work on Jewish American communities by Barbara Myerhoff (1980), Barbara Kirschenblat-Gimblett (1987), and in the work of Gregory Barz and Timothy Cooley (1997), among many others, has encouraged all of us to reconsider the interactive, dialogic nature of fieldwork and to adequately position ourselves within the cultures we study. Thus, in addition to documenting the Lubavitcher musical culture over a twenty-year period, *Music in Lubavitcher Life* also addresses some of the more recent theoretical issues concerning fieldwork as an intersubjective process, resulting in a negotiation, or mediation of power relations, as well as a context that, over time, allows for self-awareness and insight. This work, then, contributes to the current stream of scholarship that addresses issues such as the mediation of power between self and other, the role of the author/observer in narrative forms, and the need for multiple perspectives in ethnographic writing.

One of the main difficulties I encountered over the many years of working within this community was how to negotiate successfully with individuals who were frankly interested in—or saw it as their mission to—return me to Orthodox Judaism. The act of proselytizing, generally discouraged in mainstream Judaism, is a major feature of Lubavitcher daily interactions with the secular Jewish world, although most Lubavitchers bristle at this term, preferring to see their actions as bringing a soul back to its Divine source. I was regarded, as most nonobservant Jews are, especially ones who enter the community for any length of time, as a recruit. From the Lubavitcher point of view, only a person seriously interested in becoming more observant would spend so much time and effort studying in Crown Heights. And, although I was openly honest about my intentions, frequently stating that my objective was not to become more Jewish but to find out more about nigunim, there was constant pressure on me to reevaluate my life and reconsider my commitment to Jewish observance. Trying to straddle the line between open-mindedness toward Lubavitcher views and a certain justification (or, at times, defensiveness) toward my own views sometimes disoriented, annoyed, and even frustrated me.

My main concern for this book was that it would present a reasonable picture of Lubavitcher musical life, one that was understandable to an outside community of scholars and other interested readers but that was also recognizable to me and to the Lubavitchers with whom I worked. So, in keeping with the more positive, democratizing impulses of postmodern discourse, I have tried here to present the experiences I had learning about music in Lubavitcher life from many, sometimes contradictory, perspectives—through Lubavitcher writings, interviews, analytic and descriptive passages as well as through scenes, taken from my field notes, where my voice enters, often questioning, even critical. And, although it is not an especially new idea to interject the voice of the author into an ethnography, until the last decade or so, this technique functioned more or less to give the reader a sense of "you are there" rather than actually being problematized within the work itself, as it is here.

These scenes, reconstructed from my field notes and interviews and scattered throughout the book, are not meant to be confessional or self-congratulatory; rather, they highlight moments when I encountered a profound difference between my own assumptions and understandings and those of the Lubavitchers with whom I worked or indicate when I completely lost my objectivity in the face of intense Lubavitcher interest in my life as a secular Jew. In distinguishing between the "self-indulgent and experiential ethnographic modes," I took as my guide a question posed by Michelle Kisliuk that asks fieldworkers to examine whether or not "an experience changed us in a way that significantly affected how we viewed, reacted to, or interpreted the ethnographic material" (1997:39).

Sometimes, I sound combative, obtuse, or even insensitive in these scenes, and I have often been tempted to eliminate them from the book. Many of the early ones, especially, illustrate the pitfalls of my first fieldwork experiences, where I was more apt to interject my own ideas and argue with informants, especially women, about the right way to see and do things. Other scenes illustrate more mature fieldwork moments (i.e., those where I kept my mouth shut), so-called aha experiences, where I suddenly understood a fine point of Lubavitcher thinking or where I noted to myself that I had something wrong. However, it was precisely in paying attention to these sometimes bad moments of cultural mediation that I gained the most valuable insights into this musical culture, for my voice, in capturing a conflict between so-called insider and outsider perspectives, documents important moments of understanding both the other and the self.

On Organizing This Book

While thinking about and writing this book over the years, I often rearranged its parts. Indeed, it became something of a joke in my own adult family that I was at it again—reorganizing the outline. But, I thought, how is it possible to communicate successfully the richness, the intricacy, the integrity, and, at times, inconsistencies of Lubavitcher lives, as well as the many ambivalences I felt about Orthodox Judaism and Lubavitchers, without reducing them and myself to carefully constructed characters in a neatly wrapped world?

I tried to solve this problem by dividing the book into two large sections, the first of which (parts 1 and 2) deals with contexts—the academic and Lubavitcher historical and contemporary social contexts—as well as with those of the sounds, structures, and coded meanings of Lubavitcher music. In the past, this might have sufficed as a complete book on its own, an ordered presentation of the beliefs and practices of a specific group of people living in a specific time and place. But that picture bears only a slight resemblance to the often disorganized, untidy lives and musics of real Lubavitchers I know. Like a photographic negative, it lacks all of the color, bustle, and spontaneity of real life as I experienced and witnessed it during my fieldwork.

In the second section of the book, that dealing with performance (parts 3 and 4), I try to show how Lubavitcher life is actually lived, bearing in mind, of course, that as an outsider, I can only go so far. In the four chapters examining performance, I am less interested in the performance of music, per se, than in the performance of Lubavitcher social and religious identity through music. Thus, I organize this half according to four core beliefs that underlie late-twentieth-century Lubavitcher life yet are continuously enacted, refined, and adjusted on an ongoing, daily basis. This part of the book is meant to be somewhat open-ended and questioning. Hopefully, the earlier chapters, in presenting theoretical, ordered contexts for Lubavitcher musical life, will provide an overall structure or template for the later chapters, which come closer to the realities of how contemporary Lubavitchers live with music.

As I have grown in my knowledge and understanding of this community, so has the rest of the world. Lubavitchers, unlike other Hasidic groups, have become increasingly familiar to outsiders through their cable broadcasts, web sites, and, perhaps most tragically, through news of the racially motivated riots that erupted in Crown Heights during the late summer of 1991. Certainly, one of the most important recent events, well-documented on national news broadcasts and in newsmagazines, has been the death of the Lubavitcher spiritual and religious leader, Rabbi Menachem Mendel Schneerson (the Rebbe), in 1994. As I will show, this has dealt a serious spiritual blow to the community; at the time of this book's completion, no future leader has emerged. And, although I am fully aware of the Rebbe's death, I most often refer to him here in the "ethnographic present," as much of my data were collected when he was still alive.

On Collaboration and Reciprocity

The "crisis of representation" alluded to above, as well as recent postmodern literature on power relations in cultural studies, has not only forced us to acknowledge our own subject positions vis-à-vis our cultural informants (living or dead) but has also highlighted the ethical issues in doing research, issues that are greatly magnified in the ethnographic context and that we, as fieldworkers, have all faced at one time or another: How does one maintain an ethical position when fieldworker and informant openly disagree? How does one establish a fair exchange for information, especially that provided by living informants, friends, or colleagues? How much control should an informant have over his or her own words once they have been collected, analyzed, and interpreted by the researcher?

Over the years, I have shown many of these chapters or have given copies of my articles and tapes to my Lubavitcher friends and colleagues (although they have rarely asked for them and no formal agreement of exchange has ever been suggested by them or by the Lubavitcher governing hierarchy). They have at times agreed, argued, or even disagreed with my understandings and interpretations, but they have never asked me to change their words, delete them, or to stop doing my research. Fully aware of the benefits I have accrued as a result of this research, I have often asked members of the community what I can do beside giving them my work, an occasional gift, or a donation in exchange for the wealth of information, understanding, and affection they have given me. Most smile and ask me simply to continue to light *shabbos* (Sabbath) candles and, wherever I happen to be professionally, to play a nigun—at a conference, in my classes, or even in my own home. This is enough, they say. Who knows? Maybe the sound of the music can bring someone closer to God.

I am truly grateful to these people for allowing me to enter their world and for sharing their feelings about music and themselves and allowing me to share mine. Although they frequently lament that "after twenty years of talking to us and listening to our music, nothing of *hasides* [the Hasidic way of life] has rubbed off on Ellen," they know that, through music, we have come together in mutual respect and friendship.

~

Hebrew and Yiddish words used in this book have been transliterated into English spellings based on the rules outlined in the *Encyclopedia Judaica.* Occasionally, Lubavitcher spellings have been used, especially in musical titles and texts.

PART 1: OPENING

Chapters 1, "Opening Scene: A Rebbe's *Farbrengen*," and 2, "Analytical Framework," are written from the perspective of the observer-analyst-ethnographer. Although positioned outside the Lubavitcher context, they nonetheless serve as an entryway through the boundary, or fence, that separates the secularized world of the author from that of her Lubavitcher colleagues. Chapter 1 paints a picture of a rebbe's farbrengen (a Hasidic gathering), in which the main ideas and issues discussed throughout the rest of the book are presented in narrative form. Although I am present in this scene, my voice is not explicitly addressed. Chapter 2 examines the various scholarly streams that inform the analysis of the Lubavitcher musical world presented here.

1
Opening Scene:
"A Rebbe's *Farbrengen*"

It is a Wednesday evening in the late summer of 1973, and tonight I am going to my first *farbrengen* (gathering) of Lubavitcher Hasidim[1] who, in numbers ranging into the thousands, will pack into the main Lubavitcher synagogue at 770 Eastern Parkway, Crown Heights, Brooklyn, New York. This will not be an ordinary gathering—tonight the Rebbe,[2] Menachem Mendel Schneerson, will speak. At seventy he is still vibrant and vital, an inspiring leader to more than 150,000 Lubavitchers worldwide. Tonight, his talk will touch on an enduring theme in contemporary American Hasidic life: how to live as a Jew in a secular world (fig. 1).

The farbrengen will last for hours, starting at sundown, around 9:00 P.M., and will continue until 3:00 A.M. or later. The Rebbe's talk will be broken into sections of about forty-five minutes each. During the intervals where he rests, the men assembled there will sing nigunim, Lubavitcher songs, some brought to this country in the 1940s from Poland, Hungary, or Ukraine, others composed more recently as gifts for the Rebbe's birthday. Rabbi Schneur Zalman, the founder of the Lubavitcher court, often said that music was the pen of the soul and that no farbrengen is complete without it. Music has such a central role in Hasidic life that it is used not only at Hasidic gatherings in the synagogue and home but also in Lubavitcher schools, camps, and informal gatherings as a primary vehicle for expressing and teaching Hasidic concepts. Tonight, the men will repeat a song again and again, bolstered by the excitement and intensity of the music and by the vodka that passes among them.

It is after dinner now, and people are pouring out of their houses on the way to the farbrengen. No one drives; Lubavitcher homes are all within walk-

Figure 1. 770 Eastern Parkway, Brooklyn, N.Y., home of the Habad-Lubavitch worldwide headquarters (photograph by the author, 1991)

ing distance of the synagogue so that, on the Sabbath and other holidays when driving is prohibited, the community can attend services. Most of the time, the streets are safe if one walks in a group. The neighborhoods are patrolled by Hasidic, African American, and Hispanic crime-watch coalitions; but lately, no one looks up or makes eye contact with non-Lubavitcher passersby. Memories of recent clashes with the non-Hasidic population have everyone slightly edgy.

Walking up Kingston Avenue toward the synagogue, one notices an odd mixture of establishments, ranging from kosher butcher shops, Jewish book and gift shops, hardware stores, small *heders* (Jewish day schools), kosher and nonkosher eateries, fruit stands, a five-and-dime store, clothing stores selling the latest fashions, a Jewish taxi and escort service, payphones at every corner, and many other examples of contemporary, yet somehow not contemporary, city life.

It is the way people are dressed that seems out of place. It has become a joke among Hasidim that outsiders so frequently compare or confuse them with the Amish, whom they only outwardly resemble. The men wear dark suits, and one can see the fringes of their *tallit* (prayer shawls) hanging from their coats. Most of the men have full, uncut beards and pale white—even sallow—skin. Unlike other Hasidim, many Lubavitcher males do not display their *peyes* (earlocks), which are more commonly pinned out of sight under their dark, brimmed hats. Being outdoors seems foreign to them. Some are reading as they walk or are talking loudly to friends in Yiddish, Russian, or Polish—almost never English. They seem to move with a purpose, as though they are late for an important appointment, and tend to move quickly through crowds, creating an air of hurried expectation. Almost no one makes eye contact on the street, though. They seem to walk without looking, as though their minds and bodies are elsewhere.

The women also seem oddly dressed, if in a more contemporarily stylish manner than the men. In spite of the considerable heat of late summer, they are wearing long dresses and stockings, or skirts and long-sleeved shirts, buttoned to the top, and the married women are wearing wigs. Orthodox laws of female modestly (*tzniut*) prohibit the display of a woman's own natural hair and unclothed limbs except in the privacy of the home (and then only for her husband). Children are everywhere, darting in and out, almost dancing as they wander toward "770." No one, yet everyone, seems to be minding them. One gets the impression that everyone is related, that these thousands are one family with many branches.

The synagogue is part of a large complex of buildings located on Eastern Parkway between Kingston and Brooklyn Avenues. Other buildings house the administrative offices of the worldwide Lubavitcher organization, which includes, among other things, an extensive educational network, various publishing houses, and many charitable organizations. No matter what the time of day, however, a crowd is gathered near the synagogue, the symbolic center of the community. At noon on a weekday, for example, there may be only a few people standing by, hoping to get a glimpse of the Rebbe as his driver pulls the car out of an underground garage. At other times, like tonight, there is a crowd of thousands, mostly Hasidim from Brooklyn, but also from other parts of New York, as well as many "secular" Jews from Manhattan, Israel, or Russia who are here for various reasons: some to gawk at the Jewish "anachronisms," others to become inspired by their fervor.

Not counting the internal entrances used by the Rebbe and his close male associates, there are two main entrances to the synagogue: one for men, the other for women. Inside the synagogue, as in all Orthodox synagogues, the men and women are separated. Again, this practice is governed by the laws of Orthodox Judaism, especially those surrounding *kol isha* (the voice of a woman), which prohibit men from hearing the singing, and at times the speaking voices, of certain women at certain times and places.

The men's entrance, down a few steps from street level, leads directly into the synagogue proper—a large room usually divided by railings, tables, and benches into many differently sized spaces, some for prayer and gossip, others for study. Tonight, however, in anticipation of the farbrengen crowd, the synagogue resembles a small arena, with floor-to-ceiling bleachers all around the periphery and a small table in the center from which the Rebbe will speak. The men stand on the bleachers in row after circular row, with the most recent newcomers to the community, the *ba'alei teshuvah* (literally, "masters of repentance"; newly Orthodox, "returnees")[3] generally at the top. It is considered a sign of disrespect to sit too close to the Rebbe unless one is a close associate. Many hundreds are already present, and the bleachers are becoming crowded. Some children, both boys and a few toddler girls too young to observe the laws of female modesty, are running in and out between the legs of their fathers or are seated on their shoulders. There is a loud, almost deafening buzz of talk in many languages.

I enter the women's entrance, up a few steps from street level, which leads into a set of three dimly lit, interconnected rooms that almost encircle the men's area below (fig. 2). Known collectively as the women's gallery, these rooms are lined with wooden benches that are arranged in tiers, bleacher-

Figure 2. Entrance to the women's gallery (photograph by the author, 1991)

style, like the men's area (fig. 3).[4] Against the walls, numerous bookshelves hold prayer books and pamphlets considered appropriate for women. Hanging above the shelves are posters and bulletin boards announcing such things as classes for women, Jewish day care, and where to buy clothing and books. Compared to the men's section below, the space is tiny—altogether, the three rooms might hold 150 women comfortably.

All three rooms of the woman's gallery are encased in sheets of heavily tinted, but transparent, black plastic, the *mechitzah,* a screen or boundary that separates the men and women and makes it difficult for the women to see the area below (fig. 4). The plastic sheeting ensures that the men and women do not see or hear each other clearly, so that if a man is able to observe a woman praying or singing, he will not be able to identify her or to single out her voice from the others. This practice, along with many others, aims to protect both men and women from unwarranted social or sexual contact and to allow them freedom of religious expression.

Tonight, the men's bleachers are so high that they are mere inches from the women on the first tier of the gallery; standing thus, it would be difficult for the men not to see or hear the women on the other side. But the thick sheeting, with its tiny breathing space above and below, acts as a concrete,

Figure 3. Inside the women's gallery (photograph by the author, 1991)

Figure 4. The *mechitzah* (screen), located in the women's gallery (photograph by the author, 1991)

impenetrable symbol of separation. The women generally view the tinted plastic sheets as necessary for the protection of their modesty and wonder why secular women, especially the new "women's libbers," make such a fuss about this. It is not necessary for women to be public, for the men to see them, or for them to see the men, even the Rebbe: whether or not a woman is a good Jew is between her and God.

The gallery is now beginning to fill up, mostly with girls and young women, although a few older women are present also. Most of the older, married women of the community are at home attending to their small children. The women are as exuberant as the men, gesturing and talking excitedly, as though they have not seen each other for months. In reality, they see each other every day while shopping, working, or visiting the *mikvah*, the ritual cleansing bath that follows menstruation. There is some jostling for space, and some girls are pressed dangerously against the plastic sheets. There have been accidents: once, a sheet popped out and nearly caused some of the women to fall to the area below. Clearly, no one is concerned about violating the building's fire and safety codes. All in all, the scene is one of growing excitement and anticipation—even tension.

The Rebbe enters and sits at a small table that is placed to the right of the ark, where the Torah is kept. He sits in the largest chair, heavily cushioned in red, not unlike a throne. He is small, about 5'5", yet he seems larger—his body and eyes are so intense that his presence fills the room. His skin is ruddy, as though he is excited, and he walks and moves with quickened gestures. In spite of the intensity he projects, he seems serene and somehow centered.

As the spiritual leader of the worldwide Lubavitcher community and the symbol of its philosophy, *Habad,* the Rebbe is a powerful force within contemporary Judaism. Respected by world leaders and consulted on such matters as Israeli politics, American Jewish practices, and various subtle points of Orthodox Jewish law, he still remains accessible to the everyday Lubavitcher, giving council, often with great compassion and commonsensical wisdom, to those seeking advice about work, unhappy marriages, illness, an appropriate choice of mate, money problems, and a host of other concerns. Some secularized Jews say that the Rebbe has too much influence and power over his community, but Lubavitchers deny this, stressing instead the role of individual choice and the importance of free will. They say that it is up to the *benoni* (the average person), with his or her heel in the ground of the present, to try at all times to negotiate the right path from the human animal soul (located in the right ventricle of the heart) upward to the divine soul (in the head) without succumbing to the base animal soul (located in the heart's left ventricle) that threatens to obscure the holy spark residing in every Jew. The Rebbe guides, but the benoni must live on a freely chosen path.

Tonight, a visitor from South Africa is seated at the Rebbe's table. He is an important member of the Lubavitcher community there and is given this position of honor to mark his first visit to this country. Near him are two of the Rebbe's personal associates: Rabbi Yehudah Krinsky, the Rebbe's secretary, and Rabbi Hillel Greenberg, a longtime personal friend of the Rebbe and one of his musical assistants. It will be Rabbi Greenberg's responsibility to begin the nigunim that will accompany tonight's talk.

The Rebbe begins speaking in Yiddish. Later, his talks will be translated into English and various other languages, and some of his thoughts will be published for worldwide distribution by the Lubavitcher publishing house, Kehot. Tonight, the Rebbe begins with a discussion about the victory of the Israeli forces in the Six Day War. He stresses the role of strict adherence to Jewish laws in building the strength of the worldwide Jewish community, which he argues is under perpetual attack: not only by enemy troops but, more subtly, by the temptations of today's secular world. At the conclusion of this section of the talk, the Rebbe sips from a silver cup. Many of the men pass other cups around the circular tiers as the *mashke* (alcoholic beverage, usually vodka) is consumed. It is thought that the liquor helps one let go of his worldly existence, with its everyday cares and mundanities, and makes him more receptive to the Rebbe's message. The men begin to talk among themselves, commenting and praising the Rebbe's words.

Rabbi Greenberg is standing now. He, like the Rebbe, is a small man but somewhat younger, in his forties with graying hair and beard, an open face, smiling eyes, and an already intense body that seems to grow as he begins a favorite nigun, "Becho Ha-Shem" ("In Thee, O Lord").[5] The text is taken from Psalm 71 and was originally set to this melody by Rabbi and Cantor Moshe Teleshevsky in 1971 to celebrate the Rebbe's seventieth birthday. It is frequently sung at farbrengens today because its marchlike quality and uplifting text are seen as especially inspiring. Recently, the Rebbe has indicated that he wants to hear mainly happy songs at farbrengens so as not to pull his followers into sadness or despair.

Rabbi Greenberg begins to sing in a strong voice; but because of the considerable hum of speaking, only a few men standing near him hear the beginning phrase. Quickly, however, the song spreads like a growing fire through the hall, moving upward to the top bleachers. Soon, hundreds of men and boys, bolstered by the excitement of the Rebbe's talk and the vodka, are singing with an intensity that causes the entire room to vibrate.

The song continues for about twenty minutes, repeated over and over again. No instruments accompany the singing. Later in the week, however, an individual might listen to this song, arranged for the men and boys' choir and accompanied by a small band, on a recording made by the Lubavitcher music house, Nichoach, or by Rabbi Eli Lipsker or Cantor Moshe Teleshevsky, two leading Lubavitcher musicians. But tonight, one hears only singing.

Two portions of this song contain the verses of Psalm 71, but the third is sung to vocables that form rhythmic patterns such as "ai-ye-ye-yai-yai." Lubavitchers say that the wordless nigunim are more spiritual than those with texts and are better able to connect with the divine realm. Words are part of the everyday world, but pure music is the language of the heart. The men shout the pattern "yai! yai! yai!" and further reinforce it by clapping and stamping, causing the bleachers to shake uncontrollably for a few seconds. The effect is not unlike a small army marching into battle—a direct association to the Israeli war and to the more symbolic war referred to in the Rebbe's talk.

Occasionally, Rabbi Greenberg and even the Rebbe will encourage the men to even greater intensity. The Rebbe will tighten his fists and move them in a small circle, or he will stand to direct the men as they sing. If a particular section of a song seems to be especially relevant to the given topic of his talk, the Rebbe will indicate by moving his fists that the men should continue repeating this section or increase its dynamic level. Tonight, the Rebbe is standing to encourage the men, and their intensity causes a slight rise in pitch with each repetition, so that by the end of the performance, the singers are at least a minor third higher than where they began.

After a time, the Rebbe sits and gives a signal that he is ready to speak again. This next portion of the talk contains references to his visitor from South Africa and to the work he is doing there as a shaliach (emissary) to create a new Lubavitcher community. The Rebbe speaks to the community at large concerning its duty to spread the joy of *hasides* to all around them; and he exhorts each individual, no matter how committed, to be constantly striving to return ever more closely to the divine source of knowledge and power.

The men break spontaneously into the song "Uforatztoh" ("And You Shall Spread Out"). The text, taken from Genesis, chapter 28, has become the primary Lubavitcher motto, a rallying cry to spread the light of the Torah with joy and enthusiasm to all corners of the earth. Again, the men repeat the song over and over; again, there is a rise in pitch; again, the stamping of feet resounds. Many of the men sway back and forth—the vodka and persistent singing have begun to take effect—and some are beginning to fall. Another song starts while "Uforatztoh" winds to a conclusion. This one, "Ha-Aderet V'Ha-emunah" ("Majesty and Faithfulness"), was set to the French national anthem, the "Marseillaise" in the nineteenth century and is still sung today. It was common, and still is, for Hasidim to transform music of the local surroundings into nigunim. It is a way of capturing the holy sparks in the music while at the same time freeing the song from its more mundane origins. Furthermore, performing it today connects the contemporary Lubavitcher with the holy men of the past, who now reside closer to the divine head.

The next speaking portion recalls the imprisonment and subsequent freeing of the Alter Rebbe (Rabbi Schneur Zalman, the founder of the Lubavitcher court) by the Russian government in 1798. Rabbi Greenberg rests while another, much younger man, perhaps in his early twenties, standing in the front row begins a nigun *devekut* (or *deveikus*, a yearning song), "Shamil," a wordless song that recalls the unjust imprisonment of a young Russian non-Jewish rebel and his yearning for freedom. "Shamil," with its soulful ornamentation and free rhythmic quality, has come to symbolize the imprisonment of all Jewish souls in the here-and-now world and their longing for the divine freedom that comes with true *teshuvah* (repentance).

The young man is another musical assistant, Moishe Mendel Shalin, a relative of the Rebbe, who can trace his lineage to Schneur Zalman. He has a strong, vibrant voice that is not unlike an operatic baritone. At the conclusion of "Shamil," Shalin leads the men into "Napoleon's March," another wordless nigun *simhah* or *lebedig* (joyful song) that is an adaptation of a march sung by Napoleon's troops as they invaded Russia in 1812. This song is also associated with Schneur Zalman, who adopted it as evidence of the Hasidic victory over Satan.

The Rebbe's talk and the singing continue in alternation throughout the night. By midnight, the men have become more and more raucous in their singing and swaying. Some have reached a state of extreme excitement, even ecstasy (*devekut*), brought on by the commingling of the music, vodka, heat of the room, and nearness of the Rebbe. Some have fainted. They will be carried out at the conclusion of the farbrengen and taken home to sleep. Later,

Figure 5. Entrance to
Bais Chana, St. Paul,
Minn. (photograph by
the author, 1989)

Figure 6. A women's farbrengen inside Bais Chana, St. Paul, Minn. (photograph by the author, 1989)

they may recount that at a particularly heightened moment in their singing, they saw the face of Schneur Zalman or some other holy *zaddik* (saint, holy man) long since gone.

I sit in the gallery above with the women who have remained through the night. Although present all along, we have experienced a somewhat different farbrengen—no less exciting but far more modest in its expression. Many of us have been deeply affected by the Rebbe's talk. Although not all of the women, especially the ba'alot teshuvah, understand Yiddish, simply being in the Rebbe's presence creates an intensity that will carry them through the next few days of more worldly concerns.

Some of the women have also participated in the singing portions of tonight's gathering. Singing quietly, or under their breath, the women sing the familiar tunes more or less individually rather than as a chorus; but their intensity, even without the vodka, matches that of the men below them. One woman in particular, a ba'alat teshuvah, has just returned from Bais Chana, a Lubavitcher women's school in St. Paul, Minnesota, where she has been organizing women's farbrengen (figs. 5 and 6). As a classically trained musician, she is well respected and sought after as a valuable teacher and perform er. She and the other women do not seem to be upset or envious of the men's outward expressiveness—indeed, many think it is men's lack of inherent spirituality that makes them act so uncontrollably. They are happy to be experiencing the farbrengen within the confines of the women's gallery. Here, they can be free to sing, if quietly, or to express their own joys in their own ways without worrying about the men. "What is most precious is most hidden," they say.

It is now 3:30 A.M., and the Rebbe has finished speaking, his voice hoarse yet still inspiring. The farbrengen concludes with one last song, "Uforatztoh" again. It is a way of simultaneously reconnecting with the earlier portion of the Rebbe's talk and the secular world that will soon be encountered outside the synagogue. All of the participants feel renewed and strengthened for the battle with the week ahead, with all of its mundanities, trivialities, and temptations. The men continue singing, then humming, as they spill into the street. Some will remain until daylight talking and smoking. Others hurry home for a few hours sleep. Only a few women remain. We will travel home in groups, walking with the men nearby. It is a mistake to walk alone at night.

Notes

1. Hasidim are ultraorthodox Jews who follow the philosophy of the eighteenth-century teacher and mystic Israel ben Eliezer, the Ba'al Shem Tov (1698–1750). Lubavitcher Hasidim are one of the many groups (or courts) that developed after the death of the Ba'al Shem Tov and that follow, in addition to the Ba'al Shem Tov's teachings, the philosophy (Habad) of one of his followers, Rabbi Schneur Zalman (1745–1813). Lubavitchers and other Hasidim are similar in many ways to mainstream Ashkenazic (Eastern European/German) Orthodox Jews in that they follow the same liturgical calendar and share a basic history, culture, and language (Yiddish). See chapter 3 for a more detailed discussion of the history and philosophy of Lubavitcher Hasidism.

2. "Rebbe" is an acronym for *Rosh B'nei Yisroel* (Head of the Sons of Israel—that is, the Jewish people). The term "rebbe" should not be confused with the title "rabbi."

3. The four forms of this title are as follows: ba'al teshuvah (masculine singular); ba'alei teshuvah (masculine and mixed plural); ba'alat teshuvah (feminine singular); ba'alot (feminine plural).

4. This picture was taken in the middle of a weekday afternoon, when the rooms were empty. Normally, on the Sabbath, the rooms are at least partially filled with women and girls, but no photography is allowed then.

5. "Ha-Shem" literally means "the name" and refers to the Hebrew name of God when used outside a liturgical context.

2
Analytical Framework

This book is informed by a number of different, and at times competing, scholarly streams: ethnomusicology, with an emphasis on the integration of musical and sociocultural systems; the ethnomusicology of Jewish music, with an emphasis on music as a symbolic, interactive, and changeable system of sounds and meanings specific to Jewish identity; the anthropology of religion, specifically issues of boundary maintenance and interaction between American secular and Hasidic communities; gender studies, specifically issues concerning context-sensitive power dynamics between men and women; and, finally, performance theory, with emphasis on the cultural and individual performances of identity that are always inherent in musical performance. It has only been recently, within postmodern discourse, that newly developed paradigms of social and musical theory have allowed such diverse philosophical streams to intersect comfortably. And it seems no accident that conservative religious systems worldwide, including the Lubavitcher community under study here, have flourished in recent years in part as a reaction to the postmodern condition of fragmented and decentralized philosophical and social norms.

Ethnomusicology and the Study of Jewish Music

This study is related primarily to that stream of ethnomusicology, stemming from the anthropological tradition of Alan Merriam (1964), John Blacking (1973), Carol Robertson (1989), and many others, whose work focuses primarily on the interconnectedness of music and social, political, and cultural

systems. It is also informed by the more recent postmodern work of ethno-
musicologists and anthropologists, including Steven Feld (1990), Marina
Roseman (1991), Timothy Rice (1994), Jane Sugarman (1997), and others, that
deals with the symbolic, coded content of musical repertoires, their creation,
and performance. And, although none of the works cited above deals specifically with Jewish music per se, the notion of music, its creation, and performance as sounded and acted expressions of cultural values, meanings, and
identities is what connects this present work most meaningfully with those
ethnomusicological forebears.

It is beyond the scope of this book to survey the considerable historical
literature on Jewish music.[1] Of the many hundreds of sources for Jewish
music, however, few specifically address Hasidic music in any detail. Nota-
ble exceptions are the musicological works of Abraham Idelsohn (1973), who
in his monumental ten-volume *Thesaurus of Hebrew Oriental Melodies* devoted an entire volume to Hasidic music; Jaacov Mazor, Andre Hajdu, and
Bathja Bayer's collection of dance nigunim recorded in Israel (1974); Hajdu
and Mazor's article in the *Encyclopedia Judaica* on Hasidic music and philosophy (1971); Eric Werner's study of Hebrew song and chant, which discusses modal-melodic patterns found in Hasidic music (1961); Hanoch Avenary's work on wordless nigunim (1964); Fred Berk's collection of Hasidic
dance tunes (1975); and one historical work, Meier Geshuri's study of the
music of various Polish Hasidic dynasties (1952).

It is only within the past two decades that Jewish—and specifically Hasidic—music has been seen predominantly in its cultural context as a process of social interaction, exchange, negotiation, and ethnic and religious
boundary formation. The work of Jill Gellerman (1977), Philip V. Bohlman
(1989; 1993), Lionel Wohlberger (1992), Kay Kaufman Shelemay (1998), and
especially Mark Slobin (1980; 1982) has been helpful in situating Jewish music
within the context of historical and contemporary Jewish social relations and
in seeing musicmaking as a socioreligious process.

Slobin's work on the popular music of Jewish immigrants in the United
States, although not specifically addressing Hasidic music, has been especially
useful as a model for this present study of Lubavitcher music, because it attempts to integrate musical sound with social structure and religious ideology. Slobin focuses on the power of encoded symbols within Jewish music
and musicmaking that act variously as recreations of a mythic Old World,
as evocations of emotional states long associated with Jewish history and
religious practice, or as sounded metaphors for contemporary political and
economic issues. In this way, Slobin introduces the notion of music as a ve-

hicle for negotiating the intricacies of contemporary Jewish social and religious life.

My own work with the Lubavitcher community over the past twenty years has taken a variety of approaches to the problem of music and musical behavior as encodings of social and religious practices. Isolating certain aspects of Lubavitcher culture—such as compositional process (1978), performance contexts (1995), and certain gender issues (1987; 1993)—I have tried to show how specific music and socioreligious beliefs and practices are intertwined. Here, though, I am attempting a more holistic approach, one that theorizes music not as a set repertoire, or even as a system of coded sounds, but rather as a kind of generalized process by which Lubavitchers negotiate their way through a variety of social and religious interactions.

In looking at Lubavitcher life as a process of negotiation, I am introducing the idea of personal agency—that is, the role of individuals in making choices, from the most mundane to the loftiest, with some sort of intention. Lubavitchers do not, any more than the rest of us, move blindly through their lives, simply following rules; rather, they make numerous everyday choices that help resolve life's tiny and sometimes monumental tensions, using the structure of Jewish law as an overall template. For Lubavitchers as a group, the greatest tensions center on maintaining strict religious observance within a secularized context; for Lubavitchers as individuals who are attempting to live out this commitment, however, tensions may center on far more mundane matters, such as how to decide who gets the house tonight for a farbrengen, where to live after marriage, or how to play an old nigun on a new synthesizer. Thus, negotiation at many levels acts to resolve individual and in-group tensions, as well as those resulting from interaction with out-groups, however defined.

Models for the Study of Jewish Life in America

Until recently, the study of Jewish life in America was dominated primarily by sociological models that predicted or described the seemingly inevitable processes of modernization, secularization, and assimilation. Unfortunately, this model did not often address Hasidic communities.[2] When Hasidic life was mentioned at all, it was often seen as a recreation of *shtetl* (eastern European Jewish community) life in America (Freilich 1962; Mayer 1979); as a cultlike, but marginal, community dominated by a powerfully charismatic rabbi (Berger 1981); or as a system that "function[s] as a cultural constant in the life of the disoriented newcomer, as a place of haven in the stormy new environment" (Sklare 1972:44; qtd. in Belcove-Shalin 1995:14). Even the early ethnographies of Hasidic life, George Kranzler's *Williamsburg: A Jewish Community in Transition* (1961) and Solomon Poll's *Hasidic Community of Williamsburg* (1962), predicted that the new, tightly organized Hasidic enclaves in Brooklyn would eventually crumble in the face of modern America's secularism.

One problem with this model was that it failed to distinguish between the three processes of modernization, secularization, and assimilation. Conforming or adapting to new social and economic norms (assimilation) may lead to modernization; but as the recent growth of religious communities worldwide shows, it does not necessarily lead to a breakdown of traditional religious values (secularization). Likewise, making use of new technologies, living with more money, or having conveniences such as cars, dishwashers, or computers (modernization) may lead to a form of assimilation, or adaption; but again, this does not necessarily lead to secularization.[3]

Indeed, Hasidic contact with modernity did not result in secularization but rather in a strengthening of ethnic and religious boundaries within the modern context. In new ethnographic work, scholars such as William Shaffir (1995), Debra Kaufman (1991), Lis Harris (1985), Lynne Davidman (1991), Jack Kugelmass (1988), and others describe the strategy adopted by many Orthodox and Hasidic Jews as one of resistance to secularization, in effect "establishing strong boundaries with the broader culture, resisting cultural encroachments as much as possible, and setting the group up as a radical alternative" (Shaffir 1995:32).

Shaffir, for example, suggests three ways in which Hasidic communities have been able to maintain boundaries in the face of American secularization: they have maintained strict institutional control, especially in the area of secular education for their children; they have developed various negotiation strategies that have allowed them to interact with their non-Jewish neighbors and with the U.S. government, often much to their advantage; and, in the case of Lubavitcher Hasidim, they have engaged, and continue to engage, in extensive outreach programs that recruit new, previously nonobservant Jews into the community (1995:41).

Further, says Shaffir, for Lubavitchers, the very act of recruiting strengthens ideology in that it involves "witnessing," the forceful statement of one's religious beliefs in the face of resistance: "Thus it can be argued that Lubavitchers' contacts with nonreligious Jews serve, in fact, to reinforce the sect's distinctive identity and fortify members' self-identification" (1995:51). Janet Belcove-Shalin echoes Shaffir by writing that in the postmodern age, as Hasidim have been forced to coexist with many other religious, racial, and ethnic groups within a largely affluent, tolerant context, the very act of establishing nuclear families, structured, religious homes, and clear-cut gender identities can be seen as a defense against the values of American secular society (1995:16).

Thus, modernization and, to some degree, assimilation—but not secularization—seem to have taken place in a limited way within Hasidic communities in the last decades of the twentieth century. Hasidic Jews can be seen as having adapted to many of the economic and social norms of contemporary America; but their continuing adherence to strict, centuries-old Jewish law and custom has prevented their secularization and has, in effect, strengthened ethnic and religious boundaries. One of the things I hope to show in the course of this work is the dynamic process of negotiating between two seemingly fixed, yet truly flexible, ideologies, the traditional and the modern, both constructed in the present, a process that has allowed the Lubavitcher community not only to exist within contemporary American society but to flourish here. The act of negotiating is an ongoing, dynamic, and interactive process, involving creative manipulation of ideas and behaviors; the use of one strategy over another, as I will show, must therefore always be defined by context.

Gender and Performance Theory

While certain economic and political institutions have greatly benefited the American Hasidic community as a whole, Lubavitcher women have especially benefited from the general rise in social class and from the freedom that religious tolerance has provided here in the United States; they also have, as a group, developed a rich repertoire of adaptive strategies. Unlike most of their own mothers, for example, today's Lubavitcher women are likely to work outside the home, at least for a time, to receive a formal Jewish and perhaps a secular education, and to have a sense of autonomy that would have been unknown a generation ago.

It was, in fact, women's seemingly contradictory position in Lubavitcher society that led me to rethink some of my early assumptions about music and gender in the Crown Heights community (Koskoff 1993). The feminist anthropologists of the late 1960s and 1970s,[4] as well as their colleagues within Jewish feminist studies,[5] tended to locate women generally—and Orthodox Jewish women especially—within the male-dominated patriarchies of world economic and religious systems. Openly political in nature, such studies attempted to expose and change unbalanced power systems and relations; they were not necessarily looking carefully at individual women as agents in their own cultural and political worlds. Most Jewish feminists, for example, regarded Hasidic women as hopelessly victimized by strict adherence to laws that prescribed, among other things, that all Jewish men rise each morning thanking God that they had not been born women.

What I saw as I continued to do fieldwork, however, was a far cry from the picture presented in the literature. The women I worked with were vibrant, alive, joyful—not without their complaints, of course, but far from victimized. In fact, they seemed to be valorized and often praised for their strength and intelligence, and they were accorded special status by virtue of their ability to bear and nurture children. Further, they seemed to share a sense of true community with their families, their neighbors, and with other Hasidic women that rivaled the struggling sisterhoods of my own feminist experience. Was I being naive? Were they simply not conscious of their own victimization, as Betty Friedan (1963) had pointed out a generation earlier to the suburban housewives of the 1950s?

While it is certainly true that Orthodox Judaism as a religious, social, and political system is patriarchal (in that men control the religious and legal aspects of its practice) and that such control does circumscribe women's actions and behaviors and limit women's participation in public ritual and governance, there is much room for Hasidic women to attain status, power, and some autonomy within their own communities. Indeed, by the mid-1970s and into the 1980s, feminist anthropologists working in many different cultures began to look at individual contexts where women, despite their limited circumstances, were able to flourish. Works in anthropology, including Marjorie Shostak's *Nisa: The Life and Words of a !Kung Woman* (1983) and Veronica Doubleday's *Three Women of Herat* (1990), pointed to some of the benefits of patriarchy for women, such as female solidarity and a sense of pride in womanhood. As Michelle Rosaldo wrote in 1974: "By accepting and elaborating upon the symbols and expectations associated with their cultural definition, they [women] may goad men into compliance, or establish a society unto themselves. . . . [Therefore] the symbolic and social conceptions that appear to set women apart and to circumscribe their activities, may be used by women as a basis for female solidarity and worth" (Rosaldo 1974:37; qtd. in Kaufman 1991:69).

Bonnie Morris (1990; 1995; 1998) has shown that within Hasidic culture during the 1950s and 1960s, there was a tremendous growth of interest in women's activities; she suggests to her secular feminist colleagues that they "adopt the temporary perspective that Hasidism is normative, and to concentrate on *what* Hasidic women do with their lives and their influences, rather than questioning *why* Hasidic women have views or values different from those of assimilated Jews" (Morris 1995:173). She continues:

> It would be both inaccurate and patronizing to assume that ultra-Orthodox women have merely been brainwashed or conditioned by the male leadership of their respective group. Such an assumption constructs women as passive recipients of religion and shifts the active focus to the male. While male authority and control often determine or circumscribe female choice, women still retain options as ideological consumers. Religious sex-role assignments may, indeed, oppress all women as a class while still permitting individual women to attain power and status through the manipulation of the prescribed female role. (1995:173)

Most of the new research on Hasidic women has come from ethnographies of the so-called ba'alei teshuvah movement. Beginning in earnest in 1967 after the Six Day War in Israel, Hasidic communities, especially the Lubavitcher community, saw a steady influx of newly observant Jews (ba'alei teshuvah), people who had been raised within the secular American society who chose to enter these communities as adults. As Harris (1985), Kaufman (1991; 1995), Davidman (1991), and others have pointed out, Hasidic life, especially for women, provided a needed structure and safety that their families and most of secularized America had failed to provide them, and women joined these groups in large numbers.

None of the literature I found on gender issues in Jewish or Hasidic life in the United States, however, dealt with music or its performance as important ingredients in the negotiation of everyday and ritual life for women (or for men). As I was primarily interested in examining how Lubavitchers "performed themselves" through music and wanted to explore the interactions between cultural and musical knowledge and behavior, it seemed fruitful to consider Lubavitchers both as a group of cultural actors and as individual improvisers, performing their culture—that is, their shared understandings, individually interpreted and manipulated within the stage, or framework, of acceptable Lubavitcher behavior.[6]

Most literature dealing with musical and cultural performance, however, focuses on ritual, ceremony, carnival, or concert.[7] But I was not as interested in the performance or meanings of music within well-defined, easily observable social or ritual contexts, as in the notion of the personal, "ideo-performances" of everyday life, performances that were for Lubavitchers already imbued with social and sacred meaning. How did one as a Lubavitcher perform one's love of God through music? Would there be different musical performances of Lubavitcher identity for men? For women? Would there be unique performances for those born as Lubavitchers? For ba'alei teshuvah? Could one somehow negotiate Hasidic life in modern America through musical performance? What could other types of performances, such as gender or lineage performances, tell us about Lubavitcher music, musical roles, or the quality of Hasidic life as lived by real people in Crown Heights, Brooklyn?

Unexpected help came from two sources: Judith Butler's *Gender Trouble*, which, when first published in 1990, raised some interesting and controversial questions concerning the nature of gender identity and its outward manifestations through the body; and work arising from psychological anthropology, as seen especially in the writings of Roy D'Andrade and Claudia Strauss (1992).

Butler's work, drawn from the earlier work of Mary Douglas (1969) and Julia Kristeva (1980), asks if gender is "a 'natural' fact or a cultural performance?" (1990:x) and answers that to the degree that our bodies are politically constructed—that is, taught to behave in certain prescribed ways, for purposes of social order and control—we can say that our gender identity is performed (1990:136). Further, "the action of gender requires a performance that is *repeated*. This repetition is at once a re-enactment and re-experiencing of a set of meanings already socially established" (1990:140). Thus, according to Butler, gender is not a fixed, inner, or natural attribute but is rather "performed into being" (1990:140) throughout one's life, according to the rules of one's culture.

Although Butler's work focuses primarily on a theory of gender performance and derives, in part, from her work on such cultural performances as sexual parodies and drag shows, I would like to extend her theory of performance to include many other aspects of both male and female Lubavitcher identity, such as lineage and spirituality. By adapting Butler's work, however, I am not implying that all of life is essentially a finite set of learned or fixed cultural performances. We are all both constrained and enlivened by our own biology, our physical selves, and our idiosyncratic desires, motivations, and behaviors. Yet performance, or perhaps improvisation, as a metaphor for negotiating one's way through life's often conflicting choices seemed an appropriate, even apt, one for discussing music in Lubavitcher life.

D'Andrade and Strauss's work in psychological anthropology has also been helpful in understanding the ways individuals interact within specific social and musical contexts. Growing out of earlier cognitive anthropological models in the 1960s and 1970s, this work extends the notion of cultural models, or "shared cognitive schemas through which human realities are constructed and interpreted" (1992:i), by showing the highly creative, internal, and interactive processes by which people negotiate their everyday lives. Neither part of an "external" cultural system, such as a ritual, nor a specific context, such as a concert hall, cultural models, sometimes called "schemas" or "templates" (Quinn and Holland 1987), are manipulated internally, either consciously or unconsciously, by individuals within specific contexts to achieve certain goals: "The term 'cultural model' as used here refers to shared, recognized, and transmitted internal representations, not to external forms such as symbolic objectives or events. We assume that these two sides of culture are *always* linked, otherwise we would have on one side external forms without meaning or sense and on the other side internal meanings without any forms to express or communicate them. Once this linkage is admitted, it does not matter which side is called 'culture'" (1987:230).

Thus, a Lubavitcher musical performance may be considered not simply an outward manifestation of a shared musical culture but also an internal representation of an individual Lubavitcher's identity. In seeing culture as ideational and internal, as well as material and external, we can begin to understand some of the motivations that compel Lubavitcher musical and social action and allow music to be such a highly effective means of expressing and negotiating personal and social issues of religious, ethnic, familial, and gender identity within the context of contemporary America. As music carries such high value within Hasidic culture, and within Jewish culture at large, it is a natural locus for Hasidic beliefs and values to be expressed. As such, it can reveal more than just its sounds or behaviors; understanding the process of music as negotiation can unfold a rich tapestry of meanings about essential Lubavitcher beliefs and actions concerning the natures of human spirituality, human social interaction, and God.

Notes

1. See Heskes (1985) for an excellent general bibliography.
2. See Belcove-Shalin's excellent review (1988). See also Hedman (1992), Landau (1993), and Shaffir (1974).
3. See Kepel (1994) for a similar observation.
4. See especially Rosaldo (1974), Ardener (1975), Reiter (1975), and MacCormack and Strathern (1980).

5. See especially Heschel (1983), Schneider (1984), and Kaye-Kantrowitz and Klepfisz (1986).

6. See Rice (1994) for his model on the social and individual experience of Bulgarian musicians, which is similar in spirit to that presented here.

7. For example, see Herndon (1975) and Behague (1984).

PART 2: INSIDE THE CONTEXT

The following four chapters present a picture of the Lubavitcher religious, social, and musical world, a place where essential beliefs about the nature of human interaction, the realm of the sacred, and the power of music are intertwined. Each chapter deals with a specific context: chapter 3 examines the historical and philosophical context of Lubavitcher (Habad) Hasidism; chapter 4 explores the contemporary Lubavitcher social context; and chapters 5 and 6 concern the context of musical sound and structure as materialized in a core repertoire of nigunim (songs). Thus, the Lubavitcher context is seen here as a place where various core belief systems that are carried in the mind, but lived on the ground, intersect and form a space for the enactment of Lubavitcher identity.

3
The History and Philosophy of Habad Hasidism

Scene: "First Encounters with Lubavitch"

It is 1948, and I am four years old. I live in Squirrel Hill, the Jewish section of Pittsburgh, Pennsylvania. Every day, I walk to my corner and enter a large old house that is my nursery school. One morning, on arriving at the door, I am abruptly turned away by a ferocious-looking man with a great black beard and told in no uncertain terms to "Go away!" I am quite frightened and cry all the way home. A Lubavitcher family has moved into Squirrel Hill and has bought this house for a yeshivah (school). My parents are outraged—they want nothing to do with this. They are embarrassed by the Hasidim, their distinctive dress, and their quaint, old-world antics. But, as I grow older and pass this corner on my way to elementary school, I often stop to peer in the windows, fascinated by the wondrous music, by the excitement and joy within.

～

It is 1973, twenty-five years later. I am just beginning to explore the possibility of working with the music of the local Pittsburgh Lubavitcher community for my doctoral dissertation, and I have been invited to the now-rebuilt yeshivah to talk with some Lubavitchers and to perhaps meet a few musicians. I am still trying to understand exactly what it is that makes these people and their music seem so alive. But I am also ambivalent about taking on this research. On the one hand, I am curious about Lubavitcher lives, what makes them "so Jewish," what connects them to music; on the other, there is all of that proselytizing and embarrassing public behavior that I have seen and heard about all of my life. Will they want me to join this group (or, as my family says, "cult"), to become more religious, or to give up my newborn feminist consciousness?

My advisers do not know what to do with me—my training has been strictly within the boundaries of Western historical musicology, and they are hoping that I will consider working on the fifteenth-century composer Giles Binchois. My family does not know what to do with me—we are not Orthodox Jews. I grew up in a secular Jewish home—one where being Jewish consisted of (maybe) giving yearly to the local synagogue and singing the African American spiritual, "Let My People Go," at an occasional Passover seder. We do not attend services or associate too much with our Jewish neighbors. In fact, my father is amazed (maybe even horrified) that I am interested in studying this culture after he has spent a lifetime trying to dissociate himself from it. He is afraid that I will become a Hasid and revert back to the shtetl life of his Belorussian father, the first Koskoff immigrant to the United States. Why on earth am I doing this?

I now approach the familiar corner of my youth and enter the yeshivah. It is the first time I have been inside this new building, and I briefly wonder how I would appear to an inquisitive child passing by. Within a few minutes, many of the women have introduced themselves to me and have offered me something to eat. Soon they are giving me names of others in the community who "do music," and I am encouraged to call anytime to talk. I am introduced to Rabbi Ephraim Rosenblum, who is known for his wonderful voice, and we agree to talk later. But, he tells me, if I really want to learn about nigunim, I must go to Crown Heights, in Brooklyn, New York, talk with people there, and experience the music firsthand.

I am asked politely about my Jewish life, whether or not I am married, if I have a Jewish name, the Jewish name of my mother and father, and, perfunctorily, why I am interested in music. I am asked what I have heard about Lubavitchers; somewhat sheepishly, I tell them how Lubavitchers came and took over my nursery school and that this is pretty much all I know. Many of the women laugh at my ramblings; they are relative newcomers to Pittsburgh and to the Lubavitcher community, having adopted Hasidic values as adults; and, anyway, most were not even born in the 1940s.

Soon, I am being questioned more seriously about my life. Am I willing to consider becoming more observant? (I think: Aha, it's starting.) One need only take a small first step, say, lighting Shabbos (Sabbath) candles—no need to make a commitment now, just see how it feels. I am somewhat wary; but, unexpectedly, I like these women. They are not at all what I have expected.

They are nothing like the Eastern European peasants of my father's imagination. They are young, fashionably dressed, even highly educated. Some have come from liberal, "leftist" families that are much like my own. Will it really kill me to light some candles? I agree to do this; and one of the women, smiling, presents me with a small brass candlestick, branched to hold two candles. "This is for you and your family," she says. "Just start lighting—the rest will follow."

A Brief History of Lubavitcher Hasidism

Many fine books now exist that trace the historical and sociocultural developments of modern Hasidism and the religious philosophy of the Lubavitcher Hasidim, known as Habad. It is not, therefore, the purpose of this book to retrace this history in any detail or to comment critically upon Hasidic philosophy, except in that it informs this study's understanding of Lubavitcher music and its place in Lubavitcher life. What follows, then, is a brief historical sketch of the Lubavitcher Hasidic court and a general explanation of Lubavitcher religious beliefs. Certain events or beliefs may be singled out as especially important for this discussion, for they will provide a context for future discussions of music and its performance within contemporary Lubavitcher society.

Modern Hasidism, a pietistic movement that developed within mainstream, Orthodox Judaism,[1] began in eighteenth-century Podolia (then part of Poland; now part of present-day Russia) with the preachings of Israel ben Eliezer, the Ba'al Shem Tov (1698–1750), a charismatic leader and teacher who developed an approach to Judaism that emphasized the average Jew's enthusiastic love, faith, and devotion to God. Essentially a democratizing movement, modern Hasidism allowed all those who adhered faithfully and zealously to *halakhah* (Jewish law), including the *am-ha-aretz* (literally, man of the earth, the average person), to gain access to the divine realm through the mystical experience known as *devekut* (adherence to the divine).

Mystical concepts of early Hasidism had their origins in the thirteenth-century book the Zohar, attributed to Moses de Leon (d. 1305), and in the sixteenth-century Spanish kabbalist school, headed by Isaac Luria (1534–72). Luria stressed the messianic element in his interpretation of kabbalah (mystical teachings) and made certain changes in the traditional Sephardic (Spanish, North African) liturgy that were later adopted by the culturally Ashkenazic Hasidim. The Ba'al Shem Tov and his early followers developed many of Luria's ideas by synthesizing and simplifying them to fit the needs of everyday Eastern European Jews.

Spreading to various parts of Eastern Europe, Palestine, and Turkey, Hasidism quickly gained thousands of adherents; and during the next 100 years, various centers, or courts, were established in major cities and towns. Rabbi Schneur Zalman (1745–1813) of Lyady, in present-day Belarus (Belorussia), who later founded the Lubavitcher court, became attracted to the ideas of the Ba'al Shem Tov through the teachings of one of his disciples, Dov Baer (1733–1827) of Mezhirich, or Miezricz, in present-day Russia.[2] Founding his own Hasidic community in Liozna (in present-day Russia) in 1767, Schneur Zalman began to develop a form of Hasidism that he called Habad. He immediately came into conflict with more traditional rabbis and Talmudic scholars, or *mitnaggadim* (opponents), and was eventually arrested as a subversive by the czarist authorities. Taken to St. Petersburg prison, he was found innocent of all charges and was released on November 27, 1798. This date, *yud-tet Kislev*— the nineteenth day of the month *Kislev* in the Hebrew calendar—is still celebrated today as an important holiday within the Lubavitcher community.

In addition to attacks by the mitnaggadim on his new Hasidic community, Schneur Zalman began to experience personal attacks from opposing Hasidic leaders, who had established other communities in Volhynia (in present-day Russia) and in Palestine (present-day Israel). And, in 1790, he suffered the loss of his oldest and most cherished daughter, Dvorah Leah. According to a Lubavitcher legend, Dvorah Leah was renowned for her intelligence and wisdom and often acted as her father's confidante. She was aware of the hostility of the mitnaggadim as well as that of the Hasidim in Palestine, and she knew the considerable pain that it caused her father. As she became more and more certain that her father would despair and die, she resolved to sacrifice her life for that of her father and died in late September 1790, leaving her two-year-old son, Menachem Mendel (later, the third Lubavitcher Rebbe), in the care of her father.

From 1792 to 1796, certain parts of the Tanya, the literary exposition of Schneur Zalman's philosophy, Habad, began to appear, first in manuscript and finally in printed form. Still under attack from opposing rabbinical forces, Schneur Zalman was jailed once again by the Russian authorities. On his release from prison, he moved to Lyady, where he spent the next twelve years teaching and supporting the many Hasidic communities that had developed in the surrounding provinces. In late 1812, he was forced to flee Lyady before the advancing French Army, under the leadership of Napoleon Bonaparte; in 1813, Schneur Zalman died while hiding in the village of Piena, near Lyady.

Schneur Zalman's heirs and disciples continued to spread Habad philosophy after his death. His son, Rabbi Dov Baer (1773–1827), named for Schneur

Zalman's first Hasidic teacher, moved to Lubavitch (in the Poltava region of Belarus) in 1814, where he established the first Habad center. Succeeding generations of Hasidim following Habad thus came to be called Lubavitchers because of their association with this town.

Joseph Isaac Schneersohn (1880–1950), the sixth Lubavitcher Rebbe and the great-great-great grandson of Schneur Zalman, was the first Rebbe to leave Russia, moving first to Warsaw and then, in 1941, with a small following, to New York City, finally settling in Brooklyn, where he established the Worldwide Center of Habad Hasidism in Crown Heights. It was here that Rabbi Schneerson's considerable administrative ability was allowed to flourish. During the ten years that he lived in Brooklyn, he established an extensive network of Hasidic institutions, pledging a commitment to "bring about a religious revival in the United States" (Lubavitch Foundation 1970:54). To this end, he established an educational network; a series of outreach programs for local Jewish children; Bais Rivkah, a school for girls and women; the Kehot Publication Society, the largest publishing house for Hasidic literature in the world; and the Nichoach Society, which is dedicated to preserving the Lubavitcher musical heritage. In addition, Habad communities and educational and charity institutions were established in the late 1940s and 1950s in Pittsburgh, New Haven, Connecticut, Montreal, and in various other cities and towns in the United States, Canada, Israel, North Africa, and Australia.[3] On the death of Joseph Isaac Schneersohn in 1950, Rabbi Menachem Mendel Schneerson (1902–94) became the seventh Lubavitcher Rebbe. Like his father-in-law, Rabbi Schneerson continued throughout his life to develop and expand Habadic social and religious networks.

Born in Russia, Menachem Mendel Schneerson's educational path deviated somewhat from the Hasidic norm. As a child, he, like many other Hasidim before him, became recognized as an exceptional Torah scholar. However, an interest in engineering led him to the University of Berlin and the Sorbonne in Paris.

In the forty-four years that Menachem Mendel Schneerson was the Lubavitcher Rebbe, perhaps his greatest achievement was his administrative network of community services, charities, schools, women's and youth organizations, day-care centers, and summer camps. Further, taking the motto of the song title "Uforatztoh" ("And You shall Spread Out") literally, the Rebbe sent thousands of shelichim (emissaries) to cities in the United States and abroad to spread the Habad philosophy and way of life. By the mid-1980s, there were thirty-five Lubavitcher yeshivahs in the United States and 135 abroad, about 100 "Habad Houses" established at various college and university campuses, and over 35,000 children attending Lubavitcher-run schools and summer camps throughout the world (Harris 1985:106). Since the death of Menachem Mendel Schneerson in 1994, no new Lubavitcher Rebbe has emerged.

Habad Hasidism

Through his many writings and teachings, Schneur Zalman, the founder of the Lubavitcher court, developed a form of Hasidism called Habad, derived from the acronym formed from three Hebrew words, *hochma* (wisdom), *binah* (understanding), and *da'at* (knowledge). Although based on the mystical and esoteric teachings of Judaism, specifically the Zohar, and on the ideas of Isaac Luria, Schneur Zalman's Hasidism sought to balance the theosophical elements in Jewish mysticism, derived from kabbalah, with the positive aspects of Jewish intellectualism derived from the study of halakhah (law). Habad Hasidism is thus a reinterpretation of and elaboration on the ecstatic and boundless knowledge of God and grounded within the framework of Jewish law, as experienced every day by the average Jew.

Central to an understanding of Habad Hasidism, and to the contemporary Lubavitcher worldview, is the doctrine of the two souls, which concerns the ascent of the human soul to the divine realm through intense, repetitive prayer; teshuvah (repentance); *avodah* (work, divine service); and the descent of the godly soul to the human realm through the ten *sefirot* (rays, beams), the divine emanations that constitute a continuous creation. The up/down movement of souls, the in/out movement of repetitive prayer and repentance, and the near/far distancing of the souls from each other thus create a three-dimensional context for Lubavitcher life that constitutes an underlying conceptual space for all social, religious, and expressive interactions.

The following explanation of Habad Hasidism, though, cannot possibly do justice to the rich symbolism and intricate, often paradoxical, nature of kabbalistic thought. The reader is urged to read Schneur Zalman's primary text, the Tanya, for a fuller discussion. This necessarily brief explanation is presented here to merely suggest something of the philosophical context for Lubavitcher thinking about music and its creation, performance, and reception.

The Doctrine of the Two Souls

In the Tanya, Schneur Zalman discusses the doctrine of the two souls, derived from a Lurianic principle that was first presented by Hayim Vital (1542–

1620), an interpreter of Luria, and based on the biblical text from Isaiah 57:16: "For the spirit that enwrappeth itself is from Me and the souls which I have made" (Jewish Publication Society 1955:1088). This doctrine, at the heart of Habad philosophy, states that all people possess two souls, both of which are ultimately connected to the divine: an animal soul, divided into two parts, and a divine soul that assists the animal soul in its perpetual striving for God. These two souls, each with a mind and will of its own, direct all human activities, as well as the conscious and unconscious forces behind them (Mindel 1973, 2:25).

Each soul is derived from a different place, the divine soul emanating from the ten holy powers of the sefirot (the divine beams, rays, or emanations of God) and the animal soul deriving from the ten unholy powers (or, the ten crowns of profanity) emanating from the *sitra achra* (the other side). The divine soul, seen as the seat of the intellect, is indivisible, and its presence in all things can be distinguished by the brightness or dimness of its light.[4] The animal soul (sometimes called the vital soul), seen as the seat of emotions, consists of two interrelated parts: a nonhuman animal part, associated with lower or base emotions, such as arrogance and anger; and a natural or human animal part, where emotions associated with human intellect, such as self-esteem, modesty, and others that are natural to humans, reside (1973, 2:26).

The divine soul is situated metaphorically in the head, whereas the two parts of the animal soul reside in the two chambers of the heart. The divine soul extends downward and outward to the other parts of the body through the right ventricle, the seat of the human animal soul. The nonhuman animal soul, located in the left ventricle, simultaneously extends upward to the brain, where it is purified, and is redirected downward and outward again through the right ventricle by means of blood circulation (1973, 2:43). Thus, the two parts of the animal soul and the divine soul communicate with each other in perpetual circular motion, unmindful of the neutral body that houses them.

Examining the attributes of the two souls more closely, one sees a rich symbolic system unfolding, one that incorporates notions of good and evil, emotion and intellect, blind action and purposeful intention, masculine and feminine, and a host of other interrelated dualities central to Lubavitcher thinking. First, the divine soul emanates from God, as a child "evolves from the paternal drop of semen deriving from the paternal brain" (1973, 2:35), and operates through the three aforementioned intellectual powers: hochma, binah, and da'at. Hochma, the creative intellectual process, is the father, which impregnates binah, or the mother, the developmental process of the intellect; binah then produces da'at, or the child, the concluding, logical intellectual process. Da'at is connected to human consciousness and unites reason and emotion. The intellectual powers of hochma, binah and da'at become manifest through intense contemplation and meditation on the *En-Sof* (without end, limitless), the nothingness of God—that is, the unknowable God from which the process of creation unfolds (1973, 2:35)

The Ten Sefirot

In kabbalist philosophy, the ten sefirot account for the various stages through which the hidden, unknowable, unattainable, and infinite God (En-Sof) is transformed into the manifest, knowable, biblical God associated with the Creation and the finite world. The doctrine of the sefirot thus explains the central paradox of the Creation: how the world and all of its inhabitants was created ex nihilo. Often represented schematically as a set of interconnected circles in the form of a tree, the sefirot proceed in a fixed sequence, and each is said to be embedded in the other. Together, they create a structure of supreme stability and balance (fig. 7).

The highest sefirah, *keter* (crown), represents the first stage or urge toward manifestation. From keter stem two branches: hochma (wisdom) is on the right, an active, masculine grouping of divine rays; binah (intellect) is on the left, a passive, feminine grouping. Together, they produce a third group ultimately leading to *malchut* (kingdom), often referred to metaphorically as the *shechinah* (the indwelling of the divine presence).

The three highest sefirot are associated with the intellect (high, head); the next three are identified with moral attributes (mid-level, heart); and the lower three are grouped with the material world (low, heel of the foot). Malchut/shechina, the last sefirah, is associated with the Creation of the world and of the primeval Adam, the progenitor of the biblical Adam. The four subdivisions of the sefirot (3 + 3 + 3 + 1) are, in Lurianic kabbalah, and in the teachings of Schneur Zalman, referred to as the Four Worlds: emanation, creation (of formless matter), formation (of matter), and action or making (Mindel 1973:82–83).

It is in the last sefirah that the "crown" and the "kingdom" of the world are united, a union frequently expressed metaphorically in highly sexual terms. The malchut/shechina, the "symbol of eternal womanhood," is seen variously as "the daughter of light who falls into the abyss of matter," "Rachel weeping for her children," a female essence of God who is poor, who has "nothing for herself, but only what she receives from the stream of the Sefiroth" (Scholem 1961:234), and—quite literally and erotically—as a part-

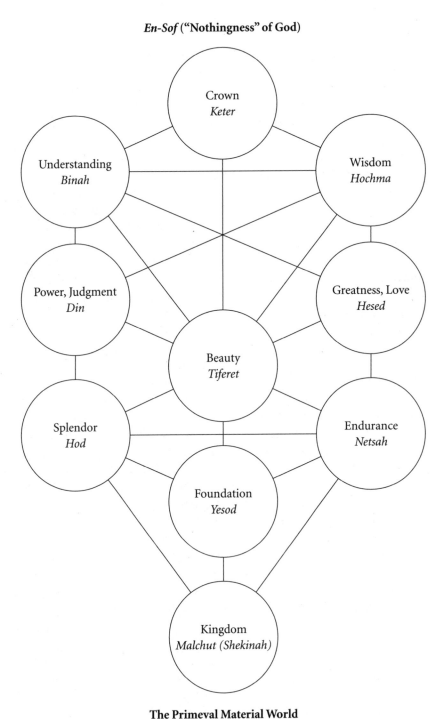

En-Sof ("Nothingness" of God)

Crown
Keter

Understanding
Binah

Wisdom
Hochma

Power, Judgment
Din

Greatness, Love
Hesed

Beauty
Tiferet

Splendor
Hod

Endurance
Netsah

Foundation
Yesod

Kingdom
Malchut (Shekinah)

The Primeval Material World

Figure 7. The ten sephirot (redrawn by the author)

ner in sexual intercourse with God. "It marks the sphere which is the first to open itself to the meditation of the mystic, the entrance to that inwardness of God which . . . discloses its secret only to those who approach it in a spirit of complete devotion" (1961:230).

Contained within each of the ten sefirot are manifestations of the En-Sof, referred to metaphorically as beams of divine light in kabbalistic thought. Before the Creation, only the En-Sof existed. As the urge to become manifest would grow, the En-Sof would contract itself into beams of light contained in vessels, leaving an empty space that was void of the En-Sof but filled instead with *kelipot* (husks, or waste products) left over from this process of contraction. Continuous expansion and contraction of the divine light of the En-Sof perpetuated an ideal state where the Creation was an ongoing process.

Eventually, a catastrophe occurred. Some of the vessels containing too much divine light became weakened and broke, scattering sparks of the light into the void, where they intermingled with the kelipot.[5] There they remained hidden, trapped within the unholy, and potentially evil, casings. The divine link between the En-Sof and the malchut/shechina was now broken, and the final sefirah went into exile, permanently separated from the unity of the other sephirot and the divine source. According to the kabbalists, the purpose of human action was to rescue the divine sparks from the husks that hid them and to restore the sparks to their holy source, thus reuniting the En-Sof with the malchut/shechina.

This doctrine of restoration (*tikkun*) lies at the heart of Hasidic thinking and action. In restoring the hidden sparks to their source by obeying the laws and precepts of halakhah (the law), repeatedly and with devotion, humans have the capacity to reconnect the broken divine link and to eradicate the potential evil that exists within the husks. Thus, when the divine spark is released through the performance of a religious act, "not only are the material things spiritualized, but the Infinite Light is, at the same time, diffused in the physical world, and the material shell, the kelipah, is dissolved in the comprehensive unity of the All. Multiplied by all the individuals performing the precepts, the entire physical world constantly undergoes a process of sublimation and spiritualization" (Mindel 1973, 2:69).

The Sitra Achra and the Ten Crowns of Profanity

The sitra achra (the other side) is also connected to, but exists far away from, the divine soul, and it is responsible for the creation of the kelipot. Also emanating from the En-Sof, the sitra achra is similarly divided into ten connected beams, the ten crowns of profanity, which are upside down, a perfect inversion of the En-Sof. In kabbalistic thinking, the sitra achra is not a separate realm; rather, it is simply in exile at the extreme end of the same processes of creation represented by the ten sefirot:

> Holiness and unholiness, or goodness and badness, essentially have the same substratum, like the two opposite poles of one magnet. . . . Being insensitive to the created force that keeps them in existence, the kelipot, or evil forces, are deluded, as it were, into thinking themselves independent and self-existent, defying the very hand that sustains them. Arrogance and humility are two basic characteristics of the unholy and holy, respectively, in their relation to the En-Sof. . . . The holy receives its sustenance direct from the En-Sof; the unholy is said to receive its sustenance from "behind the back," from the Divine "spark" that is in a state of "exile" within it. (Mindel 1973, 2:84)

The sitra achra, like the ten supernal sefirot, is also divided into the four worlds (emanation, creation, formation, and action); but because the worlds are inverted here, the sefirot that are farthest away from the En-Sof on the side of holiness are closest to the sitra achra. Thus, the three highest worlds of the sitra achra contain the totally unholy and evil kelipot, because their divine spark is completely hidden or reduced. The last world, though, contains a tiny and perceptible spark. Here is where the kelipot *nogah* (translucent or neutral husks) exist. The ten sefirot and the ten crowns of profanity thus preserve a stable unity that underlies the cosmos and all of its materializations, as well as all that is both good and evil.

The Interaction of the Souls

Both parts of the animal soul emanate from the kelipot nogah. Thus, all living creatures are believed to contain a perceptible, if sometimes tiny, divine spark. It is only humans, however, who have the capability—through thought, speech, and action (the "three outer garments")—to make a choice to follow the path inclining either toward the side of holiness or toward the other side. To the person who carefully and joyfully adheres to divine precepts, the side of holiness is always desirable and desired; the other side is merely tolerated. However, to a person ignorant of the law, or arrogant toward it, the sitra achra claims "victory," as does an army over a small city (Schneur Zalman 1968:63).

The concept of moral evil is thus defined in the writings of Schneur Zalman in terms of separateness, or distance, from the divine source and is manifested in arrogance, disobedience to God's will, untempered anger, and a host of other characteristics. As in the concept of creation, where each of the four worlds descends from its source and becomes increasingly materialized and independent of a holy spark, evil is conceived as springing from the kelipot, because these husks are not only far removed from the En-Sof, but they actively hide or obscure the divine sparks within them. The tension between evil and good is therefore seen in terms of a battle between distance and closeness, with the union of the shechina and the En-Sof as the ultimate prize.

The two souls—one existing in the head, the other in the heart—live within the neutral body and communicate, as stated above, via the circulation of the blood (Mindel 1973, 2:42–43). The baser emotions of the animal soul, located in the left ventricle, travel upward toward the brain, where they are purified. Now part of the divine soul, they travel downward back toward the heart and relocate in the right ventricle. If the circuit is completed successfully, the baser emotions fall away and do not continue to incline toward the sitra achra. If the baser emotions are too strong, having inclined too many times toward the sitra achra, the circuit cannot be completed, all is lost, and the "small city" is vanquished.

To achieve true peace, the lower emotions of the animal soul must be lulled into inactivity, extinguished, or, better, totally redirected so that the natural human emotions can be reversed and directed toward a passionate love of God. "It may be said that not only does the Divine soul desire to capture the 'small city,' and to rule it, while keeping the opposing force at bay, but it desires to incorporate the opposing force in its ranks, thereby augmenting its own forces" (1973, 2:47). Thus, the animal soul does not exist for itself but rather as a challenge to the divine soul. As such, it becomes a "potential reservoir of emotional powers upon which the Divine soul can draw. . . . For, as has been noted, the strength of the animal soul lies in its passionate nature. If it can be harnessed in the service of the Divine soul, the latter could attain a greater intensity of passionate love for G-d than it can of its own accord, since its own nature is primarily intellectual" (1973, 2:47–48).

Further, the nonhuman animal soul is said to desire being vanquished and transformed into the divine soul, for its ultimate purpose is merely to tempt the human, not to seduce him. Citing the parable of the harlot found in the Zohar, Schneur Zalman outlines his concept of moral choice: in the parable, a king hires a clever and seductive woman to tempt his unsuspecting son. In this test, she must honestly use all of her seductive powers; if the son does not succumb, both will receive a reward. Outwardly, she must convince the son to break down his resolve; but inwardly, she must desire the son not to be seduced, or her reward will not be forthcoming. Thus, although the temptations of the unholy "other side" are often desirable, even compelling, and the inner struggle is real, the divine soul must necessarily win because humans seek not to become like animals—all passion, without intellect (i.e., out of control)—but rather like God, in whom passion and intellect strike a stable and unifying balance (1973, 2:49).

The Benoni

Schneur Zalman, like other Hasidic leaders, strongly believed that achieving a unity with the divine was not solely the province of the educated Talmudic scholar but lay within the grasp of the benoni (average Jew), a person who struggled, yet never succumbed, to his or her animal passions. "The benoni is only expected to recognize his human weaknesses, fight to overcome them, and to do so with confidence, in the knowledge that he has the powers to overcome them. . . . Hence, the ideal of the true Divine servant is not to attain a state of static behavior, however good it may be; it is a dynamic and conscious effort to transcend himself, and achieve absolute mastery over his nature and habit" (1973, 2:56–57).

According to the Talmud, the human personality falls into one of five broad categories. At the high end are the *zaddik gamur*, a righteous person who transforms evil into good, and the *zaddik she-enu gamur*, a slightly less righteous person who falls somewhat short because he or she has failed to sublimate all of his or her baser (but natural) passions that can lead to evil. At the low end are two types of wicked personalities, the *rasha gamur*, who has completely lost his or her "small city" to evil (although this person's divine spark is not completely dead, simply ineffectual), and the *rasha she-enu gamur*, who is not completely wicked but succumbs to temptations, feels remorse, and does teshuvah (repentance), thus alternating between good and evil (1973, 2:51–52).

In the middle stands the benoni, the intermediate person, one who never consciously commits an evil act. Unlike that of the zaddiks and rashas, however, the animal soul of the benoni is neither eradicated nor victorious; rather, it exists in constant combat with the divine soul. Although the animal soul may exert a strong influence, it is never in a position of power because its "outer garments" (thought, speech, and action) are ultimately controlled by the divine soul. The benoni, living on the ground level, so to speak, is constantly subject to temptation; yet temptation is invariably outweighed by the divine soul. "In the benoni the animal soul is strong enough to challenge, but not actually to contest, the divine soul, and challenge it does relentlessly" (1973, 2:54).

It is possible, during moments of sincere and ecstatic prayer, for the nonhuman part of the animal soul of the benoni to become temporarily mesmerized, made ineffective by intense concentration and focus. However, when such moments are over and the mundanities and temptations of daily life are present again, the incessant tension between the two inclinations resumes. If the benoni succumbs to temptation, he or she forfeits his or her intermediate status and falls into the category of the rasha she-enu gamur (incompletely wicked person).

In the Tanya, Schneur Zalman emphasizes the vital role of simhah (joy) as the key ingredient in the benoni's struggle against the temptations, especially those of the nonhuman animal soul. One must be free from sadness or depression, as these states of mind dull the heart and lead to a breakdown of resistance (1973, 2:140). Suffering, illness, or physical pain, for example, are seen as gifts of God's grace. Even the sadness that results from remorse can be turned to an advantage if one regards it as an evil temptation, a challenge to be overcome.

Devekut

Only during those moments when the benoni is able to suppress the base temptations of the nonhuman animal soul is he or she able to achieve the state of devekut (unity with God). Devekut unites the divine soul with God and temporarily restores a holy spark from exile. It is the "ultimate goal of religious perfection" (Scholem 1961:123), a perpetual and intimate union with the divine attained through avodah (devoted and repeated service) done with kavvanah (proper intention).

Devekut can be achieved in a variety of ways: through study and contemplation, through meditation, through passionate prayer or performance of a ritual, or through the enthusiastic enactment of a divine precept or commandment. Unlike the term ecstasy, which implies an obliteration of the self, however, devekut is described by Schneur Zalman as a heightening or illumination of the self with a divine presence. Further, although this presence may overwhelm, it does not eradicate the self's identity.

In the Tanya, Schneur Zalman differentiated various grades of attachment to the divine. Devekut of a certain degree, he states, is possible to attain solely through intellectual contemplation and study; it is also possible to attain solely through enacting the Commandments or by participating in a ritual ignorant of its true meaning, provided one does so with the proper intention and passion. However, devekut of the highest sort is possible only by combining the head with the heart so that the whole person would be engaged in enthusiastic divine service (Schneur Zalman 1968:100).

Devekut is achieved in four separate stages, likened to the four worlds emanating from the En-Sof. Borrowing the metaphor of Jacob's ladder, Schneur Zalman regards the rungs or stages of the ladder as steps on which the benoni, who begins on the lowest rung, can progress incrementally upward and closer to the intellect of the divine source and inward to the depth of his or her feeling.

Climbing the first rung involves merely reciting the prayers or performing the Commandments (Mindel 1973, 2:110–11). The second rung constitutes a stage of introspection and self-evaluation, where one repents for sins committed both knowingly and unknowingly. The third stage consists of avodah (work, hard labor, service), where traits that carry with them vestiges of the animal soul—such as anger, pride, or arrogance—are worked on and refined. The fourth stage is union with the divine. Here, the material world and the distractions of the animal soul fall away while the divine soul in the human is released and "sprouts wings to soar heavenward" (1973, 2:115).

It is primarily within the area of intellect versus emotion that Habad philosophy differs markedly from other forms of Hasidism. Certainly, it is the most important point of contention that brought Schneur Zalman into conflict with both the opponents of Hasidism and with this movement's early leaders. According to Habad philosophy, the human intellect exists closest to the divine intellect, the highest of all of the powers. Therefore, for any unity between human and divine to exist, an intellectual communication is of the essence. Thus, the benoni as described in the Tanya is neither the ignorant, simple Jew of the Talmudic imagination nor the unemotional, rational scholar decried by the Ba'al Shem Tov. Rather, the benoni of Schneur Zalman's philosophy is an average, reasonably thinking person—not necessarily a highly educated one—whose love of God enables him or her to infuse each daily act, no matter how trivial or profound, with a balance of both intelligence and passion. When a person performs a divine Commandment, or precept, with a true understanding of its meaning and context within Jewish law, or when study is done with real focus and passion, like that normally saved for ritual, true union with the divine takes on an even greater significance, power, and beauty.

Perhaps the greatest contribution of Schneur Zalman's Habad Hasidism to kabbalistic thought is its emphasis on the mystic potential of the ordinary human personality, where all of the attributes of God's divine and profane emanations exist. Mystic knowledge of God, earlier seen as something outside human existence (or only for the enlightened few) became, in the teachings of Schneur Zalman, an essentially humanizing and democratizing phenomenon.

Notes

1. There are three main forms of Judaism practiced today: Orthodox, Conservative, and Reform, the last two having developed primarily in nineteenth-century Europe in reaction to Orthodoxy, or strict observance. The term "Orthodox" was not used until the eighteenth century, when it was adopted to distinguish its followers' practices from those of the Hasidim. Hasidism is considered by "mainstream" Jews to be a mystical extension of Orthodoxy, while Hasidim simply consider themselves Orthodox, or observant, in that they take seriously, and adhere to with utmost intensity, the many laws that regulate their lives. Much of the liturgy and religious practice, including music, is shared between Orthodox and Hasidic Jews. For example, Hasidim follow the same liturgical and festival calendar as mainstream Orthodox and adhere to the same basic laws as outlined in the Torah and its many commentaries. Unlike most other Ashkenazic Jews (those from Central and Eastern Europe), to whom they are related linguistically and culturally, however, Hasidim also follow the Sephardic (North African, Spanish) Jewish tradition of interspersing their own poetic texts and songs within specific ceremonies or services. For good summaries of Hasidic thought and history, see Buber (1948; 1966), Hundert (1991), Mahler (1985), Mintz (1992), Newman (1963), and Nigal (1994).

2. Many of the towns, villages, and cities mentioned here were sometimes part of Poland and Lithuania; but as a result of various partitions and treaties, they are all now part of present-day Russia, Belarus, or Ukraine.

3. See Harris (1985) for an excellent history of this period.

4. The similarity of this idea to the Neoplatonist Plotinus's theory is fully explored in Goodman (1992).

5. Lubavitchers frequently cite the big bang theory in physics as evidence for the breaking of the vessels.

4

"Here It Is Both Easier and Harder to Live": The Contemporary Community

Crown Heights lies in the heart of Brooklyn, New York, just south of Bedford Stuyvesant and east of Prospect Park. The Crown Heights Lubavitcher community of roughly 1,500 families—a family consisting of two parents and perhaps six to ten children—lives within easy walking distance of the main Lubavitcher institutions, the yeshivahs, heders (schools), the mikvah (ritual bath), various kosher eateries, Jewish-owned and Jewish-run shops, and, of course, the main synagogue and meeting place at 770 Eastern Parkway (fig. 8). The Crown Heights community is now recognized as the Lubavitcher world headquarters; and adherents, numbering around 150,000 worldwide, recognize the Rebbe, Menachem Mendel Schneerson, as their spiritual leader.[1]

The Lubavitcher court, or dynasty, is but one of many Hasidic courts that survived World War II and eventually resettled in the United States, Israel, and elsewhere. According to Lis Harris, there are approximately 250,000 Hasidim living today throughout the world, about 100,000 of whom reside in Brooklyn. Although Lubavitchers are the largest group worldwide, they are a relatively small group in Brooklyn, numbering about 15,000. Other courts, such as the Satmar (who, at 45,000, are the largest group in Brooklyn) and the Gerer, Bobover, and Belzer (numbering altogether about another 35,000), have well-established communities in the Williamsburg and Boro Park sections (Harris 1985:12–13; Poll 1962).

Lubavitcher Hasidim believe in the literal truth of the Bible and in a direct and intimate contact with the divine through devekut, the ecstatic state, described in chapter 3. The purpose of one's life as a Hasid is to be perpetually connected to the divine by adhering literally to the *mitzvot*, the 613 com-

Figure 8. A glimpse of the Crown Heights neighborhood (photograph by the author, 1991)

mandments or precepts given in the first five books of the Bible, or Torah,[2] and by following the interpretations of these precepts as set forth in various other philosophical texts.

For example, Hasidim follow a vast collection of laws, codified in the Mishna, compiled from oral tradition through roughly 200 C.E., as well as the many interpretations of these laws, collected in the Gemarra.[3] Unlike the 613 commandments that are written in the Torah, the laws and their interpretations represent roughly 5,000 years of oral tradition, those rules that observant Jews have used for centuries—and continue to use—to regulate their everyday behaviors and interactions with their families, neighbors, business associates, rabbis, and strangers. More than anything else, the Talmud is a living history of and commentary on the essential tenets of Judaism as practiced on the ground level of everyday experience.

Lubavitchers also adhere to the customs and regulations outlined in the Shulhan Arukh (1564), a text written by Joseph Caro, a sixteenth-century Spanish kabbalist, and reinterpreted by their founder, Schneur Zalman. Together, these laws govern every aspect of life—from explicit prayer practices and business ethics to the most intimate details of domestic life—and provide a set structure to the day, week, month, season, and year, as well as to all human and divine interactions. Lubavitchers also follow the standard calendar and liturgy as practiced by other Orthodox Ashkenazic Jews, with added prayers and interpolations from the Sephardic liturgy and poetic literature. In addition, they have added certain festive days that celebrate important events in their own court's history. No matter how dispersed, however, all Lubavitcher communities regard Crown Heights as their spiritual center. It is here that the Rebbe lives and prays, where the great farbrengens occur, and where one comes to marry and start a family. Being physically close to the Rebbe helps to raise one spiritually, and living in Crown Heights is something of a status marker.

Contemporary Lubavitchers, as well as other Hasidic groups, are distinguished from other Orthodox Jews and from the rest of the American population by distinctive dress, language, demeanor, and by a strict social organization that structures and regulates internal social interactions as well all dealings with the secular world. In fact, it is precisely this difference, prescribed by Jewish law, that is both a source of pride and honor within the group and something of an embarrassment to many around them, especially to nonpracticing Jews, who generally regard Hasidim as throwbacks to the peasant culture of their grandparents and great-grandparents from the shtetl. For example, although most contemporary Lubavitchers were born in this country and speak English, Yiddish, the language of Eastern Europe, is still the primary language spoken in the home, especially by males. All, except the most recent newcomers to the group, have been reading Hebrew since childhood, and many speak two or three other languages.

Lubavitchers recognize, and at times revel in, their distinctiveness. Often invoking the metaphor of the fence, they see their distinctive behaviors and appearance as a form of double protection. A fence, they say, has two sides; it protects both what is precious within and guards against the forces that threaten from without. But the fence is not solid, like a wall; it is built with spaces—not so many that the fence is weakened, but enough so that one can see through it to the outside or pull something through it to the inside. The metaphor of the fence and its importance to the lives of individual Lubavitchers are summarized beautifully in this passage taken from a Lubavitcher Internet posting, "Chabad-Lubavitch in Cyberspace":[4]

> When a gardener wants to protect his vegetables, he builds a fence around his field. The fence keeps harmful animals out of his garden. He makes sure to shut the latch every time he enters or leaves and feels confident that nothing will harm his vegetables.

The same applies to us as Jews. A person may begin to feel that he might make a mistake and not fulfill a Mitzvah properly. Therefore, he builds a "fence" to protect himself from anything that may cause him to disobey or not fulfill the Mitzvah. That "fence" will keep out anything "harmful" to fulfilling the Mitzvah. HaShem [God] created many wonderful things in this world which He wants us to enjoy and use properly. If used improperly they can cause us harm.

Take wine, for example: HaShem gave wine a special delicate taste that makes a person feel good. He commanded us to use it for Kiddush [prayer] or festive occasions. It adds to the holiday spirit. A person who drinks too much wine could become drunk and unable to think clearly. While in such a state he may do the wrong thing. A person who is worried that even a bit of wine can cause him to become lightheaded and possibly lead him to sin, may decide to build a "fence" around himself. In this way he will protect himself from going against the Torah. But how do you build a "fence" around yourself? The person who wishes to do so, decides not to drink any wine or even eat grapes. The "fence" that protects him from possibly doing wrong, is his decision not to drink any wine at all.

Perhaps the two essential features that best describe the Lubavitcher community as a whole, however, are its devotion and commitment: to Jewish law, to prayer and the fulfillment of the divine precepts, to paving a way for *Moshiach* (the Messiah), and to the Rebbe, considered both the spiritual head of the earthly community and its channel to the divine. There is no distinction in Lubavitcher life between sacred and secular, work and prayer, family and community. All of one's actions and relationships have a divine purpose.

Although most of the men and unmarried women work outside the home, they do so largely within the community as shopkeepers, real-estate agents, printers, teachers in the many Lubavitcher-run schools, or as administrative assistants to the Rebbe or other Lubavitcher leaders. Women, especially single women, have a certain flexibility in their working lives, and some commute to Manhattan or to other parts of Brooklyn to work. After marriage, a woman will continue to work, usually within the community, to support her husband's Torah study, until the care of children becomes too time-consuming. There is, however, for either men or women, no talk of career as in secular society—one's career is to devote oneself to God's purpose, to do teshuvah (repentance), and to create a stable and, hopefully, large family.

Outside Brooklyn, the Habad House—usually the house where the Lubavitcher shaliach (emissary) lives—is considered the center of Lubavitcher activity within a community. Often located on or near a college or university campus, it is a safe and openly inviting place where any Jewish person can go for a warm meal or a bed, and where visitors can come for a Sabbath meal when in the community over a weekend. Often, Habad Houses also act as places of refuge for battered women, for troubled college students, or for those with substance abuse problems.

When a newly established Lubavitcher community becomes large enough to encompass a few city blocks, its boundaries are marked by an *eruv* (border, fence): a thin wire, strung high above the streets, that creates a sacred space within its borders. The eyruv acts as both a literal and symbolic boundary, separating and protecting the community from the contaminating space of the secularized, non-Hasidic world. Within the eyruv, members of the community are free to pass without incident; and certain restrictions, such as carrying objects on the Sabbath, are eased.

Men and Women

Lubavitchers, as well as all Hasidic and Orthodox Jews, make a primary distinction between the differing roles that men and women play in relation to each other, to the community, and to God. As in many traditional societies, men and women are publicly separated in most social and religious contexts, as they are regarded as sexual distractions to each other. Within Hasidic culture, various social codes, laws, and practices have developed over time that ensure social and sexual stability within the group.

Early education and socialization of Lubavitcher children prepare them for their future adult roles.[5] Although both boys and girls receive a Jewish and secular education, and educational standards are high compared to the public school system in the United States, boys attend school for more hours in the day than girls and are expected to become learned scholars able to interpret, argue, and comment on all aspects of Jewish law. Girls focus primarily on the Bible, on Jewish dietary laws, and on secular subjects such as Hebrew and English. Most boys go on to a yeshivah, then to a rabbinical school, and eventually become rabbis, although they do not usually take on separate congregations within the community. Girls, on graduation from high school, do have the option to continue their education in a woman's seminary; but as Harris points out, "it is probably fair to say that there is no serious expectation of turning out scholars of distinction from the girl's schools" (Harris 1985:189).

Following marriage, a Lubavitcher man usually continues his studies; his wife might work in various Lubavitcher-run businesses or schools to financially support her husband's education. By the time children have arrived, most Lubavitcher men are established in their own work, often as business-men or teachers, and most women are now at home, spending any free time working on the many outreach and educational programs for Lubavitcher women worldwide. While it is true that adult men take a more active and public role in the ritual aspects of Hasidic life, women are seen as fulfilling a higher level of commandment in bearing children, in teaching them hasides, and in protecting their husbands and homes from the secularizing influences of the outside world. Because women are expected to devote most of their time to childrearing and homemaking, they are exempt from all but three of the time-bound positive commandments, such as going to the synagogue at various times of the day to pray.[6] As a result, most married women do not attend farbrengens or daily or other prayer services, as their exemption from commandments of time and place have freed them to fulfill commandments in the home that have a higher spiritual value.

Lubavitchers locate the primary difference between men and women in the body: women are believed to be inherently more spiritual—and to be in a more spiritually sensitive position vis-à-vis others—than men because of their fertility and their ability to create new life, which puts them closer to God, and thus makes them more "naturally" and powerfully holy.

Women's superior spiritual status is protected by various laws that pro-hibit sexual relations and certain religious duties during a woman's menses and for seven days afterward (the laws of *niddah*). When a women takes on the status of niddah (excluded person), she is considered to be ritually impure.[7] As such, she is forbidden to enter the synagogue, to have sexual relations, to eat with or to pass food to her husband, among many other re-strictions. Men, when they dress and bury the dead, for example, are also con-sidered niddah and must, like menstruating women, be purified by immer-sion in a mikvah (ritual bath) before resuming regular social and sexual activities.

Adult behavior is also regulated by various laws of modesty, such as the law prohibiting a man from touching a woman who is not his wife. One Lubavitcher woman explained these prohibitions this way, again using the analogy of the fence:

> A women is very precious, and just like something that is very precious, you don't want it to be mutilated and you don't want it to be spoiled in any way. A woman is not to be mutilated and, according to Torah, she's mutilated if another man touches her. Therefore she is not supposed to be in a situation

where another man (other than her husband) might want to touch her which might lead to something more. Therefore, we have a lot of laws that are really like a fence around the actual thing. . . . A woman is not allowed to be sexually taken by another man, therefore there are many laws before that yet, [like] she may not be left alone in the house because maybe something would happen and the man would rape her, or they would get to like each other momentarily, and then decide to have relations. Especially if she's married—that's the worst thing in the world. . . . These are the fences around "don't touch this woman." (Sternberg interview)

Although applying to both sexes, the laws of tzniut (modesty) are seen as being primarily women's responsibility. Debra Kaufman quotes one of her informants as saying that tzniut meant having self-respect: "It is women who teach men to have this self-respect. They [women] have always been the model for men" (Kaufman 1991:145). Further, women must be doubly conscious of these laws, integrating them into their daily lives, as it is their responsibility to pass them on to both their female and male children:

These aren't really laws, but a way of life for us. For instance I may kiss my husband but I would never kiss my husband in front of the children because they know men and women don't kiss and when they're old enough to get married they will know that husbands and wives do kiss, but other men and women do not kiss. They might be too young to understand that we are husband and wife. In a religious home the beds must be separate. The husband and wife have twin beds, we have twin beds. My children have never seen a double bed. They don't even know that a husband and wife sleep in one bed. There is the letter of the law and there is the spirit of the law, and Hasidim go beyond just the letter of the law, we go to the spirit of the law. (Sternberg interview)

And, while men are regarded as naturally intellectual and not prone to emotional excess (it is something they have to work on), women are thought to be strongly emotional—a positive attribute on the one hand, because higher emotions spring from the right ventricle of the heart, which is closer to the divine soul, but a negative attribute on the other hand, if such emotions are expressed in an improper context. Thus, women, far more then men, are cautioned always to be aware of their surroundings and to act modestly, not only for their own protection but also for the protection of their families and the community at large. In this way, women can be likened to the fence that simultaneously protects what is precious within and what threatens from without.

Concentric Circles of Spirituality

One way to look at Lubavitcher society that cuts across typical sociological categories and, in fact, comes closer to a Lubavitcher conception is to regard this community as an embedded set of concentric circles, with the Rebbe at the center. Each circle surrounding the Rebbe is measured in terms of both its closeness to the center (i.e., its amount of holiness, spirituality, and light) and, conversely, its nearness to the outside (non-Jewish, "contaminated," darkened) society. The ever-widening circles are dynamic in that they inter-act and are in constant transition; yet the structure as a whole, like that of the ten sefirot discussed in chapter 3, remains stable.

The Rebbe at the Center

One of the main distinctions between Hasidic and mainstream Orthodox Jews is the Hasidic Jews' devotion to their Rebbe. He is at the center of the community, one foot in the everyday world and the other in the divine, a man who both elevates his people and brings down the godly soul to them. Thus, he is the literal head of his community and is located, spiritually, closer to the divine head than his followers. Yet his feet must also be on the ground. He should be a part of this world, remaining completely accessible to his community, always available to answer questions of the most mundane sort. Most Lubavitchers seek his advice when marrying, choosing a job, or mov-ing to a new city. Although he previously granted interviews to anyone who wished them, he now handles all requests by mail. Many of his close associ-ates also act as secretaries, answering mail and keeping track of the many outreach and educational institutions developed during his reign.

The Rebbe is often praised for his ability to relate to all members of his community equally. Espousing relatively liberal ideas (compared to those of other contemporary Hasidic leaders) concerning the education of women, the rights of children, and the spiritual value of even those who have fallen away from the teachings of the Torah, the Rebbe is seen as a supreme communica-tor, perhaps unique in his capacity for understanding and compassion. When I interviewed Hirshel Gansbourg, one of the Rebbe's closest associates, he stat-ed that "the most interesting thing about the Rebbe is that the Rebbe under-stands exactly the life of the young people, the old people, of children—he can relate to them. You wouldn't find another leader in the world [like that]. Some can relate either to labor people, or to people in business or to people in the scientific world. Here you have a person who relates to everyone."

The Rebbe tries to remain in personal contact with his Crown Heights community on a weekly, if not daily, basis. For example, in addition to the Saturday evening farbrengens, on Sunday afternoons the Rebbe stands at the door of his office, often for many hours, handing out dollar bills to long lines of women and children waiting at the door. He does this to encourage the practice of *tzeddakah* (charity), one of the central tenets of Jewish philosophy. People from the community, as well as hundreds of others from all parts of Brooklyn or Manhattan, wait in line for the privilege of meeting the Rebbe face-to-face, if only for an instant, and having him say a blessing. Most people immediately give the dollar to one of the many women carrying tin tzeddakah cans filled with bills and rattling coins that wait outside the door. Others, especially those visiting the community for the first time, have their dollars laminated with a picture of the Rebbe and a small prayer imprinted into the plastic (fig. 9).

The Rebbe, accessible to all, and the holiest and most spiritually elevated

Figure 9. A Lubavitcher-laminated dollar bill (photograph by the author, 1999)

of men in this generation, is also viewed as inseparable from his community, belonging both spiritually and materially to his people. All that is his belongs to the community, as his role in the religious and social lives of the community far outweighs his individual, personal needs. For example, although he commands a large budget for outreach and educational activities—"'around' 50 million dollars," according to Lis Harris (Harris 1985:107)—he personally receives no salary for his work, other than a small stipend for living expenses. Thus, the Rebbe, at the spiritual center of his community, is materially much like any other Lubavitcher—hardworking and living simply.

Although the lines between the Rebbe and the community are frequently blurred, and one's holiness is often measured in terms of spiritual closeness to him, Lubavitchers also stress the importance of independent thought and action. They bridle at the common stereotype that they are sheep in the Rebbe's flock, simply following his orders, bowing to his advice, or using him as their sole link to the divine. Instead, they say that although their spiritual identity is associated with that of their Rebbe, it is one's own responsibility to find spiritual fulfillment. They distinguish themselves from other Hasidim by stressing their own individual ties with Torah learning and with everyday decision making, likening their Rebbe more to a guide than to a commander.

The Rebbe's Circle

The Rebbe surrounds himself with close advisers, those men (and some women) that he has known throughout his life and that he trusts implicitly. This group consists primarily of lifetime Lubavitchers, most of whom can trace their lineages back to the time of Schneur Zalman and the Ba'al Shem Tov. Many are personally related to the Rebbe. One might refer to this small circle as an extended family, the closest and most trusted of social and spiritual colleagues.

The members of the Rebbe's circle effectively form a Lubavitcher executive committee and work with him on important projects that involve the whole community, such as education, outreach, and various forms of welfare. The circle is also frequently involved in local, state, and federal governmental lobbying, such as the campaign in the early 1980s mounted by the Lubavitcher community and its "ambassador," Rabbi Abraham Shemtov, in Washington, D.C. The community successfully lobbied to have the federal government declare the Crown Heights Hasidim a disadvantaged group, one that had suffered "severe economic problems because of discrimination" (Severo 1984:B5) and was thus eligible for government funding, a situation that has aggravated many in the non-Hasidic communities of Crown Heights.

Esther Sternberg is one of the most influential women in the Rebbe's circle. A lifetime Lubavitcher, she can trace her lineage back to the beginning of the Hasidic movement: "I, thank God, was born to a very beautiful family, a very Hasidic family, going back all the generations, on both sides. My father is from a Lubavitch community from Russia, so he has a lineage that goes back all the way to Lubavitch. My mother does not come from a Lubavitch home, but from a very religious home, from a very famous dynasty of great Rabbis" (Sternberg interview).

Sternberg is one of the leaders of the Lubavitcher Woman's Organization, a group founded in the early 1950s, along with the Lubavitcher Youth Organization, to help in the Rebbe's outreach and charity projects.[8] The Woman's Organization, says Sternberg, is divided into a "department of the interior," which helps observant women within the community with various marital and social problems, and a "department of the exterior," which teaches newly observant women the various rules of family purity, how to keep a kosher home (complete with cookbooks), and provides afternoon tutoring sessions in Hebrew and Hasidic laws and customs.

One of this group's largest projects is the candle-lighting program that Sternberg has run for the past sixteen years. Interested in recruiting "intellectual women—lawyers, doctors, people who are busy"—the Woman's Organization routinely places an advertisement in the New York Times (paid for by a donor) that gives the proper time for lighting Sabbath candles on Friday evening and a phone number to call to get candles. As Sternberg reflects, "these kinds of women are not at home—we have to go out to them" (Sternberg interview).

In addition to living members of the community, the Rebbe's circle is also inhabited by Lubavitchers who have passed on. For example, the Rebbe regularly visits the graves of his wife and father-in-law, the former Rebbe, to whom he talks freely. He has often left books and other materials for the former Rebbe to read (Harris 1985:106). Indeed, one of the major goals of singing nigunim at farbrengens is to invoke the presence of a holy ancestor.

The ongoing and intimate relationship that Lubavitchers have with their ancestors is often expressed metaphorically through reference to the same three levels of the body mentioned earlier in the discussion of Habad philosophy. The present generation, say contemporary Lubavitchers, only rises spiritually when it has passed into history. Thus, each generation gains more and more spirituality as it moves farther away from the present and closer to past generations, such as that of Schneur Zalman—or, by extension, those of the Ba'al Shem Tov and Moses, the latter being a level seen as analogous to the head of the body. The present generation, although perpetually preparing the way for *Moshiach* (Messiah) to come, is still hopelessly caught in the mundane world, the lowest spiritually and analogous to the heel of the foot. It is only through the heart—seen as the seat of the vital, animal soul and the emotions, where the heel and head intersect in fervent and enthusiastic prayer—that the possibility of spiritual elevation and reconnection with the past exists in this generation.

The Wider Lubavitcher Community: Lubavitchers from Birth and Ba'alei Teshuvah

Many Lubavitchers now living in Crown Heights were born into Hasidism, and many come from powerful Hasidic lineages that extend back to Eastern Europe and to the eighteenth century. In this country, in the late 1960s and 1970s, Hasidism, especially Habad Hasidism, saw the growth of the ba'al teshuvah movement, which resulted in a heavy influx of new, predominantly American-born, middle-class Jews, who wished to return to Orthodoxy. Ba'alei teshuvah often describe themselves as being on a perpetual journey inward and upward toward spirituality. This journey takes years of study and contemplation; and it parallels, if on a different plane, the spiritual journey of Lubavitchers who have been *frumm* (observant) from birth.

New adherents undergo an intense and protracted assimilation process, involving total immersion in Torah, Hebrew, and philosophical studies, scholarly areas in which they are believed to be lacking. In addition, they may receive counseling and other forms of spiritual and psychological help along the way to provide for a smoother transition into observant life. Unlike the practice in contemporary cults, with which Hasidim are often compared, a new adherent is, at least theoretically, free to come and go and many remain undecided for years. Of course, there is often considerable pressure (from family, community, and, perhaps, the Rebbe) exerted on those wishing to leave. But, at any given farbrengen, one is likely to see a vast array of people at different stages of this process, from the mildly curious to those who have made a serious commitment to becoming more observant.

The relationship between the Lubavitcher from birth and the ba'al teshuvah is an interesting and complex one. Most people born into the community try not to make too much of a distinction between the groups, while many ba'alei teshuvah use it as something of an emblem. The tension between these views is relieved somewhat by the humorous nicknames given by the ba'alei teshuvah to themselves, "BTs", and to their counterparts who were born to Hasidism, "FFBs" (frumm from birth), "frummies," even "lifers." It is usually with marriage—often to another ba'al teshuvah—and the birth of children that ba'alei teshuvah are truly integrated into the community. Ba'alei teshuvah now comprise the majority both in the Crown Heights and worldwide Lubavitcher community. A Lubavitcher from birth expresses his views on the distinction:

I personally don't like it when a person walks in and introduces himself by saying, "I'm a ba'al teshuvah." And I don't like it when somebody turns around and says, "You know—he's a ba'al teshuvah." Even though it's a fact and he's proud of it, and he should be proud of it. I *should* be a ba'al teshuvah. Everybody has to do teshuvah. There's something wrong with this term. *He's* a ba'al teshuvah and I'm not? I personally don't like the wording. I wish I was a ba'al teshuvah. I have a neighbor there who's a ba'al teshuvah, and a neighbor here who is what they call a "lifer" in the community. This is the term that ba'al teshuvahs made. They call themselves ba'alei teshuvah, and that guy's a "lifer." Let me tell you, since Lubavitch has been around there was always a Lubavitcher and a guy who was not necessarily a Lubavitcher, but a different Hasid, so he would be seen as someone who came into the community. That is the distinction I make. (Schneerson interview)

Many "lifers" look on "BTs" as odd or unusual, in that they must give up so much to become religious, Schneerson continues:

They are looked upon as holier than us, because they became ba'alei teshuvah. That's the way the Talmud looks at them, the way hasides looks at them. I turn around and I see people sometimes, and I say, "Why, why would a person like that become a ba'al teshuvah? He's got it all. Why would he bring hardship on himself like that?" It's tough to be a Jew and it's tough to be an Orthodox Jew. It's tough. Everything has to be perfect. So why would anyone choose this because of all the things you have to do. He lives on Long Island, he has a nice house, he lives with decent people, why would he want to move to Crown Heights? It's a tough life in Crown Heights.

On the other hand, ba'alei teshuvah regard the lifetime Lubavitchers as privileged, lucky to have been born in an environment where learning the laws and practices of hasides are second nature, almost too much so, as seen in the following statement from a ba'alat teshuvah: "When you grow up in a family where *Yiddishkeit* [Jewishness] is new to the parents as well, you don't have the tradition, it's not relaxed—we don't know what rules are relaxed and normal and OK. People [born into it] are probably more relaxed about the laws than we are. They just relax. It's normal, but it doesn't necessarily mean that it's good" (Rosenberger interview).

Some ba'alei teshuvah, especially those relatively new to the community, resist labeling altogether:

> I'm not a *member* of this community. We don't have *members* of this community. There are all sorts of ways to be a Habad person, to be connected or involved. . . . You can be living off the energy anywhere. I sense I've been using this energy beam for a long time, but I never was comfortable and still have a hard time with one energy label. And then I comfort myself by saying, well the Rebbe always talks about just Jews, you're a Jew, everybody is a Jew, and that's when I relax because I wasn't born with a sticker around my neck. . . . For me, it's not like becoming something out of nothing. (Tampkin interview)

One important responsibility given primarily to the ba'alei teshuvah is that of outreach. It is common for the Rebbe to send a shaliach to a far-off community (e.g., Grinnell, Iowa; Durban, South Africa; Rochester, New York) to open a Habad House or to begin making a presence within the community.[9] Ba'alei teshuvah are said to have more energy; and, as they are closer to their nonobservant roots, their energy to pull away from those roots can be harnessed more easily and converted to a *mitzvah* (a blessing, such as bringing someone else closer to hasides). Further, often far removed from Crown Heights, the shaliach's secularized roots are less likely to affect the spiritual purity of the central Lubavitcher core.

Some ba'alei teshuvah, at the beginning of their journey to Orthodoxy, find it difficult to give up former freedoms, and some express difficulties with their previous families' not accepting their decision to live a religious life. One woman complained that her husband did not help enough with the children; another sat scratching her head where the elastic of her wig had dug into her scalp and groused with good humor about how hot the *sheitle* (head covering) can get in the late-summer, New York sun. A young man, clearly exhausted after a long day of "running around," complained that he now did a lot more work than he had ever done as a computer programmer "on the outside." Generally, though, most ba'alei teshuvah take their new lives more or less in stride, and complaints are generally dismissed with good humor.

Other Hasidim

The relationship between Lubavitchers and other Hasidim is ambivalent. All Hasidim ultimately trace their beginnings to the teachings of the Ba'al Shem Tov, and all share certain core beliefs and practices. Certain courts are recognized as especially pious (Satmarers), learned (Lubavitchers), or musical (Bobovers); yet all courts share a similar worldview and set of legal and moral precedents, with God and their Rebbe at the center. Major differences lie in the histories, languages, and cultures of the different courts that formed throughout Eastern Europe after the death of the Ba'al Shem Tov, in different views surrounding the political and religious status of Israel, and in attitudes toward such practices as outreach.

Occasionally, clashes in ideology result in aggression or violence. In the mid-1970s, for example, I was aware that tensions existed between the Lubavitchers of Crown Heights and their Hasidic neighbors, the Satmarers of Williamsburg. I would hear stories told with much hilarity by Lubavitchers of their "mitzvah tanks,"[10] wired up with huge speakers, sent into the Satmar community blaring Lubavitcher nigunim, much as Lubavitchers had sung their music before the invading armies of Napoleon. There would also be stories circulating in the Lubavitcher community that a Satmarer would occasionally cross the line into Crown Heights and consult an especially learned Lubavitcher rabbi (any recruitment from the Satmarer community was met with much satisfaction). The first physical attacks on Lubavitchers by Satmarers occurred in 1977 (Harris 1985:180).

By the 1980s, tensions had increased. In 1983, a Lubavitcher Hasid was stoned by a Satmarer while walking through Williamsburg, and an older, well-respected rabbi was beaten, had his beard cut off,[11] and received death threats. The main source of the tension was, and still is, the Lubavitcher position regarding the legitimacy of the state of Israel.[12] In the Orthodox tradition, the state of Israel cannot be restored until the coming of the (Jewish) Messiah. Many Orthodox and Hasidic Jews regard Zionism as a true political and religious threat. The idea that Israel could exist independently as a political entity without the Messiah is unthinkable. Lubavitchers, though, take a more middle-of-the road stance regarding the legitimacy of Israel: although they do not consider themselves Zionists, they are pro-Israel. Lis Harris quotes a

Lubavitcher spokesman as saying, "we are Jews and Israel is a land of Jews (Harris 1985:180)."

On the Fence: Secular Jews

On the spiritual border or fence that separates the Lubavitcher community as a whole from the outside are so-called secular, or nonpracticing, Jews, those people who still identify themselves as Jewish but who have, in the Lubavitcher view, fallen away from Jewish religious precepts and practices. Because Lubavitchers conceptualize all Jews as part of the same body, they regard their secularized counterparts as simply uninformed, naive, and too easily swayed by the temptations of the secular world, with its drugs, free sex, and disregard for morality. To recover a holy spark, one must return such a person to the main body of Jewry. Secularized Jews have potential, say Lubavitchers, but they must first renounce their present lives to reenter the sacred. Aiding in that process is performing a mitzvah.

Scene: "Fighting with Chaya"

It is 1975, and I am in Crown Heights for the summer. The Rosenblums, whom I first met in 1973, and with whom I have been working, have convinced me that I must live in Brooklyn for a while, and they have set me up with various hosts. I have moved from family to family, each trying in its own way to help me better understand Lubavitcher life and music. Because I am young, unmarried, and definitely not frumm, I have been sent mainly to ba'alei teshuvah homes. The BTs have more energy and patience. They can stand the constant questioning from a person on the outside.

I have lived with some "interesting" people. For a few weeks, I was placed with three young women, mostly my age, who had come to Crown Heights in various ways. One had been on drugs for a while and had been taken in by a Lubavitcher family on her college campus. One had lived for three years alone on an island eating grains and roots and had suddenly decided to give it all up and "try Lubavitch." One had been in an abusive marriage; while fleeing her husband, she had seen, just by chance, a picture of the Rebbe in an airport. She had been so taken with the compassion in his eyes that she had come immediately to Crown Heights.

Why had the Rosenblums suggested I stay here with these people? Did I seem troubled? I could understand why these women had stayed. Crown Heights offered a certain safety, a sense of community that they had lost or never had. People took you in, fed you, gave you a place to sleep, worried about your soul. It was comforting, if sometimes smothering, but it had its attractions.

Now I was going to live with a newlywed BT couple who had one child, a boy, Schmuel. Actually, Chaya,[13] his mother, had been married before, and Schmuel was from the previous marriage. After leaving her first husband, Chaya had somehow made her way to Crown Heights and had joined the Lubavitcher community. She seems happy. Her son, now about eight, is the pride of the family: he has an uncommonly strong and beautiful voice for his age and can imitate the subtle slides and ornamentations of the best adult singers with eerie perfection.

Chaya is quite an interesting person. She has a master's degree in social work and is well read, especially in the growing literature of the new women's movement. She is attractive and intelligent, with a wonderful sense of humor. Is she really happy here? She seems to understand, better than most, the tension between the secular world of her youth and the sacralized world that she now inhabits. She is firmly committed to Orthodoxy and treats my questions with respect, not the usual benevolent tolerance.

Chaya, however, is on a campaign. She is trying to convince me to marry the man with whom I am living (who is not Jewish) and come to Crown Heights to live. She says it is a sign from *Ha-Shem* (God) that I love music, because music is the quickest route to God's ear. "It's the pen of the soul," she tells me. "You're already halfway there simply because you know music. Don't you want to make the first commitment to Torah? Living with a man outside of marriage is a sin. It makes you feel bad."

I am in somewhat of an awkward situation here. I am in the middle of fieldwork and trying hard to resist the constant pressure from Chaya and others to become more Orthodox; at the same time, I am trying to maintain some sense of neutrality while absorbing ideas that are vastly different from mine (and sometimes pretty strange). I suppose I could be more tolerant if Chaya were not always trying to get me to see how empty my own life is. I am not here to question my *own* life but to find out about hers. From her point of view, though, she is trying honestly to engage me in a moral and philosophical discussion that will have ethical consequences for my life, and I am trying to interview her and her son about music. She seems hesitant about confiding in me about her musical and spiritual life because I am making no effort to move closer to spirituality myself. She is sensing that this is an uneven exchange, and I am facing my first truly awkward moment in fieldwork.

"Ellen, when you are with this man" (she never uses my partner's real name), "do you really feel whole? Honest? At peace? The fact that he's not Jewish is not the problem so much as that you're not married. When are you getting married?" This goes on day after day. It is becoming tedious. I am trying not to get angry at her constant badgering. After all, I reason, I must control myself and remain neutral if I am to continue my research. But this situation is getting uncomfortable. "Why does it matter to you so much what my lifestyle is like," I ask. "I'm not evaluating your lifestyle, I'm just trying to understand it. You're not really trying to understand me."

"I understand, all right," she says with a sly glint in her eye. "I was in your place a few years ago. I understand about sexual attraction and 'living together.' It makes you feel dirty."

"It doesn't make *me* feel dirty," I say a little too defensively. I am beginning to lose patience. "You know, Chaya, I'm getting pretty sick and tired of your incessant judging of me. I am happy living the way I am, and I don't really care what you think of me as a person." (Whoops!) "In all the time I've been here, I've never really told you what I think, personally, of the way you live. I don't have the same belief system you do. I wouldn't and don't choose to live like this. But, I've kept my mouth shut." (Until now.) "I've tried to respect your way of life, and I'd appreciate it if you'd try to respect mine!"

We are both angry. I have completely lost my objectivity, and she is beginning to sense she has lost the battle for my soul. We go on, more warily now. Soon, I move on to another house.

～

In the Lubavitcher view, the category of secularized Jews contains literally all Jews who are not Hasidic. They form a vast reservoir of Jewish potential and are the obvious targets of Lubavitcher recruitment. For years, emissaries have been sent to college campuses and busy streetcorners, shouting from their "mitzvah tanks," "Are you Jewish?" In a *New York Times* article of November 10, 1974, a young Lubavitcher is quoted as saying, "we call them tanks because they're our tanks against assimilation. With them we can knock over any obstacle in our path" (Schultz 1974:34; see fig. 10).

Startled Jewish passersby are cajoled into unwanted conversations, and some are frankly annoyed by the overt Jewishness of these young, bearded men or, perhaps, are embarrassed by their "hustling." Anyone showing the slightest bit of interest is immediately taken inside the "tank" and shown, if male, how to put on tefillin and, if female, how to light Shabbos candles. Most people hurry away. Those that remain are invited to a Habad House for a

Figure 10. A Lubavitcher mitzvah tank (photograph by the author, 1978)

Sabbath meal, and those who continue to come are urged to visit Crown Heights or to study in one of the many Lubavitcher schools.

At times, the secular and observant Jewish worlds collide in very personal ways, especially for ba'alei teshuvah. Frequently, other family members do not understand the ba'al teshuvah's need for more Orthodox religious practice. Some have been fully ostracized from their secular families, who regard Lubavitchers as akin to such cults as the "Moonies" of the Unification Church or the Hare Krishnas, while others have maintained uneasy relations with family members. Henches Gansbourg, an older ba'alat teshuvah, told me in an interview that when she visits her grown, married children, who are not observant, she must take all her food, already prepared, with her and use her own separate dishes while cooking. She says that the alternative is simply not to see her children at all.

Outside the Circle

All non-Jews are considered to be outside the set of concentric circles of spirituality, part of a world that is contaminated, impure, and to be avoided when possible. However, unlike the common stereotype of the insulated Hasid living in a world of books, Lubavitchers, more than other Hasidim, tend to interact more freely within their local communities.

Often, an outspoken rabbi can become embroiled in local or even national politics. One striking example of this occurred in Minnesota during the 1980s, when Andrea Dworkin and Catherine MacKinnon, leading radical feminists, were teaching at the University of Minnesota, in Minneapolis, and mounting their campaign against pornography. Two local Lubavitcher rabbis, Asher Zeilengold and Moshe Feller (head of the Bais Chana School for Women in St. Paul), became unexpected allies in the fight to draft a bill against pornography that focused on the civil rights of women in the workplace. Citing the effect of visual images on sexual and other behavior, Rabbi Feller stated that according to the teachings of the Torah, pornography debased the image of God; and thus, as women are created in God's image, pornography debased women (Tampkin interview).

Scene: "There Are Always Loopholes"

It is fall 1975, and I am still in Crown Heights, spending the holiday season with various Lubavitcher families. I have been placed with a nice couple, Freidi and Yitzhak, who have been patiently enduring my many questions. It is Simhat Torah, the festival celebrating the ending and beginning of the weekly Torah readings. This is the time described in the literature and pictured in so many Hasidic artworks, where the Rebbe and his followers dance wildly in the streets, holding the Torah scrolls high while shouting out nigunim.

I have been at the synagogue, off and on, for about four days, with very little sleep in between, and I am getting quite crabby. It is about 3:00 A.M., and I am hoping to walk home with a small group of people who seem to be in no hurry to leave. The place where I am staying is about four blocks from the synagogue. I can walk this myself, I reason: who else is up at 3:00 A.M.? A few people join me as I leave 770 and walk down Kingston Avenue. By the time we have covered two blocks, though, I am alone. I know the neighborhood is dangerous—I have been told this many times, but all seems quiet and peaceful in the languid fall night. I walk the third block without trouble.

I am approaching the fourth block when I hear something that sounds like chains rattling to my left. I look across the street and see a group of maybe six young boys, no older than ten or eleven. It crosses my mind that it is awfully late for these kids to be up. Maybe they are a group of Lubavitcher children also on the way home.

It is very quiet in the night. I hear one of the boys whisper in a stage voice, "Let's get her!" They race across the street and form a circle around me. I hear chains as the circle closes. I panic. This is a residential area of Brooklyn. Even if I manage to get to a door, who in his or her right mind would answer the bell or a frantic knock? These folks are too used to violent commotions outside; they will not come to the door.

There is a break in the circle, and I take it. Suddenly, a driveway appears, and I run toward a lit glass door. It is a hospital (what is a hospital doing there?), and I can see a guard. The kids follow at my heels but back off as the guard opens the door. I scoot in to safety. "Oh, God! That was close!"

"Yeah! No telling what they would do if they caught you. We have a lot of that around here. You calm down, I'm going to call the police."

The police arrive, and I give a statement. They offer to take me the rest of the way in the squad car. I refuse—it is Simhat Torah—no riding in cars. They cannot believe that I am being so stupid. Eventually, I give in and ride with them to the apartment. I crawl into bed, too upset to sleep, and lie waiting for Freidi and Yitzhak to come home. I hear the door open and I fly out into the living room, the words falling out of my mouth even before I am sure who is there. I am afraid to tell them that I rode in a car.

"How did you get home after the police arrived?" asks Freidi.

"Well . . . ah . . . the police brought me home. I'm really sorry I rode in a car! I know it's not allowed!" At this point, I break down.

"Ellen! You can always break a mitzvah [commandment] if your life is in danger! Of course it was right to ride home with the police! For these kinds of occasions, there are always loopholes!"

~

In Crown Heights, Lubavitchers share their neighborhood with African Americans, Korean Americans, and a host of other social and religious groups, and tensions between these groups have grown steadily since the 1970s. At various times, neighborhood coalitions have been formed, and attempts have been made to familiarize local police with Hasidic religious practices that may interfere with the flow of commerce or traffic; these efforts have been moderately successful in fending off much actual violence.

The whole world, however, became aware of Crown Heights in late August 1991, when a seven-year-old African American boy, Gavin Cato, was struck and killed by the driver of the Rebbe's car (Beck 1991). Within days, rioting broke out, and a young Australian rabbinical student, Yankel Rosenbaum, was stabbed to death "to avenge what [the African American community] considered a murder not an accident" (Minerbrook and Horn 1991:44). Four days of rioting ensued, with violence on both sides. Since 1991, neighborhood coalitions have been revived, but tensions still exist; and stories of the young black boy and the rabbinical student still circulate widely.

Although many Lubavitchers, especially young unmarried or recently married women, work outside of Crown Heights, friendships with non-Jews, even nonobservant Jews, are rare. Work may bring one into contact with non-Jews, but any form of interaction is limited due to stringent Lubavitcher religious and dietary practices and general distrust of non-Jews. Furthermore, nothing is taught to Lubavitcher children about other religious practices or beliefs, and most grow up with a general fear of difference.

On Becoming Modern: Negotiating the Borders

Lubavitchers make a distinction between the modern and the secular. While the secular life—with its lack of spirituality and focus-may lead to sexual freedom, drug use, violence, and other contemporary perils, modern life—with its abundance and relative religious and social freedom—contains much that is useful and desirable. Deciding which aspects of modern life pose no spiritual or social threat for the Lubavitcher community, and weeding them out from the chaotic surrounding environment, involves not only a reinterpretation of old laws in new contexts but also a steady, careful, and day-to-day negotiation with the secular.

For example, until the beginning of the ba'al teshuvah movement in the 1960s and 1970s, Yiddish was the common Hasidic language in this country. The process of learning and using English in many of the Lubavitcher-run schools can be seen as a form of negotiation, something worked out to achieve a positive, spiritual goal. To learn English, Hasidic immigrants from Eastern Europe had to associate, at least peripherally, with the non-Hasidic culture. Many non-Hasidic Jewish immigrants learned English at the same time they became Americanized. They attended English-language schools and began to intermarry and to assimilate into the preexisting Jewish culture. Hasidim, on the other hand, also learned English out of necessity, but they stopped short of total assimilation. Further, the use of English ensured the smooth passage for ba'alei teshuvah into the community. As one lifetime Lubavitcher, born in this country, notes: "There is a slight difference [today]. When we participate in our Friday night classes, we have to remember to talk in English, many don't understand Yiddish yet. My first language was Yiddish. When there is a mass meeting, there is someone shouting 'English, English.' Of course there are others shouting 'Yiddish,' because some of the older ones don't speak English. It usually ends up being English. For women it's all English" (Schneerson interview).

Living within a regulated world framed by strict observance of centuries-old religious beliefs and practices does not necessarily limit Lubavitchers from engaging with aspects of the non-Jewish, modern society of which they are now a part.[14] Indeed, the modernization of the community has been a conscious goal of the Rebbe; his relatively radical ideas (from the Hasidic point of view) concerning recruitment, education for women, and the protection of women's and children's rights have distinguished him as having pulled his community into the twentieth century.

Lubavitchers who have been born in the United States are many generations removed from the European shtetls of their grandparents and great-grandparents. However, unlike many Reform and Conservative Jews, who wish to shed their origins in this new secularized social context, Hasidim revel nostalgically in their connection to Eastern European shtetl life, often to the acute embarrassment of their more secular Jewish neighbors. In this way, they reenact and reconstruct life as they would have it be; in a very real sense, they remove the distance between generations in a conscious and deliberate attempt to integrate past and present.

Further, economic gains—in the form of more money and more opportunity for work, both within and outside the Lubavitcher community—have separated Lubavitchers in this generation from their ancestors in terms of social class, although not all families have reached true affluence. And, in creating the Lubavitcher status of the shaliach, the Rebbe has promoted a certain geographic mobility that has resulted in a vast network of Habad Houses throughout the United States. In short, rather than having weakened Lubavitcher religious practices, contact with the secular world has provided many new and creative opportunities to strengthen such practices.

One of the reasons the Lubavitcher community has been able to survive so well in the context of late-twentieth-century urban life lies in its ability to be flexible in its understanding of Torah and in its ability to reinterpret or refine ancient laws to fit new social contexts. The use of modern transportation, cooperation with local, non-Jewish crime-prevention groups, and involvement in various political issues concerning Israel and the worldwide Jewish community are not, say Lubavitchers, at odds with any of their strict religious practices.

One specific way that Lubavitchers, as opposed to other Hasidic groups, have leaped into the twentieth century has been through their creative use of modern technology. This has enabled them, like many similar groups on the religious right, to reach an ever-widening Jewish community through audio and video broadcasts and the skillful use of sophisticated computer technology. What has resulted over the past twenty years or so has been a burgeoning cable television, music, and video recording industry that imitates the slick, highly produced efforts of mainstream popular culture but stays well within the religious and social template of Lubavitcher culture. (See appendix 3 for a partial list of titles.)

Lubavitchers are frequently questioned about their obvious penchant for the latest electronic gadgets, the use of which (from an outside perspective) appears to be antithetical to strict religious observance. For example, a *New York Times* article from 1983, entitled "Rabbi Using Modern Medium in Call for Traditional Values," highlights this seeming inconsistency, stating: "Tomorrow night at 9:30, a four-hour address by the Hasidic rabbi [Menachem Mendel Schneerson] will reach electronically from Brooklyn to an orbiting Satcom satellite, where it will then be beamed to cable television systems around the country and in London and in Israel. . . . Using satellite technology poses no theological problems for Orthodox Jews" ("Rabbi Using" 1983).

Lubavitchers do not understand why the popular press finds this so amusing. Rabbi Hirshel Gansbourg explained this in an interview with me:

> Hasides goes back hundreds of years. The Gemara [part of the Talmud] says that all gold was created for the temple. That's the ultimate goal of gold. But because of that the gold is also in the world and can be used for other purposes, too. Technology was created to serve God. That means that the ultimate creation of technology or science is to do good in the world. But at the same time it could be used by people from the other side, too. TV was created to do good things. But if people do it for other purposes, that's their choice. The same thing with technology, and music, and everything.

Occasionally, the Hasidic community comes under specific ideological attack by certain political, social, or economic interest groups. At no time was this felt more strongly than when a group of Jewish feminists began in the late 1960s and 1970s to question some of the more severe Orthodox practices that perpetuated (in their view) a second-class status for Orthodox women and that effectively kept women out of the political, religious, and social arenas of Judaism. Bolstered by the consciousness raisings and the sweeping reforms of the predominantly white, upper-middle class women's movement, Jewish feminists specifically targeted Orthodox Jewish practices. Much of the literature to come out of this period dealt with various attacks on the Orthodox community and with responses by Orthodox—and even Hasidic— women to what they perceived as a gross misunderstanding of Hasidic gender politics by feminists.

The main issues that concerned Jewish feminists were centered on women's legal position in Orthodox Judaism and in their lack of participation in public ritual life. Specifically targeted were the laws of niddah (ritual impurity), including immersion in the mikvah, and laws concerning divorce and abandonment.[15] Such books as Susannah Heschel's *On Being a Jewish Feminist*, Susan Weidman Schneider's *Jewish and Female: Choices and Changes in Our Lives Today*, and Melanie Kaye-Kantrowitz and Irena Klepfisz's *Tribe of Dina* railed against what their authors perceived as antiquated and oppressive laws that prevented women from achieving their full potential and autonomy.

During the period of heightened controversy (c. 1975–85), Lubavitcher and other Orthodox women responded to feminist attacks by writing books of their own, which refuted claims of second-class status. Works such as R. S. Friedfertig and F. Shapiro's *Modern Jewish Woman: A Unique Perspective*, the Lubavitch Women's Organization's *Aura: A Reader on Jewish Womanhood*, Blu Greenberg's *On Women and Judaism*, and Mannis Freeman's *Doesn't Anybody Blush Anymore*, Charlotte Blum's *Jewish Woman in America*, and Moshe Meiselman's *Jewish Women in Jewish Law*, among others, refuted claims of women's limited status and autonomy. In these books, observant women claimed that laws regarding the interactions between men and women, especially those concerned with ritual impurity and husband-wife sexual relations, were meant to protect both men and women and have come to be wrongly interpreted as evidence for women's second-class status.[16]

As Debra Kaufman has suggested, in their original context, such laws did not imply that a person, such as a niddah, was sinful. Rather, the status of niddah was both normal and often mandatory, symbolic of death (considered ritually impure) and resurrection (recreated through immersion in the mikvah), and only became interpreted as wrongful or sinful by later Talmudic scholars. Further, writes Kaufman, such practices as wearing a wig or immersion in a ritual bath had been completely misinterpreted by Jewish feminists: "While the women understand that the perception of wearing a wig insinuates male control and possession . . . almost to a woman they spoke of the headcovering as a sign of their distinction, difference, and separation from the society at large: a sign, they claim, of their holiness and pride" (Kaufman 1991:181–81).

Although feminist discourse had a minimal effect on gender and power relations within the Lubavitcher community, Jewish feminists did succeed in opening up many more options for mainstream Jewish women. Now it is not uncommon to see among Orthodox Jews, for example, all-female Torah study groups and Sabbath services. And among Reform Jews, one often observes female Rabbis, cantors,[17] and other ritual specialists. Finally, in new forms of Judaism, such as Reconstruction, there are new prayer books and new translations of the Bible that strive for gender equality. In the end, the negotiation between Hasidic women and their secular feminist attackers did result in agreement on at least one issue: the centrality of women's position in traditional Judaism.

Rather than seeing changes for women in this generation as resulting from the women's movement, Lubavitcher women credit their modernization to America's religious and social freedoms generally, without making the connection between the two. One Lubavitcher woman described the changes between the generations this way:

> Years ago, when the role of woman was to sit at home, I would say that the Jewish woman's role at that time was to stay at home and to learn within her home all that she needed to know to prepare her for a later life as a wife and mother. But just the same way as now, in the modern way . . . the so-called "modern" woman goes out and she has to earn a living, she is not confined anymore to her own four walls. The same you find by Hasidic women. In this day and age when we are such a part of our society, there is no such thing as living in your home anymore. By way of the media, the neighborhood, where you walk, where you move, what you hear, what you read, you are by your very nature so affected by the world you live in.
>
> The Jewish woman must, if anything, prepare herself even more so, and strengthen herself by going out, getting educated in the Jewish way, of course, and going out after she is prepared and helping others in that very same way. It has become the thing to work, for economical reasons, or emotional reasons, to do more than just be at home. I would say that this trend is so strong now, I hardly know any of my contemporaries who just stay at home. (M. Rosenblum interview)

It was, in fact, this sense of being economically and emotionally secure, coupled with a certain dignity and purity proclaimed by Hasidic women, that so attracted many young, nonobservant Jewish women to become ba'alot teshuvah. Thus, the women's movement, while allowing some women to attain more economic and religious freedom, did not satisfy the needs of those who wished to retain the special status and social benefits that being women afforded them.

Much has been written recently, from both outside and inside the community, on the seeming inconsistencies or paradoxes inherent in women who were raised in the secular, postfeminist world of the 1970s and 1980s returning to a more observant (and seemingly unequally gendered) life.[18] Some have framed the question in terms of what these newly Orthodox women were seeking and finding within Hasidic (and other religious-right) communities: more structured lives, clearer sexual and social lines between men and women, greater safety from sexually transmitted diseases or physical attack, and stronger, less competitive, and more rewarding relations with other women.

Ambivalences

Lubavitchers of both genders also express ambivalences about their simultaneous participation in both Old World and New World beliefs and practices. They often say that their lives today, here in America, are both easier and harder than those of their ancestors in Eastern Europe. Certainly, the religious and social freedoms accorded to them as citizens of the United States make their lives here easier in many ways. Yet, they say, it is these same freedoms that have the potential to cause problems. The lures of American society—sexual freedom, easy drugs, and general lack of spirituality—are always there, forbidden yet enticing. Although they love America (most have been born here) and would not leave its abundant security, it was easier in Europe, they often reminisce, when the community was closer, more cohesive, and the enemy was well-known and immediate. Life during the eighteenth and nineteenth centuries—the time of the Ba'al Shem Tov and the great Alter Rebbe (Rabbi Schneur Zalman), when modern Hasidism was still young—was harder then, say contemporary Lubavitchers, with the Polish and Russian governments always at their backs. The need for group solidarity was strong. People were more strictly observant then; farbrengens were wild affairs, with the Rebbe dancing for days in the streets. In America, the enemy is everywhere, diffuse, harder to fight, and people are tired.

One lifetime Lubavitcher woman, born in Leningrad and forced to leave Russia at the start of World War II, eventually emigrated to the United States in 1955. Her childhood experiences have led her to certain conclusions about American society that she shares with many of her contemporaries:

> We were in Russia. Let's say ten families were living together in the same area. We were only friends with these children. We were never friends with anybody on the street, because, first, we were not allowed to eat anyplace. And

why? Because our parents were afraid that somebody should find out that we were religious, because this meant prison. Right? So, like I remember when my mother would *bench licht* (light candles), she used to tell me, "When you're stepping outside, don't tell anybody what you did in the house. And if they will ask you to take something, don't tell them you are not allowed to carry. Just say you don't need it. And if they will offer you something, say, thank you, you are not hungry, you cannot take it"—but don't tell them why.

Nowadays, it's easier, easier in a way that nobody tells you what to do. I mean, you're not afraid to be religious. First of all, there are no food problems. In Russia, there were a lot of problems with food. You couldn't get kosher stuff. That's one problem. Second, you were very much afraid that someone should find out if you were religious, and this meant prison. Here, you don't have to be afraid of anything. But, it's harder, too, because the children are exposed to the secular world much more than they were in Russia, and that's why it's harder. The impact from the outside world has a certain influence, so you have to be very, very strong and very, very watchful over your children. (Mrs. M. Teleshevsky interview)

Notes

1. Although I am aware that the Rebbe died in 1994, I am using the ethnographic present as a rhetorical device in the writing of the rest of this study, and I apologize for any confusion that may result. No new Rebbe has taken Menachem Mendel Schneerson's place within the community; as a result, an interesting situation has developed since his death. Some Lubavitchers continue to hold out hope that the Rebbe is truly the Messiah who will return to bring about the restoration of Israel and are opposed to finding a new leader. Others are willing to move on. However, the situation is further complicated by the fact that the Schneersons had no children, and no other family members have come forward to head the group. Further, the Rebbe left at least two wills outlining conflicting wishes concerning this matter, so the community waits, poised for a sign as to how to proceed. This situation has not changed as of January 2000.

2. The 613 commandments are divided into 365 negative commandments (e.g., Thou shall not kill) and 248 positive commandments (Thou shall honor thy father and mother).

3. Although the Talmud refers only to the Gemarra (interpretations of the Mishna), modern usage of this term includes both the Mishna and the Gemarra.

4. Although Lubavitchers spell Habad as "Chabad," I am using the former spelling as it conforms to the Hebrew transliteration rules as outlined in the *Encyclopedia Judaica* (1971–72) and to common usage.

5. I and others have written more extensively about this elsewhere. See especially Koskoff (1976), Harris (1985), Davidman (1991), and Kaufman (1991).

6. The three commandments that women must follow are lighting the Sabbath candles; immersion in the mikvah after menstruation; and burning a portion of the hallah loaf before baking it for the Sabbath meal. All these activities connect women to their homes and husbands.

7. See Kaufman (1991) and Harris (1985) for especially good discussions of the history of this law.

8. See Morris (1998) for a full discussion of this history.

9. Soon after arriving in Rochester, New York, the shaliach, Rabbi Vogel, set up a table at the local grocery store that displayed kosher items. He would sit there for hours answering questions from surprised onlookers.

10. These vehicles, usually small vans, are driven into a community and parked on the street. Passersby are asked if they are Jewish and are taken into the van to light candles or put on tefillin.

11. Male Hasidim leave their beards uncut as a sign of their special relationship to God. Thus, cutting off someone's beard is considered a grave offense to the individual as well as to God.

12. See Harris (1985:176–87) for an especially clear discussion of this.

13. Chaya and Schmuel are pseudonyms. This scene is a construction based on field notes.

14. At times, interactions between the Lubavitcher and non-Jewish secular community reach comic proportions. Recently, a National Public Radio story reported that a new Lubavitcher community forming in Texas had been looking, without success, for a place to hold services and other meetings. Finally, in desperation, they rented the only available space: the backroom of a well-known automobile service chain. The Lubavitcher shaliach chuckled to the National Public Radio interviewer that he and the others had quickly become known as "Jiffy Lubavitchers."

15. According to Jewish law, only men can obtain a divorce. If a woman is abandoned by her husband, she is not free to divorce him or remarry until it is proven that he is dead.

16. See Kaufman (1991) and Morris (1998) for excellent discussions of this controversy.

17. See Slobin (1989) for more on female cantors.

18. See the work of Harris (1985), Davidman (1991), Morris (1995), and especially Kaufman (1991; 1995).

5

Melody Is the Pen of the Soul

Music holds a central place in the Lubavitcher world. Regarded as one of the most powerful forms of human expression, it is a part of prayer, celebration, and teaching. Music and its performance have the potential to elevate the soul, inspire a student, open up the gates of joy, or bring one downward close to the other side—to coarsen one, or to cause harm. So important is the power of music to express one's innermost feelings, either positive or negative, that Lubavitchers often cite Schneur Zalman's declaration that "melody is the pen of the soul" (Zalmanoff 1948b:5). This chapter explores the Lubavitcher conceptualization of music as a spiritual process and shows how ideas about Lubavitcher social and religious identity are embedded within it.

A Lubavitcher Concept of Music as Process

Like all aspects of human life, Lubavitchers conceptualize music and its performance as inherently neutral. Deriving from the kelipot nogah residing in the human animal soul, located in the right ventricle of the heart, music as a general category exists suspended between the divine and lower animal, souls waiting for a user, a context, and a performance. Although performing, creating, or listening to music can connect one with the divine, these activities also have an equal potential to pull one toward the other side. Lubavitchers thus distinguish between the process of doing music (i.e., pulling one way or the other) from the specific entities used in this process (i.e., actual pieces of music). This is an important distinction: whether or not a specific piece of music pulls you one way or the other depends not so much on the musical sounds themselves but on an interaction between sounds and those who perceive and use them. While certain musical characteristics have, over time, become more or less associated with Lubavitcher music or musics from the outside, they are neither necessary nor sufficient for guaranteeing musical effectiveness, for it is the use of these materials by specific people within specific contexts that makes them effective, beautiful, debased, holy, or profane.

Repertoires of music that have the potential to elevate are those perceived as having musical characteristics traditionally associated with Lubavitcher nigunim, those songs that sound like or are performed in contexts similar to those of past Lubavitcher leaders. (For more on the actual sound structures found in Lubavitcher nigunim, see chapter 6.) Such repertoires are believed to be effective in elevating the animal soul because they are seen as sounded metaphors for core Lubavitcher beliefs; performing them is not only a blessing, it is a spiritual necessity. Nigunim, because of their position as the closest of all musics to the divine source, are so powerful that even a performance by an evil person, or perhaps for an evil purpose, can transform both the performer and the event into something of good.

Musical repertoires that have the potential to debase are those perceived as having musical characteristics associated with the outside (non-Jewish) worlds, in which Lubavitchers believe they, like divine sparks, are embedded. Such repertoires are seen as existing close to the lower, nonhuman animal soul; they are musics that stand at a hopelessly far distance from the divine. Although such music may contain a captive holy spark, its light is all but obscured within the coarseness or thickness of its surrounding husk and can only be perceived by a person of unquestioned holiness, such as a Rebbe. However, even if a hidden spark of holiness might be perceived in such music, it is forever encased in its husk, from which there is no escape and no retrieval—except, perhaps, by a miracle. Repertoires associated with the Christian liturgy, for example (and, by extension, all musics of other religious groups), are in this category.

It is sometimes possible for an especially holy person, such as a Rebbe, to use even repertoires closest to the lower, nonhuman animal soul to elevate himself spiritually. His level of holiness gives him the ability to see through the husk of a song's animal properties or origins and to sense a holy spark in the melody within. Further, his manipulation of the song can successfully neutralize its harmful influence so that another listener cannot be affected negatively. On the other hand, a ba'al or ba'alat teshuvah, not properly shielded against or not able to resist the harmful influences of certain repertoires, might feel that he or she is at a greater risk than a Rebbe and will be far more diligent in protecting himself or herself against musics that have the potential to violate Hasidic beliefs. Therefore, a newcomer might regard even a fairly neutral secular example, such as a song from *Fiddler on the Roof* that contains many musical characteristics associated with Lubavitcher nigunim and Jewish music in general, to be problematic and will resist listening to or performing it. (For more on *Fiddler on the Roof,* see chapter 10.)

In between these more or less agreed-upon, polarized repertoires associated with the divine (Lubavitcher nigunim at the high end) and with non-human animal souls (Christian music at the low end) lies a vast pool of musics that are truly neutral. They are seen as such in that they may contain some musical or structural characteristics associated with traditional nigunim but have other problems that exclude them from this repertoire. This middle repertoire is conceptualized as centered on the border or fence between human and nonhuman animal souls, perpetually poised and suspended, waiting to be activated through performance. Music from this repertoire must be manipulated somehow to move it away from the sitra achra, toward which it constantly drifts.

Elsewhere, songs within this middle repertoire have been called "potential nigunim" (Koskoff 1976; 1978; 1995), those pieces of music that Lubavitchers borrow from various non-Lubavitcher sources, or compose themselves, and transform into nigunim. These melodies are believed to contain perceptible (but captive) holy sparks embedded within them; when freed, these sparks allow the music to be brought inward and upward toward its holy source. It is here—in the middle, neutral area—that certain kinds of repertoires and their performances are more or less negotiated through a four-step process that I call here musical tikkun.

Scene: "Three Stories of Musical Redemption"

It is late August 1975, and I have been in Crown Heights for most of the summer. Finally back in Pittsburgh for a while, I have begun visiting Rabbi Ephraim Rosenblum and his wife Miriam again to talk about nigunim. Tonight, we talk about borrowing musical materials from non-Jewish sources. I am interested in this topic because I am noticing that some of the tunes I am listening to on Lubavitcher recordings are called "peasant tunes" or "airs" (according to the information on the record jackets; see Zalmanoff 1948a). I understand that borrowing is a natural result of cultural interaction, but this process seems inconsistent with the strict ideas concerning the non-Jewish and contaminated secular world.

In this interview, I am being very persistent with Rabbi Rosenblum—even argumentative. I do not precisely understand why some songs become ni-

gunim and others do not, and I find it difficult to understand his explanations. As he tries—with little success—to explain this distinction to me, he
eventually lapses into the following three stories, hoping I will "catch on":

EK: Okay, how do you explain songs which are borrowed from, say, not even
Jewish sources but, say, a Russian song; how do they become Lubavitcher
songs?

ER: A story is told that the Alter Rebbe, Reb Schneerson, the first of the Habad Lubavitch dynasty—I heard this story a number of times—that he
once heard an organ player, you know these organ players that sing?

EK: An organ grinder?

ER: Right, an organ grinder, sing a song which he thought was beautiful, and
he asked him to sing the song again, and he paid him, whatever, a couple of coins, whatever it was, and he sang it once, and he asked to sing
again until he learned it. And after the Alter Rebbe learned it, he asked
him to play it again, but he wasn't able to. He [the organ grinder] had
forgotten it completely. It seems that there are profound songs which,
somehow, are somewhere else too; there is profundity in other music,
somewhere else, too, either lost somehow or, like, one can speak of a lost
soul, of a soul which is lost, one can perhaps speak of a lost piece of
music.

EK: So then it just becomes Hasidic?

ER: So the Hasidim adapt it or adopt it because they feel that it has the depth
to it.

EK: There's something in it that makes it profound?

ER: Right!

EK: In the story you just told me, when Schneur Zalman asked the organ
grinder to sing the song again, the organ grinder didn't know the song.
Why is that?

ER: After the Alter Rebbe learned it, the organ grinder forgot it.

EK: Because he had passed it on? He lost it?

ER: Yeah.

EK: Well, why did he choose it? Was it the words that struck him?

ER: No.

EK: No? Only the music?

ER: Yeah, the tune. Here's another one: the Rebbe told a story, not long ago.
It must have been within the last twenty years. In Lubavitch they sing a
song which is called "Shamil's Song" [see chapter 6 for a transcription
of this song], and it seems that this Shamil was a leader of a tribe in the
Caucasian [sic] mountains, and it seems that he led a tribe, and he held
a war with the Czar, and the Czar wasn't able to capture him. He was
always free and led the tribe, and the Czar wanted very much to cap-

ture him, so with some kind of a ruse (the Czar said he wanted to make peace with him), he brought Shamil down to speak with him, and he captured him, and he imprisoned him, and when this Shamil, this chief, or prince, or king of this mountain tribe [was in jail], he always used to remind himself of the time when he was free in the mountains, was free to roam the mountains, was king over his tribe, and had this tremendous freedom, and he reminded himself. Now he's enclosed and locked up, and he would express the hope that he would be free again, and he made this tune.

Hasidim felt that this whole story of Shamil, who was free once and was imprisoned and was craving and desiring to be free again, was a very good analogy of the soul of the person which comes out of the body, because the soul is a spiritual being which is free; and, in other words, when it comes into the body, it's imprisoned in the limits of the body, for whatever reason God saw it get there, and the soul craves, or hopes, or desires to be free again. And the Hasidim would sing this song, which he sang, which embodied within it these moods, because they felt that the moods which Shamil was expressing in this nigun very well expressed the inner feelings of the soul of every Jew. And they sang it. And the Rebbe sang it and taught it to everybody, so here's a nigun which was sung by this Shamil, who was probably a profound person, it would seem, probably had some kind of very deep feeling for music, and they used the moods of the song to express the moods of the Jew. So here you have it.

There's another song which the Rebbe taught about a drunk who spends all his money and loses everything; and this, of course, was again sung perhaps with the same idea by the Hasidim. Some of us that are granted such great potential and ability, and we waste them away, and we drink them away. Reading the song with the Russian words [it says one thing], but the content was completely different. The content was the idea, the thought behind it. So the Rebbe taught the song, but the idea behind the song wasn't the drunk who wasted his money drinking. This was a person who feels like he has a beautiful life to live, and so much potential and ability, and how it's being wasted on things of naught, on things that are naught. Do you understand?

EK: Yeah, I guess so.

Musical *Tikkun*

Tikkun was described in chapter 3 as a process of restoration. All things in the universe, including the holiest of Lubavitchers or the most valued nigunim, are constantly drifting away from the divine source and continually needing to be spiritually revitalized. Lubavitcher-composed nigunim (and their performers and listeners) are revived and uplifted through simple performance; but songs outside this inner core must be more profoundly transformed so that they cease to incline toward the other side. This is accomplished through a process of musical borrowing and adaption, whereby mere song moves closer to, or becomes, nigun.

It is not unusual for Lubavitchers to borrow, adapt, and incorporate musical (but not textual) materials from outside sources. This process, a natural one of musical acculturation, is a part of all social, ethnic, and religious group interaction, especially within Jewish culture. What is unusual, however, is that borrowing is the primary form of composition within Lubavitcher musical culture and, further, that the act of borrowing and transforming a song is considered a mitzvah (blessing), one that is both spiritually motivated and rewarded.

The process of musical tikkun, like that of devekut, involves four stages: first, an appropriate person—especially a Zaddick, Rebbe, or, perhaps, a benoni—must be able to perceive a holy spark hidden in the music. That is, something about the music must arouse in him or her the properties of *simcha* (joy) and *hitlahavut* (enthusiasm) that are already present, but dormant, in the person's body and are used to awaken the proper intention (kavvanah) of the listener. Second, the song must somehow be transferred over to this person—that is, he or she must spend time learning the song, "buy" it from its original owner, "trick" the owner into giving up the song, or somehow claim it as his/her own.

Third, the holy spark in the music must be released by opening up the song to let the spark fly upward. To open the song, the Hasid, now regarded as the song's new savior/composer, must remove the coarse outer shell that imprisons it—usually, the text. Lubavitchers (indeed, all Hasidim), regard pure melody as existing at a higher level than speech, so a true nigun, one with unlimited depth and height, must be wordless. It is music, not text, that contains the holy spark; words, with their literal meanings and their connection to the everyday world, are seen as part of the coarse husk encasing the spark and must be cast away. Pure melody is thus closer to the divine, existing at a higher level in both the human and divine bodies; it is more refined, more sensitive, more open to divine influence. Rabbi Samuel Zalmanoff writes: "Words are limitations. Melody, as explained in the laws of Habad, exists on a higher level than speech. It is impossible to express in speech what it is possible to express in melody. . . . To be silent is a great merit, especially if it is an intelligent silence. But this only refers to talking, not to nigun. The melody of nigun stands on a higher level. The voice of nigun awakens the kavvanah" (Zalmanoff 1948a:24).

Finally, the holy spark must be returned to its proper place. The spark, now openly available through a new musical performance by a Lubavitcher, within the new context of Hasidic religious and aesthetic values, can be reclaimed, and a mitzvah can be accomplished. Thus, the old song is successfully removed from the territory closer to the other side and restored to its proper, more elevated place that is closer to the divine head. In this way, Lubavitchers are acting out a more general Habadic principle within a specific sociomusical context.

One, perhaps unintended, outcome of this process is that the song, now purified, can no longer waver toward the sitra achra and unintentionally influence its original composer or listeners. In its original form, with both music and words, the song was poised in the middle, neutral; but it was continuously veering off toward the nonhuman animal soul in the left ventricle. Now that its animal properties—the inappropriate words and context—have been removed, the music can no longer be tempted by or used for evil. The now-purified song, seen as an entity unto itself, can even lift its original composer/owner to a higher level, because its holy spark is now openly displayed. The original composer thus becomes dissociated with the animal properties of the music while at the same time being elevated by its divine properties.

Steps one and two of the process of musical tikkun outlined here involve both the perception of a holy spark and the ability to gain access to it. As described above, Lubavitchers regard the spiritual level of the person who is judging or using the music to be of utmost importance in the completion of these tasks. And although all Lubavitchers have the potential to fulfill these steps, those who already exist at a high spiritual level, such as a Rebbe, are believed to be less affected by the coarseness of a surrounding husk and thus have a greater ability to perceive and capture sparks that are deeply embedded in their shells.

Steps three and four involve various textual and musical manipulations as well as correct performance practices. Step three is, in effect, a kind of compositional procedure (Koskoff 1978) in that the old song is recomposed textually and musically to conform to Hasidic religious and aesthetic principles. The most common practice in dealing with an offending text is simply to eliminate it and substitute vocables, such as "bam, bam" or "oi, oi," that are believed to be the vocalization of the mystical name of God.[1] Often, new texts in Hebrew, Yiddish, or a combination of texts (so-called macaronic songs) are substituted, or the original text is kept intact but reinterpreted according to Hasidic belief.

Finally, step four can involve the manipulation of the music itself—that is, the music is made to sound more Hasidic. The newly borrowed tune must conform to at least some of the general aesthetic principles found in the basic core of the Lubavitcher nigun repertoire, those songs that define Lubavitchers musically. (The next chapter will examine these musical codes more closely to see how they are used in a variety of settings.)

What kinds of musics exist within the vast category of "potential nigunim"? Virtually all non-Lubavitcher musics (except those belonging to other religions) are regarded as potentially able to move closer to the divine soul. However, some musics must move farther to reach their goal, and some take more effort for the average Hasid to move than others. Contemporary musical examples, such as jazz, heavy rock, and rap repertoires, that start out fairly close to the sitra achra, even if used by an especially pious Lubavitcher under ideal circumstances, will move only slightly toward the divine; others, such as contemporary Lubavitcher compositions, start out much closer to the divine soul and must make only a small journey through the fence that separates historical Lubavitcher nigunim from the contemporary, "outer" musical world.

Thus, the repertoire of potential nigunim is itself divided into a hierarchy of musics that could be placed on a continuum of greater and lesser acceptability. At one end are repertoires of so-called problematic musics, which seldom reach the status of nigun, except by a miracle, because the distance they must travel is simply too far. On the other end are musics that are already closer to the divine soul and need only a small amount of adaptation to rise in status.

Organization of the *Sefer Ha-Nigunim*

The hierarchy of musical and spiritual ranking discussed above is clearly confirmed in the detailed organization of the three-volume collection of Lubavitcher nigunim, the *Sefer Ha-Nigunim (Book of Songs)*, containing 347 notated songs (Zalmanoff 1948b; 1957; c. 1965).[2] Since becoming the Rebbe, Menachem Mendel Schneerson has been interested in preserving Lubavitcher nigunim and other songs associated with his court. To this end, he established the Nichoach Society in the late 1940s, which is dedicated to notating and publishing nigunim. In addition to publishing the three volumes of the *Sefer Ha-Nigunim,* Nichoach has also been responsible for recording many of these tunes on LP records, cassettes, and, more recently, compact discs. These songs continue to be performed at farbrengens held after Sabbath evening prayers, at informal farbrengens in the home, at special gatherings celebrating the Rebbe's birthday (11 Nisan) or the anniversary of Schneur Zalman's release from prison (19 Kislev). Although some Lubavitchers say that this collection of 347 nigunim only scratches the surface of all the melodies known to the community, all agree that this set of songs represents the core repertoire.

Each volume of the *Sefer Ha-Nigunim* contains the same organizational plan. Section 1 contains "Compositions by the Heads of Chabad"—nigunim attributed to Schneur Zalman and succeeding Lubavitcher Rebbes up to the fifth generation (c. 1812–1920). These nigunim, placed at the head of the collection, are the most spiritually significant representations of Lubavitcher music and are, without question, believed to be overt manifestations of Habadic principles. Clearly, they fall into the repertoire of music associated with the divine soul. Having been composed by the founder of the Lubavitcher court (Schneur Zalman) and his successors, using Hebrew texts or vocables, these songs hold the highest, most valued place in the Lubavitcher repertoire.

Section 2 of each volume, "Traditional Chabad Melodies," contains songs attributed to various Lubavitcher composers attached to the courts of the first five Rebbes, all of whom lived in Eastern Europe or Russia before immigration to the United States (1941), as well as songs borrowed from other Hasidic groups. These songs, again using Hebrew texts or vocables, are conceived of as leaning toward the divine. It will not take much changing to push them upward through the fence.

The first part of section 3, "Chabad Melodies for Different Occasions," contains special repertoires shared with other Jewish communities: Sabbath and holiday melodies; devotional songs for the high holidays. These sections include a mixture of *zemirot* (table songs); songs for Passover, Purim, and Hanukkah; and the two nigunim mentioned earlier that commemorate specific Lubavitcher holidays. Yiddish song titles also begin to appear here, and a few are labeled "Nikolaiev" or are attributed to the Charitonov brothers, who lived in Nickolayev, in southern Ukraine. (For more on their music, see chapter 6.) Here also are two nigunim composed to commemorate special and unique events in Lubavitcher history: "Padah Beshalom Nafshi" ("He Redeemeth My Soul in Peace"), for 19 Kislev, the anniversary of Schneur Zalman's release from prison, and "Melody for 12–13 Tammuz" the birthday of Joseph Isaac Schneersohn, the sixth Lubavitcher Rebbe. Many songs in section 3 are not attributed to a composer or Rebbe, so it is difficult to place them historically.

The remaining subsections of section 3 contain a variety of songs to be used for farbrengens. Songs with Hebrew, Russian, and Yiddish titles, songs labeled "Wallachian," "Devekut" ("Yearning"), "Fonke," or simply "Nigun Simcha" ("Joyous Melody"), provide a rich sampling of common Eastern European and Russian folk-song and dance styles. Each volume concludes with a set of marches, some of which are said to have been taken from Napoleon's army in defiance of his abandonment of European Jews. The songs in section 3 thus move downward from the beginning or head of the volumes in terms of their numerical ordering as well as in terms of their spiritual ranking, with Napoleonic marches almost, but not quite, on the outside of the Lubavitcher musical and spiritual world. Table 1 shows the organization of the *Sefer Ha-Nigunim* volumes as explained above, with all three sections integrated.

Table 1. Organization of the *Sefer Ha-Nigunim*

Head of the volumes (divine, bright light)
Section 1:   *Nigunim* of Schneur Zalman
Nigunim of heads of Habad to the fifth generation
Nigunim of the Ba'al Shem Tov
Section 2:   *Nigunim* of other Lubavitchers
Nigunim of other Hasidic groups
Section 3:   *Nigunim* for special Lubavitcher anniversaries
Liturgical pieces and *nigunim* shared with other Hasidic groups
Songs that are part of the general Jewish repertoire
"Wallachian" or shepherd songs
Napoleonic marches
Foot of the volumes (animal, dim light)

The *Sefer Ha-Nigunim* and the Lubavitcher Principle of Social Ranking

The organization of the *Sefer Ha-Nigunim* volumes reflects two core Lubavitcher beliefs: the weakening of the generations, with the most important and earliest nigunim, composed solely by Lubavitchers and other Hasidim, represented by nigunim in sections 1 and 2 placed highest, at the head of the volumes; and the principle of closeness or distance from the divine, represented by the songs in section 3, most of which were borrowed, placed, in descending order of the intensity of their light, at the foot of the volumes. It is no organizational accident that the ordering of nigunim, especially in section 3, perfectly matches a spiritual hierarchy of religious and social groups with whom Lubavitchers interacted in Eastern Europe. Musics in section 1, all of which are attributed to Lubavitcher composers, stand metaphorically not only at the head of the collection but also inside, close to Lubavitcher identity; while musics in section 3, most of which are not attributed to any composer but seem to be clearly associated with outside sources, lie at the feet and (almost) outside the figurative and collective Jewish body. To better understand this ordering, it is important to look more closely at the social context in which the original Lubavitcher communities flourished in the eighteenth and nineteenth centuries and examine the notions of insiderness and outsiderness that help define the borders between these communities.

Who exactly were the people with whom Lubavitchers interacted in eighteenth- and nineteenth-century Eastern Europe? Following the death of the Ba'al Shem Tov, many of his disciples established courts of their own, based somewhat on differing interpretations of his teachings. Separated to some extent from mainstream Jewish communities, mainly in terms of their religious fervor and their strictly literal interpretation of Jewish law, Hasidim also had much in common with each other—not the least of which was their united front against the mitnaggadim—the Orthodox rabbis who challenged Hasidic practices. Individual differences, which at times could cause much strife between Hasidic groups, were often overlooked or peacefully negotiated in the face of attack from mainstream Jewish Orthodoxy and from non-Jewish sources. Certainly, much, including music, was shared between Hasidic groups (intermarriages between Lubavitchers and other Hasidic groups, for example, were frequent). Thus, large networks of Hasidic communities grew that became quite religiously and politically cohesive and powerful.

Hasidim also lived within a larger, diverse Jewish population that sustained them socially, economically, and, at times, religiously. Mark Zborowski and Elizabeth Herzog, in their classic portrayal of shtetl life, *Life Is with People*, divide this community into three "interlocking . . . yet discrete" socioreligious classes: the learned and pious rabbis—the "elite"; wealthy and middle-class burghers, who economically sustained the community; and relatively uneducated laborers (1952:157). Although all classes shared a more-or-less common worldview and perception of outsiders, they differed greatly in their economic and spiritual status as well as in their observance of traditional Jewish practices.[3]

Lubavitchers also had contact with sometimes friendly, sometimes not-so-friendly, non-Jews. Many wealthy Jewish merchants employed non-Jewish peasant servants, some of whom were proficient in Yiddish and were often helpful during an attack on a community. Synagogues employed non-Jews, often peasant boys from surrounding rural communities, to work on the Sabbath, lighting candles and performing other jobs restricted to Jews by Jewish law. And, especially among the merchant and laborer classes, interactions between Jews and non-Jews sometimes culminated in intermarriages.

At times, however, the same peasants with whom Jews interacted on a friendly basis also acted as agents of the mostly hostile governments, which sometimes arbitrarily raised taxes, forced military service, and promoted brutal attacks on Jewish communities. Further, much of the geographical area inhabited by Hasidim frequently passed hands during the eighteenth and nineteenth centuries, which resulted in changing attitudes toward Jewish communities and in new laws either allowing or prohibiting religious practices. So, while non-Jewish peasants could sometimes be trusted, and even liked, people connected with the government were uniformly despised and feared.

Given this brief summary of the original Lubavitcher social context, one can see four ordered regions, each populated by people whose connection to Lubavitcher culture lessens, or becomes more and more problematic, as the regions move outward (or downward), farther away from the central Lubavitcher core (table 2).

Table 2. An Ordered Set of Social Groups in Eastern Europe with Whom Lubavitchers Interacted

Head (high, bright, in)	Lubavitchers
	Other Hasidic groups
	Other Jewish groups
	Non-Jewish peasant groups
Foot (low, dim, out)	Government/military

Integrating the three hierarchies presented here—the hierarchy of the souls in relation to musical types; that of the organization of the *Sefer Ha-Nigunim;* and the hierarchy of spirituality associated with various social groups with whom Lubavitchers interacted in Eastern Europe—one sees a striking correspondence between the traditional and contemporary Lubavitcher's perceptions of his or her own spiritual core, the ranking of the relative spirituality of others, and the hierarchy of musical repertoires traditionally and, to this day, brought in from the outside. Thus, this collection of 347 nigunim is more than a mere presentation of tunes; in fusing this set of pieces with the doctrine of the two souls and a spiritually ranked set of social groups, the *Sefer Ha-Nigunim* becomes a material manifestation, a central locus, of Lubavitcher religious, social, and musical identity.

Notes

1. The tetragrammaton, spelled in Hebrew *yud-he-vav-he,* written YHVH, is vocalized by Lubavitchers and many other observant Jews as *Adonoi* or *Elohim,* as the original pronunciation is forbidden.

2. Actually, there are 320 different nigunim. Twenty-seven of them have been repeated.

3. See also Dawidowicz (1967).

6
Habad in Musical Sound and Structure

Understanding the religious, social, and political ramifications of the *Sefer Ha-Nigunim* will not tell us much about the musical sounds that may communicate the essence of spirituality to Lubavitchers. To do that, one must look more deeply into the music itself, its sounds and structures, to understand the multileveled musical, spiritual, and social meanings that the sounds of nigunim carry.

Jewish Musical Codes

Recent scholarly work in Jewish music, especially that of Mark Slobin, has examined musical sounds and structures from the perspective of their coded meanings: "A culture lays out its musical credo in a set of stylistic preferences: we'll use these intervals in these combinations to make these scales; here are the types of trills, shakes, and turns that will ornament our tunes, and only those basic meters will do. Not too fast except for dancing, lots of songs in the key of E minor—these and other prescriptions are part of an in-group musical language" (Slobin 1982:182).

Lubavitcher music, especially that contained in the three volumes of the *Sefer Ha-Nigunim*, contains specific stylistic and structural features that define it generally as Jewish and, more specifically, as belonging to a distinctive Lubavitcher musical culture. Perhaps the quintessential musical marker of Eastern European Jewish music (for the Western listener, especially) is the augmented 2d, a scalar/modal interval so well known that it has, in essence, become a common musical stereotype of Jewish culture. Its so-called "yearning quality" calls up visions of Jewish wandering, of shepherd's flutes, and of the pain of unfulfilled spiritual love. This interval, often highlighted in musical and performance contexts with heavy ornamentation and rubato, has become so effective in evoking Jewish culture that it has been used consciously as a staple by classical, popular, and theatrical composers for generations.

Mark Slobin's work concentrates primarily on two distinct melody-types associated with Eastern European Jewish folk songs, each of which contains the augmented 2d. Before examining these musical contexts, it is necessary to discuss the terms mode, scale, and melody-type, which will be used throughout this chapter. The terms mode and scale are often used interchangeably.[1] Here, however, the term scale will refer to a succession of pitches arranged from low to high and defined in relation to each other by steps or degrees. Mode will be defined more in the sense of its standard English meaning as a "method," or "way of being," as in the phrase modus operandi. Musically, although aspects of mode can be expressed in scalar form, mode is more than the simple list of successive pitches used in a piece or in a theoretical model; it is also, more importantly, the method or way in which the pitches are used to form melodic contours, cadential resting points or ornaments, or to move from one tonal area to another. Mode, then, incorporates pitch and contour as well as a grammar for their correct placement within a piece. Finally, the term "melody-type" as used by Slobin (1982:186) and here is defined as a group of melodies that are related, in that they all contain similar modal procedures and characteristic rhythmic and melodic contours or patterns.

There are three augmented 2d melody-types found in the 347 nigunim notated in the Sefer Ha-Nigunim, each based on a specific mode and modal contour. The first melody-type, one commonly found in Eastern European folk music, is called frigish (example 1), as its pitches derive from the Greek church mode, Phrygian (example 2),[2] which does not actually contain the augmented interval but that, like the frigish, begins with a half step (Slobin 1982:187). Characteristic of the frigish mode is the use of a specific contour that highlights the augmented 2d interval, which is located between scale degrees 2 and 3.[3] The second melody-type, which Slobin calls the "raised 4th" (♯4th) type, is based on a characteristic contour that locates the augmented 2d between the third and fourth degrees of the scale (example 3). A third common melody-type, not mentioned as such by Slobin but also containing an augmented 2d, uses the harmonic minor scale associated with many Yiddish folk songs, in which the augmented interval is found between the sixth and seventh degrees of the scale (example 4).

Example 1. Frigish mode as a scale

Example 2. Phrygian mode as a scale

Example 3. ♯ 4th melody-type

Example 4. Harmonic minor mode as a scale

Musical characteristics other than the augmented 2d are also associated with the Eastern European Jewish and with Turkish- or Arab-derived, non-Jewish repertoires of folk songs and dances with which Jewish communities came in contact. For example, there seems to be overwhelming preference for scalar, as opposed to disjunct, melodies and for heavily ornamented passages in performance—also a common improvisational practice of Turkish and Arabic music. Ornaments—such as the repetition of an important interval, a mordant, or a trill found on the penultimate beat of a cadential formula or a well-placed turn on a structurally important note—help associate this music with Hebrew liturgical chant as well as with Turkish-derived music based on the *makam* system (Signell 1986).

Furthermore, certain stylistic features and performance preferences indicated in the *Sefer Ha-Nigunim* transcriptions—such as a slow rubato or a marchlike tempo marking, frequent change of meter and mode (with an occasional appearance of the Western major scale), or the use of vocables (such as "bam, bam" or "ai, ai")—all contribute to a sound context that carried in the past, and continues to carry today, musical as well as social and religious meaning for Jewish and non-Jewish communities alike.

The Music of the *Sefer Ha-Nigunim:* Inner Core
Compositions by Schneur Zalman

Lubavitchers regard Schneur Zalman as the first and most renowned Lubavitcher composer, the one who first truly perceived and uncovered the precious sparks hidden deep within music: "If the Ba'al Shem Tov brought a spirit of life to melody, Schneur Zalman came and deepened it and revealed to many the hidden parts of the soul. And from that time onward, a new kind of melody came to Hasidism, one which was in the form of Habad melody, which is deeper and more elegant than other Hasidic music" (Zalmanoff 1948b:20).

Thirteen of the 347 collected melodies are attributed to Schneur Zalman. In addition, he is credited with the third section of another nigun, "Nigun Shelosh Tenuot" ("The Nigun of the Three Movements"), placing him last in a compositional lineage that includes the Ba'al Shem Tov, believed to be the composer of the first section, and Dov Baer (the disciple of the Ba'al Shem Tov and the teacher of Schneur Zalman), the putative composer of the second.

It is not clear whether or not Schneur Zalman or any of the early Hasidic leaders were the actual composers of these tunes, in the sense that we usually understand the term "composer" today. Indeed, they were probably not the songs' individual creators. As mentioned in chapter 5, it was the custom in Lubavitcher culture (as well as in Jewish musical culture as a whole) to borrow and adapt melodies that were already part of the larger repertoires of Jewish and non-Jewish musical cultures. But once adopted, a nigun usually became associated with, or is said to have been composed by, the person who first introduced it within the context of a Hasidic gathering. What is important here is that this body of thirteen songs, whether composed or adopted by Schneur Zalman, provides a significant and highly valued inner core within an already established canon of songs from which one can extrapolate salient musical characteristics, as well as notions of Lubavitcher value and aesthetics, that together can serve as a template for all Lubavitcher music.

Example 5 is a transcription of "The Rav's Nigun," also called the "Alter Rebbe's Nigun" or the "Nigun of the Four Stanzas," which is in many ways the most important Lubavitcher composition and, as such, can be used as a

Example 5. "Rav's Nigun" (reprinted from Zalmanoff 1948b:1)

model of a generalized Lubavitcher musical style. This nigun, believed to be a musical essence of Habad philosophy and history, is performed only at the beginning of Elul (the last and holiest month of the Hebrew calendar, just before the New Year), at significant life-cycle rituals (such as circumcisions, bar mitzvahs, and weddings), or on the anniversary of Schneur Zalman's release from prison (19 Kislev) (Stambler and Stambler 1962).

From its very beginning, "The Rav's Nigun" highlights the augmented 2d characteristic of the frigish melody-type. Further, each stanza, except the fourth, emphasizes this interval at its cadence, an important structural point. The fourth stanza actually ends with the third stanza repeated, bringing the augmented 2d cadential formula in at the end. Further evidence of the importance of this interval is its consistent ornamentation, especially at cadential points.

Clearly, the use of the frigish melody-type not only marks this song as part of an established Jewish musical repertoire; it also signals the importance of the frigish melody-type to Lubavitcher culture in particular. After all, its composer, Schneur Zalman, the founder of Habad Hasidism, chose this particular melody-type, with its quintessential "yearning" interval, to be his signature nigun. It is the most important Lubavitcher melody, the first one notated in the *Sefer Ha-Nigunim*, and the only one of all 347 to bear his name in its title.

But there is far more than mere association that links this song's musical structures to important Habadic principles. For example, Lubavitchers note that this song contains four stanzas, each of which is repeated entirely, and that it contains a repeated section (the stanzas are clearly indicated in the title and in the *Sefer Ha-Nigunim* score, an unusual Lubavitcher practice). Many Lubavitchers refer to this song as the "Nigun of the Four Worlds," as its overall structure is believed to incorporate the essence of the "four-ness" associated with the tetragrammaton of God's name, the four worlds of the ten sefirot, and the four-stage process of devekut.

Further, each stanza either extends its range upward or is placed at a higher range, with stanza four reaching its peak on G, a 10th above the tonic E. This rising pattern clearly follows the upward trajectory of the process of devekut and resonates with the core Lubavitcher metaphor of movement from the heart (the beginning of the song at the E–A mid-range level) to the head (the high G peak). The lowest note, a C♯ below the tonic, E (the "heel" of the song), only appears briefly in the fourth section, quickly rising to the stable mid-range level at the end (i.e., the song returns to the heart). What makes the song both musically and spiritually interesting, though, is its constant falling patterns (measures 5, 9, 15, and at cadence points). Creation, restoration, and adherence to the divine are conceptualized as continuous processes in Lubavitcher thinking. One is continuously falling and rising again.

To continue, each stanza is repeated, and stanza three is repeated again as the second half of stanza four. In stanza three, the fragment G♯–F–E (the essential falling augmented 2d pattern) is repeated three times and occurs again at the end of each stanza at its cadence. The beginning of stanza two is a repetition of measures four and five of stanza one; these measures themselves are a filling out of the original motive that begins the song: four repeated notes introduced by a pickup. Clearly, repetition at many different structural levels is significant in this music, just as it is in the neverending, constantly repeated processes of creation, devekut (adherence), tikkun (restoration), and avodah (constantly vigilant work).

Finally, this song contains no text and is performed using various vocables that are phonemically consistent with Hebrew, Russian, and Yiddish, the languages spoken by a majority of Eastern European Hasidim. Often referred to by outsiders as meaningless syllables, these vocables, on the contrary, carry much meaning for Lubavitchers. First, they are believed to symbolize the four letters of God's name (YHVH); second, their use emphasizes the middle-level status of nigun, existing between the material, everyday world of the body and the world of the divine; and, finally, their connection to the everyday and ritual languages of Eastern European Jews reconnects the present-day performer and listener with the past and with the more holy generations.

What about elements of time in the music? Although notated in the *Sefer Ha-Nigunim* in common time (4/4), the direction *Adagio molto religioso* is given at the beginning of the piece. This is, in a sense, an invitation to performers to add an ornament here or there, to linger on a high note, to emphasize an important interval, all performance practices considered to be not only important religiously but also aesthetically pleasing. A nigun performed in this style is frequently referred to by Lubavitchers as a deveikus (devekut) nigun, a nigun of cleaving to or yearning for, a clear reference to the four-stage process referred to in chapter 3. Devekut nigunim are generally regarded as the deepest, most spiritually fulfilling nigunim in the repertoire.

Extending the analysis to Schneur Zalman's other compositions, a clear compositional style begins to emerge. Of the thirteen nigunim attributed to Schneur Zalman, all use an augmented 2d melody-type throughout or in at least one section. Ten nigunim use the principle of four-ness at some structural level, all repeat at both small and large structural units, and most retain the familiar "peak and fall" melodic contour. Six of the thirteen nigunim attributed to Schneur Zalman are not texted; five contain a Hebrew text from Psalms and other books of the Hebrew Bible; and two are partially texted, using Hebrew texts. Nine of the thirteen nigunim are notated in duple meter (4/4 and 2/4), while three are in triple meter, and one is a mixture of duple and triple. Finally, all thirteen songs are to be rendered slowly: six are marked explicitly as *Adagio molto expressivo* or *Lento, religioso molto expressivo* by their Lubavitcher transcribers.

Before moving on, examine the song "Shelosh Tenuot" ("Nigun of the Three Movements") (example 6), whose third movement (measures 12–15) is attributed to Schneur Zalman. In his movement, Schneur Zalman continued the compositional practice set up by Dov Baer: namely, repeating measures 4–6 of the Ba'al Shem Tov's original melody a fifth higher than Dov Baer, who had himself raised it a fifth.[4] Thus, an octave and a sixth (B♭–G) and three separate tonal areas (B♭ minor, F minor, C minor) separate the three movements. One interesting point is that the Ba'al Shem Tov's first movement encompasses seven measures (in this notation); Dov Baer's movement, which repeats only part of the first movement, is six measures long; but Schneur Zalman's movement is only four measures. The beginning of the devekut process, say Lubavitchers, is often hampered by inertia—one sometimes needs an extra push at the start. Further, repetition is not only evident in the overall structure of the piece but at the tiniest motivic level as well (as are the repeatedly rising and falling lines). Finally, marked *Adagio molto religioso*, notated in duple time, and performed using vocables, this nigun obviously belongs to the devekut type.

Example 6. "Shelosh Tenuot" (reprinted from Zalmanoff 1948b:15)

Taking the thirteen (and a third) nigunim as a whole, five basic compositional principles are found in Schneur Zalman's music: (1) there is an overwhelming preference for the augmented 2d melody-types, including the harmonic minor mode; (2) four is an important structural number at the motivic, verse, and sectional levels; (3) repetition at many levels is essential; (4) nigunim are to be performed religiously—that is, at a slow tempo, with much expression, heavy ornamentation, and a liberal sense of time; (5) true nigunim are textless and performed using vocables, but a Hebrew prayer or biblical passage is sometimes used in a texted or partially texted nigun.

Compositions through the Fifth Generation (c. 1920)

Also included in section 1 of the three volumes of the *Sefer Ha-Nigunim* are eleven other compositions attributed to the "Heads of Chabad," given in chronological order by the composers' dates. By the twenty-fifth song, all of the Rebbes from the first to the fifth generation are represented, either by their own compositions or by those composed at their court. The fifth generation represented here is that of Rabbi Sholom Dovber (1860–1920), the last Lubavitcher Rebbe to die in Russia. With minor exceptions, the eleven compositions of the Heads of Habad resemble the prototype compositions attributed to Schneur Zalman in almost every respect.

Before leaving this discussion of the Lubavitcher core repertoire, it is worth examining the compositions attributed to the Charitonov brothers, Sholom and Asher, who lived in Nikolayev, a Habad center in southern Ukraine located on the Black Sea plain. Placement of their compositions begins in section 2 and continues into section 3 of the *Sefer Ha-Nigunim*, marking them as spiritually near, but not central, to the inner core.

Favorites of the fifth Rebbe, Sholom Dovber, and his son, Joseph Isaac Schneersohn (the sixth Rebbe), the Charitonovs are cited more than any others as the most important Lubavitcher composers by present-day members of the community. Blessed, they say, with beautiful voices, exceptional compositional talent, and unquestioned piety, the Charitonov brothers composed some of "the most delicate[,] . . . meaningful, and inspirational nigunim" in the Lubavitcher repertoire (Sharitonow 1973).

There are nine melodies in the *Sefer Ha-Nigunim* attributed to either one or both of the Charitonovs, including some simply labeled "Nikolaiev Nigun." Below are two nigunim, one by Asher Charitonov (example 7), the other by Sholom (example 8). Asher's nigun conforms almost totally to the stylistic framework already established by previous Lubavitcher composers,

Example 7. "Nikolaiev Nigun," by Asher Charitonov (reprinted from Zalmanoff 1948b:53)

while Sholom's is a distinct departure: notated in 6/8 time (highly unusual for a Lubavitcher nigun), its structure resembles a typical nineteenth-century, Western European folk song. It has four lines, each repeated once; a repeated motive (the arpeggiated D minor triad) used at the beginning and at cadences); and no augmented 2d. Conforming somewhat to the Lubavitcher model (the song is wordless; its third line is at the peak pitch level),

Example 8. "Nikolaiev Nigun," by Sholom Charitonov (reprinted from Zalmanoff 1948b:61)

in overall character, the nigun is distinctly influenced by Western European—not Turkish, Eastern European, or liturgical—styles. It is, rather, tonal, tonic-oriented, and periodic in structure. Its obvious stylistic connection to the art or salon musics of mid-eighteenth-century Western Europe marked it for earlier Lubavitchers as a "modern"—that is, a Westernized—composition.

One last nigun attributed to the Charitonov brothers, "Der Benoni" (example 9), is found at the end of section 2 in the first volume of the *Sefer Ha-Nigunim*—essentially, the middle of the volume ("intermediate," heart level). With its title a mixture of Yiddish, the spoken everyday language of Lubavitchers, and Hebrew, the language of the Torah, and with its placement at the end of this series of divinely inspired tunes, it symbolizes both the importance of the average person, as described by Schneur Zalman, as well the more general Hasidic notion that such a person exists near the foot of the divine body.

Musically, "Der Benoni" incorporates every one of the coded structures recognized as significant spiritual and ethnic markers by Lubavitchers: the use of the raised fourth melody-type; the four-part structure; heavy ornamentation; an opening percussive and marchlike motive at the head of each

Example 9. "Nikolaiev Nigun: Der Benoni" (reprinted from Zalmanoff 1948b:37)

section; and the characteristic rise in the second and third sections. So successful is this piece in using these codes that one might almost see it as a stereotype of Lubavitcher music.

The *Sefer Ha-Nigunim:* Moving Outward

Songs that exist on the fence, or the border between in and out, are defined here as those that were commonly shared between the Lubavitcher and other Jewish communities. These songs, although probably not specifically composed by Lubavitchers or for a Lubavitcher Rebbe were, nonetheless, considered musically and spiritually valid enough to be incorporated into the collection. Certain repertoires—such as the daily and holiday prayer cycles, liturgical formulas, Yiddish songs and dances, ballads, lullabies, and other folk musics—were known to all communities and were frequently shared. Occasionally, words were eliminated or new words substituted, but the tunes remained relatively stable. Familiar and widespread songs—such as "Ashreinu"; the Yiddish song "Essen"; and "Nigun Rikud," a combination of two Passover songs, "Chad Gad Ya" and "Dayenu"—were clearly part of a wider community of shared songs and dances. Musically, they closely resemble the Lubavitcher models. It is in the music borrowed from non-Jewish sources that one sees a more creative manipulation of textual and musical materials.

Romanian, Hungarian, Russian, and especially Ukrainian folk songs frequently entered the Lubavitcher repertoire, along with newly composed nigunim and with musics shared with the wider Jewish community. Not so different musically, they were generally able to convey many of the same musical (if not spiritual) codes as Lubavitcher-generated songs. Such songs, however, had to undergo a considerable spiritual transformation. They had to be removed from their non-Jewish performance contexts, changed significantly, and reinterpreted within a Lubavitcher context to take on their new form as nigun—that is, they had to undergo the process of musical tikkun.

As discussed in chapter 5, many songs in section 3 of the *Sefer Ha-Nigunim* were taken from the surrounding non-Jewish peasant musical culture and refashioned as nigunim by their borrower-composers. Labeled variously as "Wallachian Airs" (brought in from Wallachia, now part of southern Romania) or "Shepherd Melodies," these tunes suggested images of peaceful, pastoral contexts and of the wandering shepherd, long a staple metaphor of the Jewish diaspora, who was conceptualized as a relatively benign, friendly, and nonthreatening figure, forever free but always searching and longing for a divine purpose.

The "Wallachian Airs" found in the *Sefer Ha-Nigunim* are of special musical interest in that they combine elements from both the devekut and simhah styles. Thus, they are both similar to and different from the core Lubavitcher repertoire. First, their original texts have been removed and vocables have been substituted; each begins with a relatively long section, often divided into four parts; each uses most of the stylistic features described above as characteristic of Lubavitcher compositions and performances: the augmented 2d scalar melodies, heavy ornamentation, and free tempi in performance.

Each of the beginning phrases is further characterized by a triplet figure or a rising, dotted, rhythmic pickup motive. However, near to the end of each of these tunes, there is a sudden change of key and character, with more regular phrases and repeating, syncopated rhythmic patterns predominating.

One melody, "Shamil" (example 10), illustrates the Lubavitcher tendency to expose the hidden, allegorical meaning in a common song (i.e., its spark), thus revealing its potential as a true nigun. This tune and a now-missing text (as introduced by Rabbi Ephraim Rosenblum in the preceding chapter) are said to have been composed by a Georgian (non-Jewish) soldier as he wasted away in a Russian prison. His story is repeated in the *Sefer Ha-Nigunim* and on the record jacket of the Nichoach recording (volume 4). The interpretation of this is provided by Rabbi Zalmanoff: "The soul descends to this world from the heavens above, clothed in the earthly body of a human being. The soul's physical vestments here are really its prison cell, for it constantly longs for spiritual, heavenly fulfillments. The soul strives to free itself from the 'exile' of the human body and its earthly pleasures by directing its physical being into the illuminated and living paths of Torah and mitzvos" (Krinsky 1973).

One of the many techniques of borrowing and adaption mentioned above is that of keeping an existing text but reinterpreting its meaning (Koskoff 1978). Russian or Ukrainian folk songs about such mundane subjects as drinking or eating too much, visiting public taverns, and other excesses are reframed into Lubavitcher allegories more in keeping with Hasidic teachings. For example, the Russian song "Nye Zhuritze Chloptze" (example 11) is about

Example 10. "Shamil" (reprinted from Zalmanoff 1965:90)

Example 11. "Nye Zhuritze Chloptze" (reprinted from Zalmanoff 1948b:98)

drinking, as this translation of its text shows: "Don't worry fellows, about what will become of us; we will travel to an inn—over there will surely be vodka." But this worldy song has been reinterpreted to symbolize the Lubavitchers' deep devotion to their Rebbe, who will let them drink from the "well of Torah and Chassidism" (Zalmanoff 1961).

Lubavitchers also sometimes lived surrounded by unfriendly or even hostile non-Jews, such as landowners, Russian and Polish armies, and, in the early nineteenth century, the Napoleonic Army, all of whom at different times led raids against Jewish settlements and established communities. Some of these events were parodied in songs that eventually became nigunim. For example, tunes in the *Sefer Ha-Nigunim* marked "Fonke" (from *fonye*, meaning a non-Jewish Russian or a Cossack) mimic the yelling and screaming of the Russian military with their high, sharp, repeated figures, marked in the *Sefer Ha-Nigunim* score as to be heavily accented in performance.

A final example, taken from the end of section 3 of the *Sefer Ha-Nigunim*, is "Napoleon's March" (example 12), an actual French tune taken from the advancing troops of Napoleon's Army.[5] Squarely in major, with its simple, regular, unornamented phrases and strict march tempo, "Napoleon's March," placed at the foot of the collection, bears almost no musical resemblance to the intensely wrought nigunim of Rabbi Schneur Zalman, which appear at the head. Symbolically, however, this tune, recalling the treachery of Napoleon's abandonment of the Jews, also signals the ultimate defeat of Napo-

Example 12. "Napoleon's March" (reprinted from Zalmanoff 1948b:142)

leon's power through the mystical transformation of his army's music and its redemption as a nigun.

Musically, then, the nigunim presented in the *Sefer Ha-Nigunim* follow the same model as found in the collection's overall organization. As the tunes travel down the table of contents (metaphorically, the Jewish body)—from the head, to the heel, and outward to the sitra achra—the melodies become dimmer and dimmer. That is, they begin to shed their brightness, or "Hasidicness," in the form of musical structures that for Lubavitchers are spiritually encoded. As the sparks dim, the music becomes more and more like music from outside the Jewish body, such as folk or art songs from the non-Jewish population. That these outside songs are nonetheless considered nigunim—after all, they have been included in the *Sefer Ha-Nigunim* collection—is musical evidence for the real and lasting restoration of a divine spark.

Thus, the printed repertoire, notated by Lubavitcher musicians and transcribers and preserved in the ways of Western culture—in book form—is seen as having value in and of itself, in that it is a material preservation of core beliefs. The *Sefer Ha-Nigunim,* however, has almost no value as a prescription for musical behavior. Almost no one uses them to learn the nigunim, to study their compositional features, or to provide examples for arranging, teaching, or performing. Indeed, very few Lubavitchers read music or even own the *Sefer Ha-Nigunim* collection. The living essence of nigunim for contemporary Lubavitchers is in their performance.

Notes

1. See Powers (1980) for an excellent article on "mode."

2. Although the church modes (e.g., Dorian, Phrygian, etc.) are usually referred to as modes, they are not modes as defined here; they will be presented in this work as scales.

3. The frigish mode is also related to the Jewish prayer mode *ahavah rabah*, where the augmented interval also occurs between the second and third scale degrees. According to Eric Werner, the ahavah rabah mode was "supposed to be the perfect expression of penitential contrition and deep lament—the theological ideal of a cantor's effect upon the worshippers" (Werner 1976; qtd. in Slobin 1982:187). Finally, the frigish melody-type resembles the Arabic mode (maqam) *Hijaz*, with its augmented interval also placed between the second and third degrees.

4. This "fifth construction" is typical of folk songs of Hungary and other parts of Eastern Europe.

5. The French national anthem, "The Marseillaise," was also adapted by Lubavitcher Hasidim, who eliminated the text and added a Hebrew prayer and vocables (Koskoff 1976). It is still frequently sung at farbrengens in Crown Heights.

PART 3: INSIDE THE PERFORMANCE

In introducing the Lubavitcher world, its conceptualization of music, and its core repertoire, I have presented a philosophical, historical, and social context that endows nigunim with tremendous, almost magical, power, as well as a context of musical sounds and structures that symbolically signify the essence of Habad Hasidism and Lubavitcher social relations. So far, however, I have concentrated on an idealization of Lubavitcher culture, one that sets forth a coherent religious, social, and musical system that, when integrated, presents a recognizable, framed picture of Lubavitcher life.

But how is this intricate system acted out, or performed, by real people living, so to speak, on the everyday, untidy, ground level of culture? The next four chapters isolate four central beliefs in the Lubavitcher world and show how each of these beliefs is materialized or given form through music and musical performance. In this way, music becomes more than just its sound; it becomes the means by which Lubavitchers perform their core beliefs into being.

7
Performing the Past in Music

The Past as Spiritual

One of the most important core beliefs in Lubavitcher culture is that true spirituality is irrevocably linked to the past. As seen in the metaphor of the weakening or coarsening of the generations, those who pass on move upward and inward toward the divine head, while those that remain are destined to live downward and outward at the level of the calloused heel. While both the past/head and present/heel are necessary for the body as a whole, it is the idealized past that is seen as a time of spiritual giants. Any connection one makes in this lifetime with that spirituality is counted as a blessing. So strong is this connection that it occurs as a perennial theme in the Rebbe's talks:

> The Rebbe always asks us the following question: If we are spiritually weaker—then why should Messiah come in our days, if he hasn't come before? So it's explained to us that we are like dwarfs, and in the past great people are like giants. Giants! If the dwarf, though, is placed on the giant's shoulders, then we are higher than the giant—not by our own powers but by going in their ways. By using what they have already done, we can achieve greater heights. In other words, when we say that we are weaker spiritually, it means that our own, new creative powers are less, but we have much more to build on. If we build on the past, this gives us a higher thing. There's such a strong connection in Yiddishkeit between the present and the past. They merge, and they use each other to get further. (Gurwitz interview)

This belief in the spiritual ideal of the past is one of the most important underlying concepts that governs contemporary Lubavitcher musical aesthetics and performance practice. It is crucial that today's Lubavitchers perform and compose songs that somehow link them to the past, and it is precisely this interaction with the past that allows their spirituality to grow in present times.

In chapter 6, I introduced the idea that certain musical structures—such as the augmented 2d scalar-melody type, embedded repetition, and "four-ness"—carried symbolic, coded meanings of Jewish ethnic and religious identity, in essence creating musical stereotypes known to both Jews and non-Jews alike, and that these codes lay within the musical structures of Lubavitcher nigunim themselves. Performances, too, carry coded meanings. For Lubavitchers, simply singing a nigun might be of some minimal spiritual value; but to create a channel to the divine through the past, one must observe specific traditional performance practices that, from the outside, might seem extreme. Indeed, such practices as swaying, drinking alcohol, screaming, and fainting continue to bring harsh criticism or derision on Lubavitchers and other Hasidim from their critics today. This chapter explores the present-day performance of nigunim as a form of musical negotiation with the idealized, spiritually elevated past.

The Past in Musical Performance

Although nigunim and other musics are frequently sung on a variety of occasions, nowhere are they more enthusiastically performed than at a farbrengen, that quintessential Hasidic gathering of men (or women) who come together to pray, study, and celebrate. At a Rebbe's farbrengen at "770," performances can become quite spirited; but even in one's home, listening to recorded performances, the ideal of hitlahavut must be a palpable presence in the recording, which becomes, in essence, a symbolic performance of past musical occasions where devekut, the underlying motivation of all Hasidic action, was accomplished.

Here, I will concentrate on two kinds of performance contexts: live performances at farbrengens; and recorded performances, which are used predominantly for teaching Hasidic concepts or as a form of entertainment in the home. In live performances in the synagogue, such as at a Rebbe's farbrengen, no instruments are permitted (commemorating the destruction of the Second Temple (74 C.E.); on Lubavitcher recordings, however, nigunim are frequently arranged using a variety of instruments and structural features, each of which carries special meaning within Jewish musical culture.

Live Performance: Today's Farbrengens

Although today's farbrengens (especially those held since the death of the Rebbe in 1994) are usually exciting and rousing events to an outsider, contemporary Lubavitchers describe them as pale shadows of the raucous gatherings of the past, where the Rebbe and his followers were able to call up the spirits of past Rebbes and communicate directly with them. Lubavitcher folklore is filled with many tales that attest to the role nigun plays in achieving a spiritual union with the holy men of previous generations.[1] This is especially effective if the nigun being performed is known to have been associated with or composed by an especially revered ancestor. Martin Buber has collected a tale recounting a conversation between Schneur Zalman and a friend: "In the Palestinian Talmud we read that he who says a word in the name of him who originated it, must—in his mind's eye—conjure the author up before him. This is only a fancy, but he who sings a melody another devised— that other is really with him while he sings" (Buber 1948:272).

Another tale relates an incident that occurred one night at a farbrengen during the time of the previous Rebbe, Joseph Isaac Schneersohn. According to this anecdote, a man suddenly jumped up and began singing a song that was known to have been composed by the third Lubavitcher Rebbe:

> Everyone stood up and joined the singing. When they got to the place that was well known to them, where the words are, "Happy are they who will not forget Thee," everyone became ecstatic—so much so that their faces became enflamed and on their cheeks tears began to flow. You could see that these people were experiencing that holy moment [when the Rebbe first sang this song], and there was no shadow of a doubt that everyone there knew and felt that he was standing near the Rebbe, and was seeing and hearing how the Rebbe prayed. (Zalmanoff 1948b:25)

Clearly, then, the ideal contemporary performance is one that is not only associated with past generations but also with past performance events and behaviors. Thus, today's Lubavitcher performers must create the past anew each time a performance takes place in the present. Both the music and its contemporary performance, in essence, act together as mediators negotiating between two worlds: the idealized past and the spiritually weakened present, both of which are constructed in the context of a contemporary musical performance. How, specifically, is this accomplished?

The Musical Performance of *Devekut*

One way in which Lubavitchers bring forth the past in the present is to connect musical performance to the essential four-step processes associated with the spirituality of the great Hasidic leaders of the past, especially the four worlds of the sefirot and the four stages of devekut, which include kavvanah (awakening the proper intention of an action); mesmerizing the animal soul; separating the divine and animal souls; and devekut (ultimate adherence). These four stages (awakening, self-evaluation, work, and union) are used as general behavioral guides to be realized in all actions of the everyday and ritual world; they are also useful in creating an aesthetically pleasing, powerful, and effective musical performance.

The four stages of musical behavior that correspond to the stages of devekut are: (1) awakening: choosing the correct nigun according to specific criteria; (2) self-evaluation: marked expressive gestures, such as heavy accenting of beats, ornamentation, repetition, and the ingesting of alcohol; (3) work: swaying, screeching, sharping the pitch, speeding up, and the performance of extraordinary gestures (such as weeping and raising arms); (4) devekut: swooning, unconsciousness. Table 3 shows the four stages of devekut, the four general actions, and the four musical actions aligned.

Table 3. The Four Stages of *Devekut* Aligned with the Four General and Musical Actions

Process of *Devekut*	General Action	Musical Action
1. Awakening the *kavvanah*	Any action	Choosing correct *nigun*
2. Mesmerizing the animal soul	Introspection, self-evaluation	Expressive musical gestures (accenting, ornamentation, repetition, drinking)
3. Separation of the souls	Hard work, effort	Extraordinary musical gestures (wild bodily movements, screaming, drinking)
4. Union with *devekut* (the divine)	Total absorption in task, focus on divine	Swooning, unconsciousness

Stage 1: Awakening (Musical Choice)

This preliminary stage involves awakening the intention of the performer, who must choose an appropriate nigun. If the correct nigun is not chosen,

any positive actions brought by the singing of such a song remain suspended. As choosing the correct nigun is crucial to the awakening of the proper
intention, only the Rebbe, those who are directly related to him, or men who
know him well are trusted with this responsibility in a group performance
such as a farbrengen.

The choice of a nigun must be made taking into account the general as
well as specific context. For example, around 1975, the Rebbe began to dis-
courage the performance of devekut nigunim, proclaiming that with simhah nigunim, joy opens the gates. Under certain circumstances, such as the
anniversary of a previous Rebbe's death, however, devekut songs are still
performed in the main Lubavitcher synagogue at 770. More specifically,
someone must choose a song with the correct spirit—that is, the choice must
come from text taken from a specific biblical verse just mentioned by the
Rebbe in his talk, or it must be a song without a text, but one closely associated with a spiritually elevated ancestor mentioned by the Rebbe in his talk,
an ancestor who was known to have composed or favored it. As the talks at a
farbrengen are improvised on general themes, the people responsible for
choosing the nigunim must know both the Rebbe and the repertoire well,
so as not to choose badly. Most songs sung at a Rebbe's farbrengen today can
be found in the third section of the *Sefer Ha-Nigunim.* Only occasionally are
newly composed songs performed unless there is a specific occasion to do
so, such as the Rebbe's birthday (see chapter 9).

*Stage 2: Self-Evaluation: Mesmerizing the Nonhuman Animal Soul
through Expressive Musical Gestures*

This stage is marked in musical performance by the exaggeration of certain
musical parameters (such as strong accents on every beat, ornamentation,
and repetition). Singing the song with feeling allows the nonhuman animal
soul to become temporarily hypnotized, suspended, and ineffectual in its
perpetual conflict with the divine soul. Drinking small portions of vodka or
other alcoholic beverages is also encouraged to help the nonhuman animal
soul to "go to sleep." It is during this stage that self-reflection and evalua-
tion take place, as the performance of nigun is believed to be a primary vehicle for self-knowledge.

Example 13 is a transcription of the beginning of a typical nigun, "Nye
Zhuritze Chloptze," which was previously introduced in chapter 6. Recorded live at a Rebbe's farbrengen around 1980, the performance shows many
of the features earlier described as crucial to this second stage of musical

❀ = foot stomp

Example 13. First statement of "Nye Zhuritze Chloptze," performed by the Lubavitcher Choir of Men and Boys (Chabad-Lubavitch, tape 1; transcribed by the author)

devekut: repetition, heightening the augmented 2d interval—especially in its descent to the second and first degrees—and marked accenting.

Stage 3: Work: Separation of the Two Animal Souls through Extraordinary Musical Gestures

In stage 3, the nonhuman and the human animal souls separate, and the human animal soul rises upward toward the divine soul, located in the head. The human soul, however, still needs the body to continue its work to help keep the vestiges of the nonhuman soul from attacking the more elevated human soul as it rises. This stage is realized in musical performance through an exaggeration of performance gestures. Here, the musical and bodily behaviors extend to loud clapping, shouting, thumping, sharping, speeding up, swaying, and, at times, dancing. Arms begin to flail, drinking becomes more obvious, the Rebbe's fists become more tightly clenched as he cues the men to sing faster and with even more force. Stage 3 must be realized through physical bodily effort. Various features—such as a noticeable sharping, an increase of tempo, and more of a pushed, harsh vocal quality—are becoming obvious here (example 14). These performance characteristics are seen as musical equivalents of the repetitive actions of avodah (sustained work), which is needed to keep the two animal souls separated.

❀ = foot stomp
+ = hand clap

Example 14. First repeat of "Nye Zhuritze Chloptze," performed by the Lubavitcher Choir of Men and Boys (Chabad-Lubavitch, tape 1; transcribed by the author)

Stage 4: Devekut *(Union)*

After many repetitions, many sips of vodka, and wilder and wilder bodily gestures, swooning or unconsciousness may take place. It is not uncommon to see one body slump onto the shoulder of another, slowly sinking to the step of the riser, or onto the floor in exhaustion. The men on either side may attempt to hold up their neighbor, especially if they are located on one of the top risers, as falling from that distance can cause serious injury. These behaviors are inevitably interpreted as overstimulation in the face of the divine, and those who achieve unconsciousness are treated with special deference. Below is the end of the second repetition of "Nye Zhuritze Chloptze," as recorded on the farbrengen tape (example 15). Notice the further exaggeration of performance gestures discussed earlier.

The live performance practices cited here serve a dual purpose: their energy helps lift the spiritually weakened Lubavitcher from the inertia that he or she feels from having been mired down with the week's trivial cares; and their association to past practices helps provide a literal connection to the generations that exist at a higher level and that are, in a sense, helping to pull participants upward and inward through the fence separating past and present worlds.

Recorded Musical Performances

The recordings of Lubavitcher nigunim made by the Nichoach Society provide a better representation of the wider repertoire than the live farbrengen performances today. Examples from all three sections of the *Sefer Ha-Nigunim* appear on recordings, each arranged for solo voice or for male choir and various small instrumental ensembles. Such arrangements, like the

✿ = foot stomp

+ = hand clap

Example 15. Second repeat of "Nye Zhuritze Chloptze," performed by the Lubavitcher Choir of Men and Boys (Chabad-Lubavitch, tape 1; transcribed by the author)

specific musical codes discussed in chapter 6, also give clues as to the nigun's symbolic spiritual and social distance or closeness to Lubavitcher core beliefs or notions of otherness.

The Nichoach Society, formed in the late 1940s to research and collect nigunim, began recording them in 1958. The singers were selected from the best of the Lubavitcher musicians, including Cantors Moshe Teleshevsky and Eli Lipsker, as well as many men and boys from the Baumgarten and Gansbourg families, among others. Non-Lubavitcher (but in most cases observant) Jewish musicians were hired to make the musical arrangements and, in some cases, to perform instrumental parts.

The recordings have continued on and off from that time to the present and are easily available at Drimmer's Judaica, a store located around the corner from the synagogue on Kingston Avenue. In addition to Lubavitcher-produced media, there are a number of other recordings and videos available for the Hasidic and Orthodox Jewish communities of Crown Heights. These include recordings and videos for children, for women, and many nigunim and other songs recorded by observant Jewish musicians. Originally pressed onto vinyl LPs, they are now available in tape cassette and CD formats to the Lubavitcher community as well as to interested outsiders.

The majority of songs recorded by Nichoach are taken from the core repertoire, but occasionally a song newly composed for the Rebbe's birthday or one introduced by an important visitor will be included. The recordings are frequently played in the home, especially among newcomers to the community, who find them a pleasant way to absorb Hasidic values, and at Lubavitcher-run schools and camps, where children are taught the basics of Jewish and Habad philosophies. What is significant here, though, is the way in which these recordings relate to the construction of the spiritually elevated past in the present.

First, as the recordings are made primarily for commercial use, every care has been taken in their production. For example, all of the volumes have been recorded in a professional recording studio, only the best male voices have been used, and the songs have been arranged. Indeed, it is precisely in the arrangements that the songs, now separated from the spontaneity of live performance, can successfully connect to the past. The arrangements, although made from the late 1950s onward to the present, universally conform to an idealized musical sound associated with eighteenth- and nineteenth-century Jewish instrumental performance practice.

For example, certain instruments long associated with Eastern European klezmer bands (such as the violin and clarinet), as well as instruments associated with nineteenth- and early-twentieth-century "pioneer" music in Palestine (such as the accordion), feature prominently in these recordings. A pronounced vocal style, recalling traditional Jewish liturgical practices, and controlled harmonizing, associated with nineteenth-century Eastern European folk materials, are also universally present, as are the strong rhythmic accents and stereotyped patterns of traditional Polish, Russian, and Lithuanian dances.

In addition to standard, ethnically coded instruments, the accompaniments themselves fall into two distinct styles, the first of which is associated with the spiritually elevated, wordless, and slowly moving nigunim (devekut, deveikus nigunim). The second is associated with nigunim used for happier occasions or for dancing (simcha, *lebidig* [happy] nigunim, or nigunei *rikud* [dance]). Devekut nigunim tend to be accompanied by simple chords, moving in streamlike progressions, outlining principle notes in the melody. There is no attempt at arrangement (in the standard musical sense) of either the tune itself or its accompaniment: that is, there is no vocal harmony or instrumental independence, no obligatos or ornamentation other than that provided by the melodic line. Nigunim, which fall into the category of joyous or dance songs, are usually arranged on these recordings for a small ensemble, consisting of piano, violin, bass, and clarinet. Here, there are frequent obligatos (or other independent instrumental lines) and simple vocal harmonies.

Performance practices associated with the four stages of devekut are also present, if less obviously, on recordings. Example 16 is a transcription of the nigun "Nye Zhuritze Chloptze," near the end of the second repeat of verse 1. By the third repetition of the song, the choir (but not the instruments) is sharping, and the men are beginning to shout, somewhat like the live performance discussed earlier. Furthermore, the repetitions of various melodic contours outlining the augmented 2d interval are becoming more and more accented, and the tempo has increased from ♩ = c. 100 (found at the beginning of the recording) to ♩ = c. 130. Altogether, this recorded arrangement captures many of the spiritually and musically significant performance practices heard in live performance.

One final example will illustrate the limits of Lubavitcher nigun arrangement. Here, there is an opposite secularized pole from the solemn, contemplative, and unobtrusive, chord-stream accompaniment found in most re-

Example 16. End of the first section of "Nye Zhuritze Chloptze," performed by the Lubavitcher Choir of Men and Boys, 1960 (transcribed by the author)

corded performances of devekut nigunim. "Hop Cossack" is perhaps the best example of the marching and joyous quality of nigunim that were also used as dance tunes. It is attributed to a Lubavitcher, the Shpoler Zeidi (Shpoli Grandpa). Unlike the pious and deeply serious devekut nigunim, this one is meant to be amusingly ironic, as it refers to an highly unusual incident where a Hasid bested a Russian nobleman. According to the record notes for *Chabad Nigunim,* volume 6:

> The "pritzim", the nobles ruling the villages in old Russia and Ukraine in those days, used to make sport on the Jews subject to them, by dressing them up in bearskins and forcing them to dance with a Cossack. When the Jew failed to keep step with the tune, he would suffer lashes with the whip. Once, a Jew who had rented an estate from the "poritz" [sing.] was imprisoned for failing to pay his rent on time. When his turn came to dance in the bearskin, the Shpoler Zeidi managed to take his place and perform the dance for him, which culminated in the Zeidi's gaining the upper hand over the Cossack. (Zalmanoff 1966)

All of the delicious humor of tricking a Russian (conceived as stupid, thuggish, and potentially dangerous) is presented in this song as a form of musical parody. The introduction (example 17), played by piano and violin, sets the tone with a humorous, marchlike, staccato rhythm punctuated by chromatic and scalar ornamentation. By the second section of this rather com-

Example 17. Introduction to "Hop Cossack," performed by the Lubavitcher Choir of Men and Boys, 1966 (transcribed by the author)

Example 18. Second section of "Hop Cossack," (transcribed by the author)

monplace Russian tune (example 18), set squarely in a major tonality, both the soloist and choir have sped up and sharpened considerably, imitating with a mannered ornamentation the quickened dancing step of the grandpa as he attempts to outdo his Cossack dancing partner. That these ornaments are usually associated with musical devekut only adds to their comedic effectiveness here. The second section also introduces a high "shouting" motive commonly found in many of the spirited Lubavitcher marches.

The third section of this song (example 19) becomes even more "Hasidic" as it switches abruptly to the augmented 4th scalar melody-type. The soloist performer, Eli Leib Rivkin, lets us know, though, that the spiritual/ethnic code introduced by this switch is to be regarded as a stereotype—that is, a parody of Jewish musical culture. Twice, his voice breaks over the augmented 2d interval as he exaggeratedly imitates the quintessential yearning figure. After all, this is a playful song being performed for an in-group audience, who will not only get the reference but delight in it. The song ends with a boys' choir playfully shouting, "Hop Cossack," their young taunting voices emphasizing the Shpoler Zeidi's victory and utter humiliation of his Cossack rival.

The songs presented here in their recorded arrangements show a clear and unmistakable progression away from the divine/head sound associated with heightened spirituality and an inner, core repertoire (streamlike chords, free

Example 19. Third section of "Hop Cossack," (transcribed by the author)

rhythm, etc.) and toward the mundane/heel sound associated with the secularized, non-Jewish repertoire (instrumental arrangement, parody, major tonality, etc.). However, their very presence in the *Sefer Ha-Nigunim* and in recorded volumes of Lubavitcher nigunim inverts this outwardly moving progression. For Lubavitchers, placing them here in this spiritual and musical context has also elevated these songs, bringing them inward from outside the fence and upward toward the divine source. In this way, the circle of negotiation between the inside and outside is complete.

One other set of recordings is worth mentioning here. The musician Rabbi Eli Lipsker (fig. 11), long recognized by the community as a prominent Lubavitcher singer and performer of the old style, has recorded more than twenty albums, including all 347 nigunim in the core repertoire. Recorded in his home, more for purposes of preservation than commercialization, Lipsker presents this core repertoire in a straightforward and unassuming way, using almost none of the stereotyped musical performance practices found in live performances or on the recordings.[2]

Lipsker is unusual in that he is one of the only professional musicians in the community who is also a lifetime Lubavitcher. Born in the former Georgian Republic of the Soviet Union, he was one of fourteen children raised in a rather poor but religious family. Unable to afford formal music lessons, he taught himself how to play the accordion by ear and soon was proficient in performing Lubavitcher nigunim for family and friends. Immigrating to the United States in the late 1940s, Lipsker was able to attend the Manhattan

Figure 11. Eli Lipsker at
his home in Crown
Heights (photograph by
the author, 1991)

School of Music, an educational path that was highly unusual for a young
Lubavitcher immigrant. His parents, fearing that he would turn away from
Judaism if he pursued a career in music, asked the Rebbe for advice. The
Rebbe told them "to encourage him and even give him any money he might
need toward that end. . . . thereby encouraging other observant Jewish mu-
sicians to find their niches" (Levin 1990).

Lipsker has continued to perform and record traditional Hasidic music
throughout his life, stating outright his disdain for the new Jewish music of
today that uses contemporary musical arrangements (see chapter 10). He
believes that "too many of the contemporary Jewish musicians have betrayed
their ethnic roots [and] criticizes this tendency of the Jewish music world to
imitate the fashions of contemporary music with their adaptions of disco and
rock music" ("'We'll Bring Moshiach Now!'" 1981).

The nigunim recorded by the Nichoach Society, Eli Lipsker, and others are often lovingly criticized as old-fashioned by younger Lubavitchers, many of whom have attempted to integrate new, mainstream popular song forms, harmonizations, and vocal styles into nigun performances and recordings. That they are indeed old-fashioned, though, is intentional. Being old gives them a certain spiritual status that is denied the music of the younger generation. And it is precisely because they are "fashioned old" that they are so effective in evoking the Lubavitcher historical and spiritual past in contemporary performance.

Notes

1. See Staiman (1994) for an excellent collection of stories.
2. Rumor has it that Lipsker made these recordings while at home during the day while his younger children were napping, which is why they sound quietly introspective.

8
Performing Gender in Music

Scene: "Visiting a Lubavitcher Home"

It is summer 1973, a few months after my initial foray into the Lubavitcher community, and I have been invited to the Rosenblums' for a Shabbos dinner. Rabbi Rosenblum had talked with me for quite a while on that first encounter and eventually invited me to his home to meet his wife and family. Approaching the house in the somewhat noisy Squirrel Hill neighborhood, I am immediately struck by the clutter. The porch is overflowing with old furniture, children's toys, and bicycles in various stages of dilapidation. Boxes line the edges of the porch; an old school desk, like the one I used in the 1950s, rests near the steps; a battered car, with its muffler half-off, lies exhausted in front of the house. Is this really the right address? Perhaps these people are just moving in? Or are they moving out?

I knock tentatively. Miriam Rosenblum comes to the door. She is a pleasant-looking woman, about my age, wearing a cotton dress and a kerchief on her head.

"Welcome, welcome," she beams. "You're early! Come, you can help me in the kitchen. Call me Miriam. Yosie, Freidi, twins, where are you? Time to get ready. Come, Ellen, you must wash your hands. Now, do you know the prayer?"

Prayer? I think. There's a prayer for washing your hands? There is so much I do not know—will I ever understand all of these rules?

"I'll help you," says Miriam, watching my blank face. "You must say it out loud after me."

I am wondering where Rabbi Rosenblum is. After all, he's the one who invited me. I wander into the kitchen, passing through the living room. All the lights are on, although it is still bright and sunny outside. The furniture is old but still comfortable, and bookshelves line the walls. I see a twenty-volume set of the Talmud and many other religious texts—no novels or magazines, no television. The room looks lived in, homey, clean, but cluttered, like the porch. On the wall are the most remarkable pictures, all of the Rebbe, peering out from under his brimmed hat with eyes that really do follow you around the room. This is somewhat unsettling to me. Why is his face so stern?

Rabbi Rosenblum rushes in. "Ah, you're here! Good!" We have a short but pleasant chat. I explain the nature of my research, what I am interested in studying. I tell him of my first encounter with a Lubavitcher at my nursery school. He smiles and tells me that if I am really interested in nigun, I must go to "770" in Crown Heights to get the true flavor.

It is sundown, and the candles are lit. I mumble the half-familiar passage with Miriam, embarrassed that I have never really learned even this simplest and most basic of prayers for women. There are more prayers. We eat: chicken, of course, and vegetables, great hallah bread, wine. Then Rabbi Rosenblum tells his six children seated around the table that I am interested in music, and the singing begins. This is great: it is what I came for.

A familiar tune pops up. Miriam is humming quietly. I begin to sing along.

"Shh," Miriam leans over and whispers in my ear. "Stop singing."

"Why?" I whisper back.

"I'll tell you later. Just be quiet."

The singing continues into the night. Rabbi Rosenblum has a beautiful baritone voice and sings with tremendous feeling and gusto. He and the children are really enjoying themselves.

"So: why can't I sing?" I prod Miriam later. I know women and men cannot sing together in the synagogue—but does that extend to the home as well?"

"The idea is that a woman's voice is beautiful. It has a lot of qualities that would be enticing to a man. This is a fact known anywhere. So, it's better that you don't sing. It would distract my husband."

I think to myself: am I really that attractive? In addition to thinking about my dissertation, I have become interested in the literature that is flowing out of the new women's movement. This conversation is beginning to sound like the male-induced rationalizations I have been reading about. Maybe Miriam needs some consciousness-raising. Are the Rosenblums unaware that there is a virtual revolution happening right outside their door? Of course, I realize that if I am really going to continue with this research, my opinion concerning Lubavitcher gender issues will only get in the way, but I cannot resist.

"Wait a minute," I suggest, my defenses up, "I might think that the sound of your husband's voice is enticing, so why is he allowed to sing in front of me?" I can see by her face that I have missed the point.

"Ephraim, Ellen wants to know why she can't sing in front of you, but you can sing in front of her." They both smile patiently at me as though I am a willful but lovable child. "Because the Torah forbids it, that's why," says Rabbi Rosenblum. "And the Torah is the will of God. We must all do the will of God."

On the one hand, I can accept this; it is the Lubavitcher way of thinking. But on the other hand, the budding feminist in me is not happy with this explanation. I begin, once again, to protest.

"Ellen, this is the way it is," Miriam explains. "It's been looked over a lot because liberated women are pushing away all of their ideas about being different. But for us in the Torah way, it is like this. Woman is woman, and man is man. Women have certain aspects which are appealing to men, and they cannot be taken away. Now, one of the *halakhic* (legal) considerations is that when a women sings, it has a very appealing aspect to a man who is not her own husband." She finishes with a look that says this conversation is closed.

I know it is counterproductive, but I am becoming annoyed. The topic of what men and especially women can and cannot do is like a red flag to me. I have been struggling with this issue in my own life, with my own family and friends. My dissertation research and my "real life" are beginning to merge uncomfortably here. Maybe working with Lubavitchers is not such a good idea. Maybe it is time for me to go home and think about this a little more, to make a clear choice. I pick up my purse to leave.

"You cannot carry on the Sabbath," Rabbi Rosenblum chides.

"What should I do, then?"

"Leave it here and pick it up tomorrow after sundown."

"No, I think I'll take it now." All these rules are beginning to get to me.

"Remember, God is watching," says Rabbi Rosenblum.

"I'll take my chances," I say, with an edge.

⌇

Two days later, I interviewed Miriam Rosenblum about this incident:

EK: I knew I shouldn't have done it [sing], and I remember turning to you and saying, "I know I shouldn't be singing, but I don't know why," and then you explained it, and then I said . . .

MR: You got on the defensive.

EK: No, I didn't, I said that a man's voice is just as enticing.

MR: "You're not gonna make me religious," you said (*laughing*).

EK: No, no, that's not what I said.

MR: It came around through what you said, I think (*still laughing*).

EK: I said to you, "But a man's voice is just as enticing," and you laughed.

MR: I guess it's not.

EK: It is to me.

MR: Yes, I guess that's—well—that's why we won't take you, okay?

Men and women live fairly separate but parallel lives within Hasidic society. Men spend much of their time working, studying, and praying, largely in the company of other men. Once married, women may also work, but their primary responsibility is raising children and maintaining an observant Jewish home. In addition, women's groups, such as various charity organizations and candle-lighting programs, eat up the time left over from home and childcare responsibilities. Even within the sanctity of the synagogue, men's and women's social and ritual spaces are clearly separated.

As first mentioned in chapter 1, and again in chapter 4, Lubavitcher gendered behavior is regulated by various laws of family purity and modesty, most of which are for the protection of women against their own sexual power and against an assumed, natural sexual aggression in men. These laws, like all of halakhah, act as a necessary fence surrounding both women and men, a fence that both protects what is precious within—a proper and ordered sexual relationship between men and women—and what threatens from without (possible male sexual aggression; unwanted pregnancy).

Nowhere is the performance of gender so clear as within the performance of music. Performing music as a Lubavitcher woman or man involves a separate set of behaviors, attitudes, even aesthetics that both reflects and regulates established gendered norms. This chapter explores the differences between Lubavitcher women's and men's music making and the underlying beliefs and assumptions that give rise to gendered musical behaviors.

Gendered Performance Contexts and Repertoires

Much Jewish law is written for and about men and deals with religious, familial, social, business, ethical, and other issues that affect men's daily and religious lives. There are, of course, laws for women also, such as those concerning marriage, prayer, modesty, and ritual purification. Both men and women are regarded positively as sexual creatures, and both are seen as responsible for their own sexual behaviors. However, as I first suggested in chapter 4, women are believed to be spiritually superior to men and are given the added responsibility of protecting men against their own aggressive sexual behavior.

Music is regarded by Hasidic culture, as in most world cultures, with a certain ambiguity. Intensely powerful, music, like sexual stimulation, can arouse either the human or the nonhuman animal soul. Music associated with liturgy, prayers, holidays, and other religious activities is regarded as an emotional and spiritual necessity, whereas that associated with non-Jewish culture, mixed public performance, and secular contexts is regarded as coarse and unseemly, something to be avoided.

Lubavitcher men and women are considered to be equal in their emotional connection to music and to the divine; and in the proper circumstances, with the proper musics, both have many opportunities to express themselves, often with the same repertoires. Problems arise when they do so together. Because women are generally conceptualized as naturally sexually alluring (whether they intend to be or not), and men are conceptualized as naturally sexually aggressive (whether they intend to be or not), adding music—an already powerfully loaded expressive medium—to the mix would, in the Lubavitcher view, certainly result in a breakdown of social and sexual norms. Therefore, music, when combined with an embodied female sexuality and a potential for male aggression, can become so overpowering that it can lead to inappropriate sexual relations, a very grave transgression. Music performance is thus strictly regulated within Lubavitcher society.

As most of the previous accounts of Hasidic music and musical performance contexts have focused on men's activities and concerns, many fine books already exist in the literature that describe the enthusiasm and excitement of Lubavitcher male performance practices. Authors such as Abraham Idelsohn (1973) and Jaacov Mazor, Andre Hajdu, and Bathja Bayer (1974) have beautifully captured the essence of Hasidic music making through vivid accounts of men dancing in the streets, through photographs of wildly exciting male farbrengens, and through musical transcriptions of male performances.

From these accounts, one can see that Lubavitcher men's religious performance contexts are many and varied, but their repertoires are fairly limited to nigunim and other songs shared by the general Orthodox Jewish population. At a farbrengen only nigunim are sung; but in other, less formalized contexts, such as teaching situations, summer camp retreats, or informal gatherings, especially with children, adapted popular songs are performed that teach basic Hasidic values. Generally, though, men consider adapted popular songs to be too "light" to truly express their own intense personal feelings.

Women, too, freely engage in many of the same musical activities as their male counterparts, but their choice of repertoires is far more varied, at times extending outward to include adaptations of popular or commercial musics. It is not uncommon, for example, to hear women, while at home lighting Sabbath candles, singing all sorts of music, from nigunim (such as those found in the *Sefer Ha-Nigunim*) to popular Israeli folk tunes that have been adapted to fit this context. At a woman's farbrengen, or in the context of the *forshpil* (a party given to a young woman on the Sabbath evening before her wedding), women will use a variety of repertoires to arouse themselves to the point of exhaustion:

> I remember my own forshpil. They [my friends] even had me up on the chair, the way they do with the bride, and they were dancing wildly, and I was exhausted. I was literally exhausted at the end of the day, and it was very good. It was a kind of, you know, great release. What is very beautiful is that they time the wedding periods. I don't know if you've noticed. There are certain months that you don't get married, and certain months that you do get married. So each time that there's a forshpil, it's like a new experience. . . . This is the woman's farbrengen, in essence. Because how often do they get to come together like that? (Thayler interview)

What most clearly differentiates men's and women's musical performance is neither their emotional connection to music nor the abandon of their performances but, rather, context and, as seen above, repertoire. Although men may freely sing in the presence of other men and women, they are prohibited from hearing women sing. Therefore, in contexts that are defined as female—such as the home, a birthday party, a forshpil, or a woman's convention, and so on—women are free to sing, but men must not listen (indeed, they are generally not present or are in another room). And in contexts that are male defined—such as the synagogue, the Rebbe's table, a public business context, and so forth—women, if present, simply refrain from singing. These behaviors are regulated by a set of dicta concerning the sexuality of a woman's voice and when she may speak or sing, who may listen, and in what contexts she may perform music. Understanding the gendering of Lubavitcher music is only possible through an understanding of the intricacies of this prohibition, its history, and current practice.

What follows is a discussion of the prohibition of kol isha (a woman's voice), merely one law out of hundreds that are the hallmark of Jewish philosophy and life. What emerges from this discussion is far more significant than a mere listing of rules; rather, in carefully untangling the web of often conflicting interpretations of kol isha, one may glimpse the complexity of the social, political, and cultural history of Judaism itself as it negotiates, with an elegant flexibility, the many and varied contexts of historical and contemporary Jewish life.

Kol Isha

The dictum of kol isha[1] states, *kol b'isha ervah* (literally, a woman's voice is a sexual incitement). Therefore, the rule that follows is that men may not listen to a woman's voice under certain circumstances (such as while they are reciting prayers). In current Orthodox practice, this ban extends primarily to men who hear the singing (not speaking) voices of women who are forbidden to them—that is, Jewish women who are menstruating, who are married to other men, unmarried Jewish women over the age of twelve, and all non-Jewish women. Most rabbis agree that a man may hear the voice of his own wife, that of a prepubescent daughter, or that of any other nonmenstruating female under the age of twelve. Why is such a law necessary, and how did it develop? Why do contemporary Lubavitchers adhere to this in an age where issues of women's economic, political, and expressive dependencies are being challenged, even within the Hasidic community itself?

The authorship of the dictum of kol isha is attributed to a sixth-century Babylonian Talmudic scholar, Samuel, who, in commenting on the biblical passage Song of Songs 2:14 ("Let me see thy countenance, let me hear thy voice, for sweet is thy voice and thy countenance is comely"), states: "the voice of a woman is a sexual incitement" (Jewish Publication Society 1955:1932). Later Talmudic scholars cite Samuel's dictum on two occasions, each time within a completely different context. Further, a third reference in the Talmud to the sexual properties of a woman's voice appears in a discussion concerning performing music at feasts, but Samuel's dictum is not cited.

The history of kol isha begins with a controversy concerning which version of the Talmud is to be taken as the final legal source. The Babylonian Talmud (of which Samuel was an early commentator), cites the above passage from Song of Songs as the source of this prohibition; the Jerusalem Talmud (in tractate Halah 2a, not found in the Babylonian version), however, cites the following passage from Jeremiah as the original source. The passage is taken from a conversation between God and Jeremiah, during which God explains why he has punished Israel, using the metaphor of the harlot to signify Israel's fickleness or adultery toward him: "and it came to pass through the 'kol' of her [Israel's] harlotry, that the land was polluted" (Jer. 3:9). In the passage, the word "kol" is spelled without the middle vowel (*vuv*), a common practice in the writing of Hebrew. The word "kol" without the vowel can be translated as "lightness," so that the phrase would read: "and it came to pass through the lightness of her harlotry." In referring to this passage, the compilers of the Jerusalem Talmud did not accept this translation, instead inserting the vowel, thereby clarifying the meaning of "kol" as "voice." Thus, the passage was now translated: "and it came to pass through the voice of her harlotry." This last version provided, for these scholars, a more concrete materialization of "harlotry" than "lightness." So any ambiguity posed by the Babylonian Talmud's implicit statement that a woman's voice is sweet (not necessarily a sexual enticement) becomes explicit in the Jerusalem Talmud's clear merging of the woman's voice with harlotry or with forbidden sexual arousal in the man.

The Three Talmudic References

The first citation of Samuel's dictum comes in the first section of the Babylonian Talmud, tractate Berakot 24a, the section dealing with prayers and benedictions. A question is raised as to whether or not it is permissible for a man to recite the Shema, the most holy of Jewish prayers, in the presence of a nude (female) person.[2] Would the man be able to concentrate sufficiently on this important task if he also heard her voice? The scholar answering the query cites Samuel's statement, kol b'isha ervah, as a reason not to allow a (male) person to recite the prayer in the presence of a nude (female) person. Thus, the element of sexual distraction, while performing a primary religious duty, is first introduced into the discussion.

The second reference is found in tractate Kiddushin 70a, a section dealing with marriage laws and genealogies. Here, kol isha is cited in the context of a discussion between two rabbis: Rabbi Judah has been brought to trial on a charge of slander; and Rabbi Nachman is the judge in the case. To impeach Rabbi Nachman's authority, Rabbi Judah begins to question Rabbi Nachman on the tiniest elements of Jewish law, hoping to trick him into making an error, thus proving he is not a competent judge. When the questioning stops, and Rabbi Nachman assumes that the testing period is over, the two men have the following exchange:

Rabbi Nachman: Will you send a greeting to my wife, Yalta?
Rabbi Judah: Thus said Samuel, "a woman's voice is a sexual incitement."
(Berman 1980:46)

Here, the element of "warm greetings" as a prelude to an illicit relationship is introduced.

A third Talmudic reference to the arousing quality of a woman's voice occurs in tractate Sotah 48a, which deals with laws concerning adulteresses, murder by strangers, and war. Although Samuel's dictum is not cited, the connection between women's voices and sexual arousal is made clearly here. The tenth-century Rabbi Joseph, commenting on the prohibition against singing at feasts, especially in a mixed-gender group, states: "When men sing and women join in, it is licentiousness; when women sing and men join in, it is like a fire raging in flax" (1980:46). This third reference resulted in banning female performers (as either vocalists or instrumentalists) from performing at festive gatherings of men. Here, the notion of women's power to lead, coupled with the arousing qualities of music itself, is introduced.

The three references to the sexuality of women's voices subsequently brought up different issues and questions, each reflecting the initial context of the citation. All were hotly debated in the centuries following the codification of the Talmud (c. 500 C.E.). The arguments both for and against the law of kol isha took three different streams, which did not merge until the early nineteenth century.

Stream 1: Distraction

The first citation of Samuel's dictum is made within the context of a man reciting the Shema, a task that must be done without distraction, especially sexual distraction. The Talmudic scholars, assuming that a nude female body would already be something of a distraction to a man praying, further ensured the man's compliance by equating women's voices with their uncovered bodies. In doing so, the voice itself becomes embodied with sexuality. Now the voice, coupled with the already sexual, nude female body, becomes a force too powerful for a man to resist.

Two questions arose: Was the voice ervah (sexually arousing) to men all the time or only when reciting the Shema? And, what kind of voice was ervah: the speaking voice or merely the singing voice? (Berman 1980:47) The first generation of scholars interpreting and answering these questions agreed that the prohibition should extend only to reciting the Shema, although one dissenting opinion extended the prohibition to the study of the Torah as well. Concerning the speaking or singing voice, the early scholars declared that only the singing voice was problematic, thus linking once and for all the notion that music (but not speech), when performed by a sexually embodied female voice (the assumption being that all female nude bodies are naturally sexual), is, in itself, ervah.

In an interesting argument, Rabbi Eliezer ben Samuel of Metz (c. 1115–98), known as the Rabiah, introduced the notion of accustomedness, writing that an unmarried but menstruating woman (whose hair is customarily exposed) is not considered ervah. Therefore, a voice is not ervah if one is accustomed to it. Furthermore, the Rabiah stated, the voice of a woman was prohibited not only because it was inherently sexual but also because of the ban against staring at women. After all, it would be normal for a man to stare at a woman while she is singing.

Later scholars, concerned with the equation of the voice with the nude body, ruled that a voice, if hidden or altered in some way, could be separated from the female sexual body and therefore no longer be prohibited. If, say, a woman sang behind a *mechitzah* (screen) or in a group of women, where her individual voice and body would be hidden or obscured, her voice, now separated from her body, would be allowed. Thus, a woman's voice could only be ervah if it were accompanied by the visual stimulation of her body.[3] In the twelfth century, Rabbi Isaac ben Moshe agreed that the voice alone was not the problem, arguing that the voice must be put in the real-life context of a man reciting the Shema, with all of the visual and other stimuli inherent in this context. Only then was hearing the voice prohibited. If it were only the voice that were ervah, he reasoned, then a woman could not recite the Shema herself, because she would be listening to her own voice and become sexually stimulated (Cherney 1985:67n.43). In a twentieth-century interpretation, Rabbi Eliezer Waldenberg stated: "Since the voice cannot be seen it cannot be considered as ervah, and so should not be prohibited" (1985:67n.43).

Stream 2: The Character of the Relationship

The context for the second citation of Samuel's dictum is that of the exchange between Rabbi Nachman and Rabbi Judah, where Rabbi Nachman asks Rabbi Judah if he would like to send greetings to his (Rabbi Judah's) wife, Yalta. Here, the reasoning is that warm greetings sent to a man's wife through another man forbidden to her might cause her to send warm greetings back, thereby moving the two inexorably toward an illicit relationship. Thus, the character of any relationship between a man and a woman would inevitably alter through an exchange of warm greetings. Clearly, this context relates to the speaking voice, since it would be unlikely that the wife would respond to a warm greeting from a man by breaking into song. So, the question of the speaking voice versus the singing voice is once again raised. However, the notion of distraction is missing here; a man hearing a warm greeting from a woman would most likely not be simultaneously engaged in a religious duty. The Talmudic scholars responding to this citation of the dictum decided that a proscription against the speaking voice was appropriate; but this prohibition would be during greetings only and not during regular conversation, because there is a clear expression of warm friendship in a greeting.

Around the thirteenth century, Rabbi Menahem Ha-Meiri took up the strain of warm greetings, stating that Samuel's dictum may not be applied to a man who knows in himself that he will not be inclined to become aroused. Thus, a subjective, individual decision could be made through each man judging his own tendencies.[4] In an interesting reversal, Rabbi Judah He-Hasid of Regensburg (d. 1217), anticipating a feminist argument that would not surface for another 750 years, proposed the notion of *kol ish* (the voice of a man) as constituting the same sexual problems for women as kol isha did for men. Unfortunately, this argument was not adopted or even subsequently addressed by later scholars.

This second stream of discussion raised questions concerning the kind of woman to whom one could not extend a warm greeting. Did the prohibition, for example, include unmarried women? Nonmenstruating women? A woman who alters her voice to extend a greeting? Could a man who trusted his good intentions be allowed to hear a woman's warm greeting?

Perhaps the most important commentary on this stream of discussion is that of the great scholar, philosopher, and medical doctor Moses ben Maimon (1135–1204), also known as Maimonides or Rambam, who took up the strain of a relationship's character in his *Code*, compiled in 1180 (Maimonides 1965), where an entire section devoted to "Forbidden Unions" clearly outlines the kinds of relationships that can and cannot be formed between Jewish men and women and between Jews and non-Jews of both sexes. Maimonides's interpretation of kol b'isha ervah, though, took an interesting turn, shifting the emphasis away from the inherent sexuality of the voice and toward the illicit sexuality of a forbidden woman.

Maimonides cites the biblical negative commandment number 353, which prohibits a man from approaching a woman forbidden to him in marriage (e.g., a non-Jewish or married woman) because it might lead to an illicit relationship. He saw the word ervah as referring to the woman and to the context, not specifically to the voice. In his commentary on kol isha, he preceded the word ervah with the Hebrew definite article *ha* (the) so that the original dictum by Samuel was now interpreted as *kol b'isha ha-ervah* (the voice of the illicit woman is prohibited). In the fifth book of his *Code*, in the section titled "Forbidden Intercourse," he states:

> Whoever indulges in [having intercourse with an illicit woman] lays himself open to the suspicion of forbidden unions. A man is forbidden to make suggestive gestures with his hands or legs or wink at a woman within the forbidden unions, or to jest or act frivolously with her. It is forbidden even to inhale her perfume or gaze at her beauty. Whosoever directs his mind toward these things is liable to the flogging prescribed for disobedience. He who stares even at a woman's little finger with the intention of deriving pleasure from it, is considered as though he had looked at her secret parts. It is forbidden even to listen to the singing of a woman within the forbidden unions, or to look at her hair. (Maimonides 1965:133)

The word ervah in Maimonides's interpretation referred only to a woman of the "forbidden unions"—that is, one who was not likely to become a marriage partner, one with whom a man might establish an illicit relationship. Maimonides in effect shifted the emphasis from the inherent sexuality of women and their musical voices to the context of a potential illicit relationship between a man and a prohibited woman. Sexual stimulation in itself was not prohibited (nor was the voice, per se); rather, it was the potential to create a context of sexual stimulation that was restricted. Therefore, using Maimonides's interpretation, men may listen to the singing (and speaking) voices of their wives and premenstrual daughters. This is allowed in the first case because the couple is already married and in the second because it is believed to be unlikely that an illicit relationship will develop between two close relatives, especially when one is a child. In addition, unmarried women, with whom a marital relationship could be possible, as well as one's wife while she is menstruating—because sexual intercourse will soon be possible—are also excluded from this prohibition.[5]

Streams 1 and 2 Integrated

The first generation of Talmudic scholars seemed to ignore the question of the speaking voice (raised in the second citation of Samuel's dictum), while many later scholars ignored the question of sexual distraction during the performance of a religious duty (that raised in the first). Considering both statements of Samuel's dictum together posed a problem: if, as in the first context, only the singing voice were prohibited, how could one interpret the second context, clearly a reference to the speaking voice?

The first scholar to connect these two statements, Rabbi Abraham ben David (c. 1125–98), known as the Rabad of Posquieres (Provence), did so by taking a stricter view of the problem of kol isha than previous rabbis: he included a woman's speaking voice as well as her singing voice, expanding the prohibition beyond the recitation of the Shema to the performance of all religious duties. However, he did permit the speaking voice of one's wife, because a man would be accustomed to it and not become aroused, and he defined the speaking voice as the one used only in warm greetings, not in casual conversation. In connecting the two statements of Samuel's dictum, the Rabad and succeeding rabbis who followed his decision in essence created a third category of woman's voice (the warm greeting voice), one that carried a mid-level sexuality between the conversational and the singing voice.

Three further, much later rulings were made concerning the notion of visual stimulation. In the late nineteenth century Rabbi Moshe Schick (1807–79) ruled that vocal stimuli alone would not cause illicit thoughts unless the man were acquainted with the woman. Later, in the twentieth century, Rabbi Ovadia Hadaya (1891–1969) went even further, defining an acquaintance not only as a person one actually knew but also as a person one could come to know through photographs. Finally, Rabbi Mehashe Klein concluded that it was permissible to listen to a woman vocalist on the radio "since the sounds emanating from these devices are not voices but mechanical reproductions" (Cherney 1985:69). But if a man were to listen to a woman sing on the radio or on a recording while looking at her picture, he could become aroused, so this was prohibited (1985:68).

Stream 3: Mixed Singing

One of the greatest and most influential of the Talmudic interpreters, the eleventh-century Babylonian scholar Rabbi Shlomo Yitzhaki of Troyes (1040–1105), also known as Rashi, was also one of the first to comment on the third reference to the sexuality of a woman's singing voice. He states: "The one who leads does not pay attention to the one who is answering, therefore, even though the principle of kol b'isha ervah applies, it is not as volatile a situation if the men lead. However, if men are answering, they pay close attention to the voice of the leader (in this case the women), so there is greater danger of sexual incitement" (1985:59).

Here, the issue concerns a man paying attention to a woman's singing voice and not merely hearing it. In this context, the woman is in control not only of her own musical voice but also of the musical performance. Therefore, the notion of inherent sexuality in the woman, or in her singing voice, becomes less significant than the issue of men paying attention to women and music, both being sexually loaded entities. Thus, singing in mixed groups, especially when women lead, becomes the musical equivalent of staring at women (an even graver prohibition).

Two of the most significant discussions of the prohibition against mixed-gender group singing did not come until 1814, the year of the Congress of Vienna, and even later in the mid-twentieth century. Rabbi Moses Sofer (1762–1839), the head of the Viennese Rabbinate, was asked to give permission for a mixed choir to perform at a reception for conference dignitaries. He prohibited this form of performance by citing Samuel's dictum, but the decision caused something of an uproar with the more liberal-minded Viennese Jewish community (Berman 1980:62). In the twentieth century, Rabbi Yehiel Weinberg was asked to rule on whether young girls and boys (under twelve) could sing Sabbath zemirot together. He allowed this form of performance, reasoning that one could not single out one girl's voice from many at the table and that at Sabbath meals (hopefully), no one is thinking about sex. Rabbi Weinberg, not especially happy about his own ruling, justified it nonetheless by writing: "In countries like Germany and France, women would feel disgraced and see it as a deprivation of their rights if we prohibited them from joining in the rejoicing over the Sabbath by singing Zemirot. This is obvious to anyone familiar with the character of women in these countries. The prohibition could drive women away from religion, God forbid" (qtd. in 1980:64).

In looking at the many strands of kol isha, it is clear that the ban was deemed necessary for three important, yet unrelated, reasons: to prevent a man from succumbing to the danger of not fulfilling his religious duty; to prevent him from forming an illicit relationship with a woman forbidden to him; and to prevent women's inherent sexuality from controlling a situation in which musical performance is occurring. All three reasons share an underlying assumption that a woman's voice, in certain circumstances, is inherently sexual, whether or not she intends it to be, so sexual as to be overpowering to a man. What still remains ambiguous, however, is precisely what is ervah: The woman? Her voice? What is performed? How it is performed? The context?[6]

Contemporary Lubavitcher Attitudes toward Kol Isha

The Lubavitcher position follows that of Maimonides and other rabbis who took a fairly strict, but not completely prohibitive, view toward the question of kol isha: men are prohibited from hearing all women over the age of nine sing; a man may hear his wife sing only if he is accustomed to it and is certain it will not arouse him; and kol isha refers only to the singing, not the speaking or "warm greeting," voice.

Most contemporary Lubavitcher women and men regard the restrictions of kol isha as necessary for women's protection—not only against prohibited men but also against their own inherent sexual power. Like the fence that protects from two directions, following this prohibition prevents graver offenses from occurring. The notion that a woman's body and voice are precious and valuable gifts is also a common theme in contemporary Lubavitcher women's understanding of kol isha. Precious gifts, if displayed all of the time, become commonplace; one must keep them hidden and protected, bringing them out only on certain special occasions.

Rather than seeing these regulations as signs of impurity or as somehow degrading, however, most women view them as a sign of their special status in Lubavitcher society, a position that sets them apart from men in a positive, spiritual way: "I definitely know that any mitzvah that separates man and woman is done not because of any kind of inferiority on my part. Perhaps it's because of my superiority; you know, women have the power of distraction or attraction or whatever you want; and therefore, I'm not in the least insulted. I'm flattered by it" (Gurwitz interview).

Perhaps the best way to capture the essence of kol isha for the contemporary Lubavitcher woman is to present part of an interview, conducted in 1991, that shows the necessity for, and the difficulties with, the prohibition of kol isha. The woman being interviewed, Rus Dvorah Shatkin, is a ba'alat teshuvah and a trained musician, one who received a bachelor's degree in voice from the Cincinnati College Conservatory of Music. I have chosen a ba'alat teshuvah because lifetime Lubavitcher women do not often think consciously about this prohibition. They have known no other way. Those who have chosen an observant life only as adults, however, often must and do question such rules.

~

EK: Tell me a bit about kol b'isha ervah.

RDS: A lot of people think this is a very stupid and foolish thing. I think the reason is, especially in America, that people have become so desensitized sensually and sexually that nothing is a turn-on. You're constantly exposed by radio, by TV, by books, by brochures, by billboards, by advertisements to sexuality. . . . So you're always stimulated, but you're never stimulated, there's always a stimulus, but you're never stimulated, and so something that could be very stimulating to a person who is pristine, like the moving of a hand, or a kiss on a cheek, or a touching of fingers—something very simple like that—is no longer stimulating. So, when a person says, "What? You're not allowed to shake a man's hand?" You know, every time you meet a colleague, and you shake his hand, and you say, "Hi, How are you," and what you really mean is: "This is a formality, I have to say 'How are you,' now let's get down to business." These things have become so habitual that there is really no real expression of sensitivity or sensuality, so we come to the point where we're desensitized.

Religious women and men are not physically together until they're married, and so that allows for a sensitization, that allows for people to remain physically, sensually sensitive. When people marry, what happens, thank God, through family purity laws, is there's always the sexual novelty because of the absence of coming together, because of certain restrictions. So that's just a little introduction [to kol b'isha]. When a person, say, meets someone at a party and kisses them, and "Oh, it was just a kiss. It was just a kiss on the cheek, it was just platonic. It didn't mean anything!" Or shakes their hand and says, "Ach, I didn't feel anything!"—that's sad. According to a Hasidic perspective, that's sad. You should feel something when you kiss someone, or when you shake their hand or hold their hand. There should be some kind of exchange of physical, sensual, psychic, emotional energy between the two people. . . .

[When I starting becoming more observant,] I stopped going out with men, I stopped watching certain movies and stopped reading certain books intentionally, not because the Torah prohibits it. This is the spirit of the Jewish law. The Torah does not say, "Thou shall not read sexual novels." Hasidim are ones to go beyond the letter of the law, and what does this mean? Not making new laws, but taking the laws and putting fences around them and being sensitive so that you don't even come near to breaking down the fence. . . .

So, when the Torah and the Talmud and the Shulchan Arukh, the code of Jewish Law, talk about the nakedness or the lasciviousness of a woman's voice, it's real; but for an American, it's not, because I [the American] hear Madonna and nothing turns me on. That's sad. Nothing turns you on?

EK: The feminist might ask, "Why not a man's voice?"

RDS: Probably if you were to look at Masters and Johnson, tests and censuses and all of the psychology and human sexuality texts, probably there would be some statistics to say that it's much harder for a man to control his sexuality. The protection that is in the Torah is for the man. Protection not only for himself, because he is a religious being, but protection also for women. You don't usually find sexual crimes committed by women. Women are not the aggressors, historically. So, it's to protect women and to protect men, religiously. So it's not to say that men's voices are not attractive. The Torah talks to the majority, the normative society. . . . The Torah cannot be time limited, because we believe the Torah is eternal, infinite. The Gemara is talking to the ideal society, where women are more in control, where men, unfortunately, the way God made them, [are] less in control. We must protect them, sensually and sexually. (Shatkin interview, Sept. 1990)

Shatkin went on to describe four different levels of kol isha, following the rabbinical argument concerning visual stimuli. Although this ruling was made centuries ago, Shatkin was able to apply it readily to contemporary situations, where microphones, videotapes, and other technical equipment would be used.

RDS: Now, getting to kol isha: seeing a woman physically onstage, with this lovely voice, and maybe with her hair also could be very stimulating for a man, and, to use the euphemism, "he spills his seed," so he's committed a biblical prohibition. This is not just a rabbinic decree. So, a live women with no sound-dubbing devices, just, live without anything, a woman right in front of you, a soloist—then you could say that's kol isha.

EK: What about a chorus of women?

RDS: Live, choral performance is no problem, because you can't distinguish one voice. If it's really a good choir, even if it's a cappella, if it's like one voice and has a good conductor, and he got them to pronounce their vowels, and they're in the same pitch, and they're all together, then there's no problem.

EK: So, do men ever come to concerts of finely trained women's groups?

RDS: Some men will. Fewer Hasidic men will, although it might be permissible. But again, what is Hasidic? It's trying to go beyond the letter of the law to its spirit. Each man knows his own conscience, and he's the only one who knows if he's sensitive or not. Whether he'll be stimulated or not. In this place in Minnesota the rabbis know, "this school is for women, so it's tough luck for me. If I hear the women's voices, I can't tell them to stop singing. I either go out of the room, or I'm not stimulated by it. This is their school." So, in these women's schools, in New York, in my program in Russia, in Minnesota, if the rabbi is there, it's his tough luck—and he knows it. He made it for women, so if they sing, he either walks out, or he closes his ears—he closes his sensitivity. You would never find in such a place a man who was a truly learned Hasidic rabbi who would say, "Stop singing." You would never hear that.

So there are two distinctions: there is a single soloist woman and a woman in the context of many voices. That's kol isha, and that's not kol isha. Then there's a live performance with some kind of electronic device, like a microphone, all sorts of instruments, a reverb, some kind of change in her voice through the microphone, that's the next level. It's not really her voice anymore. Then, if you don't see the woman, but she is live, you don't know where that voice is coming from.

EK: What if it's not being manipulated by any kind of device, like she's singing behind a screen, and you can't see her?

RDS: Right. [That's OK.] Why? Because when you hear a voice, and it's connected to that "body," . . . or, you would have someone who's on a recording, someone you don't see, there may be other voices with that person, even if it's only three or four or five voices.

EK: What about videotape?

RDS: On videotape, you're seeing the person. I would think that would come before the recording in terms of stringency.

EK: You're seeing the person, but it's not live? So it would be higher than a recording but not at the top?

RDS: Right. (Shatkin interview, Sept. 1990)

Finally, she concluded with a story from her college days that concerned her own singing voice and the steps she took to integrate her love of music with her growing observance of Jewish law.

RDS: Let me tell you a story. When I was in college, I became religious. And there was a question. Here, I was a vocal concentration, so what do I do now with my boards [i.e., juried professional exams]? What do I do now in front of my professors? What do I do now when I have to sing in an opera or sing in a madrigal choir? At that time, it was the beginning of my Yiddishkeit, so at the beginning, you have to know your rabbi, and your rabbi has to know you. He has to know how sensitive you are and at what level you're able to receive. You can't stuff a steak down a baby's throat. The steak may be a very rich and wonderful food, but some people may not be able to eat it. You can't stuff the whole halakhah down prematurely. So, he said I could sing in the choirs, no problem, and I could sing for my boards, if I knew there were no male judges (and there were none), so that was really wonderful. What I had to do was to change the type of music I sang. My vocal teacher was very sensitive. She was Catholic, and she really appreciated this. She didn't give me any Christian music to sing. The literature abounds with Christian music, Bach, etc. I didn't sing any Bach. Ninety-nine-point-ninety-nine percent of Bach's [vocal] music is religious, commissioned for the Church. So, I didn't sing any religious, Christian music. But she gave me some Yiddish songs and some Jewish music that was from the literature—Ravel and so on. Once you become familiar enough with the laws, you realize there's much more leeway. (Shatkin interview, Sept. 1990)

∾

Two new contexts have developed for women's music making over the past twenty-five years or so: the woman's farbrengen and the women's convention. With this flowering of women's musical voices, new repertoires have developed that reflect the concerns and values of Hasidic women in relation to God, their families, and each other. Although these will be discussed more fully in chapter 10 (as they are closely related to the modernization of the Hasidic community), it is important to stress here that despite the proliferation of solo singers, such as Ruthie Navon, and of various Lubavitcher women's musical groups, the law of kol isha remains intact. In fact, it is precisely this adherence to the principle of the law within the context of contemporary life that provides the flexibility for these rules to remain alive and relevant.

Gendered Performance Behaviors Today

As discussed earlier, Lubavitcher men are believed to have a certain positive aggressiveness—that is, a certain intensity, boisterousness, or fervent enthusiasm that imbues all of their activities, from prayer to casual conversation. Indeed, the noted Jewish writer Elie Wiesel, in his book about Hasidim, *Souls on Fire* (1972), captured even in his title the intensity of the Hasidic experience as one of all-consuming love and attachment to the divine.

Women, too, share in this intensity. But what differentiates men and women in music making and other forms of religious expression is how intensity is materialized through the body—that is, how it is performed. Women must be constantly aware of their surroundings and behave in accordance with the laws of modesty; they must match their bodily responses to the proper context. This does not mean that they must limit their intensity, which, in many cases (such as at the forshpil), rivals that of the men. It means that they must be self-conscious and conscious of others, always aware of their social and religious context, not only for themselves but also for their children and husbands.

As men have no laws of modesty pertaining to musical performance, there is a certain autonomy and freedom in the performance of their intense feelings toward the divine and, indeed, toward all aspects of life through music. Of course, men, like women, must behave in accordance with many social and religious laws as outlined in the Torah and the Talmud, but they are given relative freedom, as was discussed in chapter 7, to shout, scream, screech, drink to the point of fainting, sway to the point of falling—in short, to express their spiritual feelings without physical limitation, even within a mixed-gender, public context.

Lubavitcher men and women speak of the difference between their emotional lives as the difference between "deep feeling" (male) and "sensitivity" (female). Men are believed by both sexes to feel more deeply; therefore, they must express themselves with more outwardly physical intensity. Women are more open to their own and others' feelings. Therefore, they must behave and treat others with inward sensitivity and delicacy. Men can sing anywhere, can burst spontaneously into song. Women must be aware of their surroundings and can sing only for and among each other. The following comments—the first from a male Lubavitcher, the second from a female Lubavitcher—perhaps sum up these differences, as applied to music performance:

[He said:] My personal opinion is this: let's assume that you take a woman and a man, who are both musical, and attempt to sing certain nigunim. I'm sure that nine out of ten people would tell you that the men are singing with more feeling, and I'm not talking about trained singers—I'm talking about laymen. I've heard women sing. Let's say I was home. There was a comedy show here. I couldn't help that I was home, so I just overheard their singing. It's not with deep feeling. It's just singing, just to get a song through with and get to the next song. You can see [the men], if you ever were by the farbrengen. They take a nigun, and they sing. It's with a lot of feeling, and it's much more than women would sing. (Moshe Teleshevsky interview, 1975)

[She said:] When men sing, it sounds definitely different [from us]. The men sing completely on cue of the Rebbe—you might have noticed that—and a lot of them screech. I mean, you know, there are some who are very delicate singers, but a lot of them screech. This is their only way to show their great, great love, by belting it out, and for the women, it's definitely more delicate. The same nigun sounds completely different. The women harmonize and take a gentle approach. I really believe it's because the woman does not sing with the men—you know, generally speaking, they don't sing as much. They listen and take so deeply into themselves the song, that when they do get an opportunity to sing, it's just going to come out differently. It has a different level of appreciation. (Thayler interview, 1976)

Notes

1. I am grateful to Rabbi Saul J. Berman (1980) and Rabbi Ben Cherney (1985) for their articles on the development of the intricate body of laws surrounding kol isha; they were invaluable to me in the writing of this chapter.

2. There is no assumption here of a male nude body. Homosexuality is absolutely forbidden in Jewish law.

3. As Sawa (1987) points out, an almost parallel situation occurs in writings on Arabic women's voices.

4. For example, there are often men present at women's formal gatherings, carrying in chairs, setting up tape recorders, and so on. When questioned about their presence, I received this reason as an explanation.

5. Maimonides's (1941) rulings on kol isha are further emphasized in a passage where he is asked if one can listen to Arabic music. He replies with five reasons why one should not listen to any music, the fifth of which is that if hearing the speaking voice of a forbidden woman is prohibited, then surely her singing voice is also.

6. Debating the ambiguities of kol isha continues. Judith Cohen, an ethnomusicologist and contemporary performer of traditional (primarily Sephardic) folk songs, recently told me that one of her performances had been canceled due to a new, strict rabbinical ruling in Toronto (personal communication, Oct. 1996).

9
Performing Lineage in Music

Scene: "The Rebbe Sings"

It is 1976, and I am in Crown Heights, attending a Rebbe's farbrengen. The bleachers are packed with men and boys, and the women's gallery is more crowded than usual. Actually, the bleachers have been stacked so high that I am at eye-level with the men on the top riser; all that separates us is the (nearly see-through) sheet of tinted plastic. My friend Dvorah slides into the seat next to me. She is about my age, a teacher in one of the Lubavitcher day schools. She is unusually excited.

"I hear the Rebbe is going to sing tonight!" she says breathlessly. "He usually doesn't—out loud, that is. Wait till you hear him, Ellen. You will not believe it! His voice is so beautiful, so holy! It will take you out of yourself!"

The assembled crowd quiets down, and the Rebbe begins to speak. He is concerned about the political situation in the Middle East, and his talk addresses the plight of Israeli Jews. There is a break, and then the singing begins. It is "Ashreinu," one of my favorite songs. I start to sing—quietly. Suddenly, I get a sharp poke in my sides. "Watch! The Rebbe is standing! He is going to sing!"

I look down to where the Rebbe is standing. He is quite old but still steady on his feet, like a rock whose bottom half is buried in the ground. He is near the microphone he uses for his talk, and his voice can be clearly heard above the rest. This is unusual. At a large farbrengen like this one, it is almost impossible to hear one single voice, but tonight the Rebbe's voice shines through. However, it is nothing like the booming operatic tenor and bass voices I can hear from the bottom bleachers. Although strong rhythmically, the Rebbe's singing is unexpectedly soft, cracking, pushed, and tight. It is difficult for him to reach the top notes of the tune; furthermore, he is getting more and more intense as he progresses, his face reddening as the verses go on. I fear he will suffer a stroke.

I turn to Dvorah. She is crying with joy. She looks at me expectantly: "What do you think? Doesn't he have just the most beautiful voice?"

I am the musician, and I am being asked to give a musical judgment here. Can I tell her the truth—that the Rebbe is not a great singer—without upsetting her? Is it at all relevant what I really think? "Well," I hesitate, not really understanding the motivation behind her question, "He's really old, and, of course, his ability to sing is somewhat weakened now." I go on diplomatically: "I see what you mean about his intensity, though, but to be totally honest, Dvorah, you know, this is not such a great performance—from a Western classical music point of view, I mean."

Dvorah's eyes narrow, and her mouth tightens as she peers directly at me. "What do you mean, 'This is not such a great performance?'" she hisses over the singing. "This is the best performance you will ever hear of this nigun! It is the best simply because the Rebbe is singing!" she concludes with a look that tells me that I am probably the most insensitive person she has ever encountered.

The Importance of Lineage in Lubavitcher Music Making

In chapter 4, I used the metaphor of concentric circles to describe the Lubavitcher social hierarchy, placing the Rebbe, his assistants, and lifetime Lubavitchers within the inner circles and ba'alei teshuvah and nonobservant Jews within the outer circles. Those within the inner circles are Hasidic by birth, many of them able to trace their ancestry back to Rabbi Schneur Zalman or other Hasidic leaders. And although some individuals may be regarded as more spiritually elevated than others due to their own personalities or special acts, all lifetime Lubavitchers are seen as inherently spiritual simply because they have been "born into the life."

Those living within the outer circles are seen as returning to a more observant life. True, all Jews possess a godly soul and a spark of holiness; but like the divine light caught deeply in its husk, the spark of the returnee must be liberated slowly, over time, so as to be ready for the burden of its freedom. Those who have stayed within the community for some time (ten years or more) have married and had children there are regarded as seriously committed to an observant life. But, at any one time, there may be hundreds of people attached to the community who come and go through the invisible fence separating sacred from secular.

Lubavitchers from Birth

The main distinction between the two groups is that of a proven lineage. Lifetime Lubavitchers are able to show a real and unbroken connection to the past by their genetic relationship to previous Lubavitcher Rebbes or to the Ba'al Shem Tov, the founder of modern Hasidism. Ba'alei teshuvah, although they may have had a Hasidic grandparent or great-uncle in their past, have fallen away from this inheritance and must spend a great deal of time and effort returning to their rightful place to claim it.

The importance of lineage in the social organization and in the aesthetics of Lubavitcher musical performance should not be underestimated. As illustrated in the scene that began this chapter, the beauty or effectiveness of a performance has little to do with Western classical notions of musicianship (such as the ability to project one's voice or to sing in tune). Lubavitcher musical ability is, rather, defined solely in relation to one's closeness to the living or historical Rebbes, to one's knowledge of hasides, and to the context in which one has learned the repertoire of nigunim.

The following excerpts from two interviews illustrate how the themes of proper lineage, reverence for the past, and correct musical transmission are intertwined within the context of Lubavitcher music making. The first excerpt is taken from an interview with Rabbi Hirshel Gansbourg, a longtime associate of the Rebbe and one of the Rebbe's musical assistants. The second is from an interview with Rabbi Menachem Mendel Schneerson, a thirtyish real-estate broker, a direct descendant from the same line as the Rebbe, and also one of the Rebbe's musical assistants.

Rabbi Gansbourg is one of the most honored men in the Rebbe's inner circle. Gansbourg, a lifetime Lubavitcher, can trace his connection to Hasidic culture back to the early eighteenth century. He was born in Russia in 1928, the son of a stationer-photographer who was a member of a small but vital Lubavitcher community there. The family moved to Palestine in 1938, where Gansbourg was sent to the yeshivah of the former Rebbe (Joseph I. Schneersohn) in Lubavitch. Gansbourg followed the Rebbe to New York, and there he continued his studies in the newly formed Lubavitcher community in Crown Heights. He moved to Canada for a time, returning to New York in 1957. He currently owns and runs his own printing business.

Rabbi Gansbourg is part of a loosely formed group that oversees musical activities in the community. Although he professes not to be a musician, his reputation as a close associate of the Rebbe and his own assertions ("I have chutzpah") have enabled him to become a musical assistant to the Rebbe. Along with Rabbi Joel Cahn and the young Rabbi Menachem Mendel Schneerson, Gansbourg frequently chooses specific songs to be sung at farbrengens and other musical events. In addition, he helps other members of the committee choose appropriate music for the Rebbe's musical birthday gift each year: a setting of the specific numbered Psalm of the Rebbe's year.

In a 1991 interview, Gansbourg describes how he came to be important in Lubavitcher musical life today and how past and contemporary Lubavitcher musicians compare:

EK: How did you become a person who starts a nigun at a farbrengen?

HG: First of all, I'm born in Lubavitch. My father played instruments. He was a musician. But the real reason was that I helped make the first *Sefer Ha-Nigunim,* the one Rabbi Zalmanoff did. He was the Rebbe's official *hazzan* [cantor]. Then Rabbi Zalmanoff moved to Israel, and the singing stopped, so the Rebbe asked to his secretary, "Maybe something could be done." And a group came together and decided how to sing and recorded it. And, actually, there was a whole group to start, but little by little they fell off. [Laughing.] That's how it was, that's true. And besides, I had the chutzpah to start. They were all ready to sing but not to start.

EK: How did you come to be one of the Rebbe's musical assistants?

HG: I'm not a musician. But I was born into it [the Lubavitcher community]. There were people who were singing much better than me, much better, who know the nigunim better. I have chutzpah—I told you before.

EK: When you're at a farbrengen, how do you select a nigun to start? How do you know which one to select?

HG: Sometimes I make mistakes. It depends on the mood and the words of the Rebbe. The last years, the Rebbe has only wanted to sing joyous nigunim because the Rebbe spoke last Shabbos about a rabbi in Israel who came out with a statement: "The Holocaust happened because God was angry with the Jews, and the accounting, when the time comes, He hits. And it happened, and it will happen again, and that's only because the Jews are not observing the Sabbath and are eating pork and other things." And the Rebbe was very angry about it, and he said, "God is mostly a God of mercy. How can you say that He killed children because people ate pork?" The connection here? The Rebbe says that the most important thing now is that in no way, even if we want to bring the Jews back to Judaism, it's only with kindness and with joy. Because otherwise, we turn away people. The Rebbe feels now that whatever happened years ago, it doesn't reflect on now, because now we are before the period of the coming of the Messiah, and you have to be joyous to know you were in that period. See, the Rebbe speaks nowadays only about joy. It started years ago, maybe more than twenty years ago.

EK: During the last fifteen or twenty years, what kinds of music have come out of the community?

HG: Every year, we take a chapter of Psalms that is the same as the Rebbe's age. He's eighty-eight now, so we take Psalm 89 (because he's in his eighty-ninth year). Some of the people here, they compose music to that, although I don't like it.

EK: Why don't you like it?

HG: Because, first of all, it's not music of Habad. Secondly, it's not joyous enough.

EK: Why is it not music of Habad if it's composed by a Lubavitcher?

HG: Well, most of the nigunim they composed previously, I would say until the 1920s, were composed by people who were deeply into Habad philosophy, learners who worked on themselves, and they came out with something that came from the inside. I would say that the same thing probably happens in the world, too, with people who are deeply working. It comes out from the inside. But when you compose just because you do something for other people, it's just a repetition. That's the way it looks to me. Maybe I'm mistaken.

EK: So to truly be a nigun, a song would have to have been composed before the 1920s?

HG: No, it could be now, too, but we just don't have the people. Most of these people are not the type of people who compose. It also depends on acceptance. Don't forget that now when you come into 770, most of the people were not born to Lubavitch. The greatest majority now are the ba'alei teshuvah. They've come back. And the people who decide on the nigunim now are boys in the yeshivah. Young people. They like it, that's all. Every year, there is a committee that has to select what to sing, but they [the boys] don't listen to the committee. Whatever be decided [by] Baumgarten, me, Lipsker, they don't like it! The boys don't like it, they like something else. I'm not going to fight with them. But that's how it is.

Born in Newark, New Jersey, in 1958, Rabbi Menachem Mendel Schneerson proudly traces his lineage back to Rabbi Schneur Zalman through his beloved daughter Dvorah Leah:

The Alter Rebbe had a daughter, Dvorah Leah. She had a son, the Tzemach Tzeddick, who had seven sons; the oldest son was Reb Baruch Sholom. Reb Baruch Sholom had two sons; he had Reb Levi Yitzach and another. We come from Reb Levi Yitzach. Reb Levi Yitzach had two sons: Reb Baruch Schneur, which is the present Lubavitcher Rebbe's grandfather; and he had Reb Menachem Mendel, my great grandfather. Reb Menachem Mendel had my grandfather, Reb Schneur Zalman, who had my father. I am the seventh generation from the Tzemach Tzeddick. (Schneerson interview)

Unlike Rabbi Gansbourg, Schneerson considers himself to be musical— or at least from a musical family. His main distinction, he says, is that he was taught nigunim by his father, whom he considers a true expert. In the following passage, not only is his father's expertise cited, but in true Hasidic fashion, Schneerson tells a miraculous story of his father's musical abilities (present even in infancy), a story that validates his connection to the past, to Russian persecution (both a real event and a coded ethnic marker), and to the importance of music in the context of spiritual deliverance, all positive values in Lubavitcher culture:

> I know a lot of nigunim. I don't know if I know a lot, but what I know, I know correctly. My father taught me the nigunim correctly. He himself investigated the nigunim, and he asked around. My father had a photographic memory; and whatever he read, he could repeat. It was not difficult for him to repeat a telephone book after he had read it. He didn't even have to bother to learn, because he knew. People would tell me that. He never learned, but he knew everything. [He would say,] "I know nigunim." Not like me— he was a real Schneerson. Nigunim—that was his pet peeve, as he would say. Everyone would know when he was coming home [from work] because he would be singing from the beginning of the block. . . .
>
> He heard nigunim from many, many, many people. He was with my grandfather in France after the war—they were at the place where everyone gathered when they came from Russia, Poland, wherever they came from. And they all passed through his house in France. My grandfather was very much involved in the rescue work there. A person told me that when my father was a year-and-a-half old, he couldn't speak. My grandfather, after *davening* [praying], would set him in a big chair for *kiddush* [Sabbath prayer]. And the Hasidim would get together; and afterward, they would sing. He couldn't talk—but if someone made a false move in the song, he would with his finger go, "Enh, enh." He couldn't talk! They took him to doctors because he was over two years old, and he didn't speak yet, and the doctor said, "If he will stop singing, he will learn to talk."

My grandmother told me that story about when my grandfather was arrested in Russia in 1934: they busted into the house, as was customary. They were looking for my grandfather, and they were taking him away. (He got out later, and he left for France.) And my father was standing in the crib, and he was singing. He was holding onto the crib, and he was jumping and singing. And the arresting officer asked what he was singing. He just happened to be singing a song with this text: "From the horns of the evildoers, I will raise the Zaddick." They didn't want to tell him that, so my grandfather said, "He's just singing childish stuff." But my grandfather knew that he would come home alive because of the song my father was singing.

One aspect of his father's musical expertise highlighted by Schneerson was his ability to sing nigunim correctly, which meant singing the sections of a nigun with appropriate ornaments and, even more importantly, singing each nigun's sections in the proper order (i.e., the order in which they were originally composed and passed down to the next generation). If, along the way, a person were to rearrange the sections or forget one, then the musical lineage would be broken, and the singer's knowledge could be questioned, as Schneerson stated in the interview:

When my father taught me [nigunim,] he would not deviate an inch from the way he thought was right. My grandfather knew a lot of nigunim, but he didn't know them as correct as my father. They would have differences of opinion. The first song my father ever taught me, my father would say, "A Hasid of the Alter Rebbe, Reb Moishe, he made the song." And my grandfather would say, "No, it's Reb Pesach." My father is right, with respect to my grandfather, because he [my father] investigated it. He had a tremendous voice, but he won't sing anything he can't sing correctly.

There shouldn't be a right way to sing the nigunim, but there is. The previous Rebbe wrote in the *Sefer*, "Music is the pen of the soul," so if you want the soul to come out correctly. . . . What is correct? In a symphony, if one deviates, he gets thrown out. I need it to be perfect. For example, if someone tries to sing one verse before the other, that's too much. Also, a lot of people try to polish and try to add "curve balls" [ornaments] that might sound right to them—sometimes it turns my stomach. . . . It's maybe the way we've been brought up, learning the Talmud, which is about splitting hairs to a certain degree. I'm a little too radical. . . . I'll tell you what it's all about. [Laughing.] It's about *I* know the song better than *you*, and I heard it correctly, and don't tell me how to sing the song! "Correct" is how the composer made the song. Rabbi Charitonov, he was here only fifty years ago. My father heard it from a person who heard it *directly* from Rabbi Charitonov.

Until recently, lifetime Lubavitcher women did not usually take an active role in music making, especially after marriage. Busy with home and child-rearing responsibilities, many saw music as a somewhat frivolous, male activity. However, within the past twenty years or so, women's musical activity has increased, and it is now not uncommon for married women to hold women's farbrengens at their homes, during which the women gathered there will sing far into the night. The recent growth of modern Lubavitcher women's musical performances and repertoires will be discussed more fully in chapter 10.

Ba'alei Teshuvah

Those who have entered the community as adults, the ba'alei teshuvah, are generally regarded as being far more consciously aware and energetic than their lifetime counterparts, aware of the minute nuances of Jewish law and possessing unbounded energy to live them. They are often highly motivated to learn quickly, to catch up for a lifetime of being on the outside; thus, a certain heartiness of approach, as well as precariousness, characterizes their actions. Rus Dvorah Shatkin gives the following analogy:

> A Zaddick in the temple, when he went to do his service, he would ascend on a ramp, a very steady, inclining ramp. He would go up this incline very gently. And that is the service of a Zaddick. It's always up, it's always gentle. There's always an incline, but it's modest, it's very subtle, it's very consistent. But the service of a ba'al teshuvah is like going up a ladder. There's space between the rungs, it's straight up and down, the ascent is much greater. It's much more extreme. The steps have space. There's always the fear of coming down a rung, because you're afraid to take that step. And when you go up a rung, the distance that has been traversed is much greater than that distance the Zaddick has been traveling on. So the energy is much greater. You have to take a step. It's not just an itty-bitty baby step, it's a real big jump, and at one point, there's always one leg off. (Shatkin interview, Dec. 1990)

The energy that characterizes ba'alei teshuvah is often channeled into music making, especially if the person entering the community has had musical training and experience in his or her former life. In fact, musical ba'alei teshuvah have special roles: they are seen as ideal musical emissaries, reaching outward toward the secular community in ways far more effective than lifetime Lubavitchers. They are familiar with the secular world, only recently having left it; yet they are far more aware of its seductive influences and often feel the need to be far more vigilant against its power to contaminate.

Scene: "What Am I Doing Here?"

It is 1988, and I am living in Rochester, New York, teaching ethnomusicology at the University of Rochester's Eastman School of Music. Recently, a Lubavitcher family, the Vogels, have moved to Rochester, and I have been in touch with Rabbi Vogel, who occasionally comes to the Main Hall of the school and sits at the center table with information about observant Jewish life. He is a pleasant, handsome man, with a soft English accent, and he is willing to talk with anyone who passes the table or expresses any curiosity.

One day, he tells me that his wife, Masha, will be calling to ask me a favor. She has organized a woman's farbrengen at the university's River Campus and wants to know if I will come and introduce the nigunim. She has asked the Eastman School's All-Girl Klezmer Band, made up of observant Jewish female students, to play and hopes I will participate as an "expert."

I am uncomfortable with this. While I am pleased—in fact, honored—that she has asked me to do it and flattered that she thinks me enough of an expert to be the emcee at this gathering, I do not want to be seen as a Lubavitcher or, even more importantly, as a recruiter for the Lubavitchers. I hesitate on the phone. "Who will be there?" I ask. "Oh, just women from the community. Any Jewish woman who wants to come. You know, Ellen, there are some recent immigrants here, straight from Russia. They'd love to hear the old songs. Some of them haven't heard them in years. Come, it will be fun!"

"Well, I don't know. I'm not a Lubavitcher, you know, and I don't want to be in a position of being a spokesperson for Lubavitcher beliefs or music—you know what I mean?"

"Yes, I know what you mean—just come and do it. It will be fun!"

I give in, mostly because I am so grateful to this community for being so unendingly kind and generous to me over the years: how can I refuse them this one little thing? So, although I am a bit uncomfortable, I can deal with it. Indeed, the night is fun, the All-Girl Klezmer Band is great, there is dancing, the Russian women cry, and no one mistakes me for a Lubavitcher.

I am feeling pretty good as I leave Hubbell Auditorium, women trailing after me into the night. The next day, I read in the *Campus Times* that a group of young male University of Rochester students has protested not being allowed to attend this all-female gathering on the basis of sexual discrimination! Sometimes, it is difficult being both an ethnomusicologist and a feminist.

The Four Levels of *Ba'alei Teshuvahness*

There are essentially four levels of ba'alei teshuvahness, each of which carries particular musical responsibilities for both males and females. Although these levels and musical activities are not really formalized within Lubavitcher culture, years of observation show them to be real markers of social and musical activity. I present them here, moving from the outside and inward, toward the inner core.

Level 1: Outside

The first level consists of people who are marginal to the community—those who perhaps live in Crown Heights, Manhattan, or elsewhere—who regard the Rebbe as an important spiritual leader but have not taken on the responsibilities of observant life. Such people move easily back and forth between the Lubavitcher community and a more secularized one, testing to see if they truly want to (or can) make a commitment to hasides. This social flexibility is often seen as useful in situations where Lubavitcher outreach extends to a secularized environment, such as a community center, a professional recording studio, or a college campus, as in the story presented above.

Two such people are Bob Dylan, the well-known musician and poet, and Ruthi Navon, a singer popular for the past twenty years or so in the United States and Israel. Both are professional musicians, both have experimented with religious life, and both have attachments to the Crown Heights community. While Bob Dylan's experience with Lubavitcher Hasidism was fleeting, Ruthi Navon has become increasingly religious with time; and in 1988 she released a cassette, *Ruthi Navon: Lead Me to Your Way (A Production for Women and Girls Only)*, in which she included the following letter to her audience:

> To My Dear Jewish Sisters!
> This album is brought to you with hesitance and yet with enthusiastic joy. Fifteen years ago, I would never have dreamt that I would someday record this type of music and for women only. Having started my musical career as a contemporary singer with no conscious connection of the true spiritual power inherent in music, I have traveled a long soul-searching

journey to discover the roots of my Jewish soul and its expression through the Divine gift of music. My journey is far from over but I present to you my dear Jewish Sisters at this station the fruits of my spiritual labors which [have] enabled me to reach upward through the medium of Jewish song.

Although the beat may be in the modern idiom it is my fervent hope that the songs herein will inspire you to the beauty of our Jewish heritage.

May the song in my Soul touch yours.

Ruthi (Navon 1988)

Not quite firmly committed to Hasidic life yet moving in that direction, Ruthi Navon thus acts as a powerful spokesperson for Jewish, and especially Jewish women's, values. Reaching large audiences through her recordings and public appearances, she is something of a hero inside Crown Heights, and her music sells well at women's conferences and other gatherings.

Level 2: The Fence (Up to Ten Years)

At the second level are people who have made a firm commitment to observant life but who are still relatively new to the Lubavitcher community. Full of energy, they are seen as the most important link to the outside and are often found leading farbrengens in their homes for friends or family, many of whom still live on the outside. Like a fence that divides two fields, people in this group face both directions at once, often seeing beauty on both sides. One man described this period in his musical life as like standing on the threshold between two worlds, each of which offered something important, with himself as a translator or mediator negotiating between them:

Basically, I felt I was on a threshold of being aware of non-Jewish music and appreciating it very much. Loving rock, loving all kinds of music that was emotional and good, and, on the other hand, seeing Jewish music. There was not a lot of music on the Jewish scene that I liked. [In] contemporary Jewish music, sometimes there was an attempt to take Jewish songs and copy them in rock style or something. I really didn't like that at all. To just take a nigun and jazz it up in a rock style usually was a bring-down. The threshold that I was in was seeing these nigunim as very, very beautiful, very musically relevant, but they were not really happening. Mostly they were being documented on a shelf in book form, or documented in tape form, or sung once in a while by certain people who knew them. . . . I felt the nigunim were floating off into some kind of a nonrelevant oblivion. They were just floating off somewhere, but actually they are totally musically inspiring and relevant. (Burston interview)

Women musicians figure prominently in this group of ba'alei teshuvah. One woman, Rifka Miriam Tampkin, who is relatively new to the Lubavitcher Crown Heights community, having lived there for about three-and-a-half years at the time of my interview with her, has been involved with Jewish music since she was a child in Cleveland, Ohio. She frequently holds women's farbrengens in her house. Many kinds of women come to the farbrengens, some of whom are formally connected to the Lubavitcher community, some of whom are not. For her, and for many of these women, the farbrengen is a time when women can be free to express themselves without the normal restrictions of their daily lives, whether or not they are observant: "When people come here, you know, we're all friends. We greet each other, we schmooze, we hug, we whatever. We raise energy together. We share energy together. . . . There are certain women I just start to sing around! There are women who really love to sing nigunim and are passionate about it. Last May, we had quite a gathering—it lasted until two in the morning. Women coming in and out!" (Tampkin interview).

Recently married, Tampkin describes a conversation she had with her husband, in which they negotiated who would have control of the house on Saturday evening after Shabbos, a conversation that many modern Hasidic women would not imagine their mothers having. Pointing out to her husband that men have far more opportunities to gather and express themselves, she argues that she has more right to the house than he:

> This Saturday night—we already discussed it before—he's going to try to find somewhere else to sleep. I don't think it will go until two in the morning, but he likes to go to bed early. One day, God willing, we'll have a two or three-story house, and we'll be able to insulate everybody from what they don't want to be around. I said to him, "Look, you know, the guys have a lot more environments where they can just farbreng, until whatever hours you want." They've got their options lined up. The women have got to be a lot more ingenious to create them. When I saw this place, my first thought was people can dance here. I want space for people to be able to move, dance, and sing. Knowing how precious these spaces are for women in the community, it meant a lot to me. So I said to him, "Look, we need this. You've got a lot of resources at your fingertips that I don't have. That doesn't mean that I don't have a lot or can't maneuver a lot of things, but there are a lot of things that I have to maneuver for a lot more than you, so step aside, this is our night." And he does.

Level 3: Inside (Ten to Twenty Years)

By the time they have adjusted to religious life, have married, and started families, many ba'alei teshuvah take on new musical and social activities. Some are placed as teachers in the many Lubavitcher-run day schools, where young Lubavitcher and other Orthodox children go to receive a Jewish education. Occasionally, a person is chosen from this group to perform an especially important role, such as teaching hasides in the newly reorganized Jewish communities of Russia and Ukraine.

Rus Dvorah Shatkin, a trained musician and ba'alat teshuvah for about twelve years, explained how her commitment to music, teaching, and Judaism eventually led her to such a position in a Lubavitcher-run school for young Russian girls in Ukraine. Originally wanting to become a cantor, Shatkin studied voice at the Cincinnati College Conservatory, choosing Cincinnati, Ohio, as much for its music as for its Jewish community. After leaving college, she moved to Brooklyn and began teaching music in an Orthodox Jewish day school. At the same time, she was learning more about Habad Hasidism and gradually began to connect herself to the Lubavitcher community in Crown Heights. She soon earned a reputation for being an unusually gifted and effective teacher. Combining her love of Habad nigunim with her abilities as a musician, she began to arrange nigunim for her students, often making "Orffestrations"[1] of favorite nigunim that she performed in concerts.

Eventually, she began freelancing as a woman's farbrengen organizer, traveling to over thirty cities in the United States, Canada, Israel, and Russia to bring young women and children together to sing, tell stories, and discuss Jewish topics. About this time, the Rebbe opened up a Habad center in Ukraine, and Shatkin was asked to go there to teach. She arrived with songbooks she had developed while working in the Catskills, where the music and texts were printed in English with Hebrew transliterations. Knowing almost no Russian at the beginning of her journey, she began to communicate through the tunes.

> I had made these songbooks. In Russia, there was this language barrier, not only in the music, but with general communication. The girls I brought didn't speak any Russian, I spoke a little Russian. Whenever I taught Habad nigunim, they asked, "Let's sing wordless songs." This became, like, the *ideal* mode of communication. There was melody without words, and this is what they loved. Even though I had the words in front of them in English letters, they always

went back to the wordless nigunim. This was a Habad-run program in Ukraine, where Hasidim started. It was really divine providence, like a circle: we came from here, and we came back to here. (Shatkin interview, Dec. 1990)

Another ba'al teshuvah, Chaim Burston, who was born in Pasadena, California, had been, at the time I first met him, living in the Crown Heights community for about eighteen years. An avid rock musician in high school, playing with musicians who eventually became professionals, Burston planned to make music his career. But on traveling to Israel and visiting the Lubavitcher center there (Kfar Habad), he began to realize that simultaneously being a rock musician and a religious Jew would be impossible. After moving to Crown Heights in the early 1970s and starting a family there, Burston stopped performing until he was asked to get involved in a community recording, playing keyboards. Realizing that he could merge his love for popular music with his current observant life, he began to work with children, teaching them newly arranged nigunim on his synthesizer. He has continued working with children to the present, as well as organizing music classes outside the Crown Heights community, where he performs nigunim using New Age harmonies for audiences of men and women who are beginning to be curious about Hasidic life. (Musical examples of Chaim Burston's arrangements will be discussed more fully in chapter 10.)

Older than Shatkin, and with children of his own, he describes how difficult it sometimes was to find time to work on his music when he initially became observant: "At one point, my wife had gone into labor while I was at one of these sessions, so between tracks either she was calling me between her contractions, or I was between tracks calling her. It was totally ridiculous. After the session, we went to the hospital and had the baby. That's how insane the whole thing was, trying to put together a recording and finding a time to do it" (Burston interview).

In this same interview, Burston stressed that he played the nigunim correctly, even though he played them on the synthesizer, a modern electronic device, an instrument that even his wife hated and found "unnatural." He saw that this type of performance could be useful and instructive to people who loved music as he did:

I was very excited about making nigunim a relevant part of the life of people who wouldn't necessarily go to a synagogue or to a speech but who are interested in music. So to go to a musical happening, they could say, "Yeah, I can see that. I'll go hear some music, and maybe I'll hear someone talk about it." So I felt that standing by a keyboard and playing and talking would be more appealing for myself and for others than just hearing a class. It's a good feeling to do this with music. But, I want to do it exactly [correctly]. These are holy and part of the Torah itself. I will be free in the sounds or chords that I use, but I would never change the melody.

For example, the first nigun I played [tonight], I took it from a record that was recorded in 1948 that was sung by a very respected Hasid from the [court of the] previous Rebbe, so I felt he sang it this way, so I can rely on his way of singing it. So I felt confident having this as my source. Usually, I have a source for whatever I am doing. I can say, "I heard it from this Hasid, I heard it from this source," but when it comes to sounds and chords, I feel I have some leeway.

It is at the third level that issues such as correct performance practice and one's connection to the past begin to become truly important. It is also here that pure melody becomes separated from its musical surroundings (i.e., its harmonies, which are still connected to the secularized world).

Level 4: Near the Inner Core (Over Twenty Years)

Those ba'alei teshuvah who have lived most of their adult lives as Lubavitchers are more or less integrated into the inner core of those who have been Hasidic from birth. And, not surprisingly, their musical roles mirror those of their lifetime counterparts. Men are usually more active musically than women but less active than either men or women at the outer levels of ba'al teshuvahness.

Ephraim Rosenblum has been a Lubavitcher for over thirty years. He has lived most of his adult life as a teacher in the Lubavitcher yeshivah in Pittsburgh. (Examples of his compositions appear in chapter 10.) Although he is quite talented musically, he rarely uses his musical abilities to teach Hasidic values to his students, nor does he usually arrange farbrengens in his home. These activities, he says, are for the younger and more energetic. He is more likely to sing at his own Sabbath table with his children, or perform with other men in their homes, or stand on a lower bleacher at a Rebbe's farbrengen in Crown Heights, lending his powerful voice to the performance. As a well-respected musician within the community, he has participated in many of the recordings of Lubavitcher nigunim made by Nichoach and has even created songs of his own that he sings for his family and friends, although none of them has been officially adopted by the Rebbe at a farbrengen.

Old Musics in New Lives

Ba'alei teshuvah, especially those who have either been musically trained or have had previous musical experience, sometimes find it difficult to reconcile their former musical loves with their newly observant lives. Most find creative ways to merge the old with the new or are eventually able to give up musics to which they had previously been connected.

As illustrated in the quotations below, some ba'alei teshuvah initially solve this conflict by imbuing their former musical favorites with spirituality. This process, however, is not done without certain ambivalences, as the following woman states:

> I also have to admit, from time to time, I listen to . . . Bob Dylan. . . . I mean, what can I say? A little Bach, a little Dylan. . . . Okay, they say that, technically, you're supposed to only listen to someone who is a religious Jew, because anything that he expresses will carry his intent with him, so if you listen to melancholy music, the person who authored it meant to make you feel melancholy, and you will feel melancholy, so there are certain subtle influences that people, if their head isn't in the right place, it will come through their music and affect you. But I mean, personally—you're asking me—I think Dylan is religious. He's a Jew. He has this component to him that we are all bound with, a special connection to God, and so he's a little off the track, but every once in a while, he also has glimmers of Judaism. I know he's been interested. He's been here. He comes to see the Rebbe at farbrengens. He's been here for Simchas Torah, and this and that, and he was here for Shabbos and. . . . So, I know he, personally, is also religious in his expressions. There are certain songs—like, the whole *New Morning* album is very religious, so I would say there are things that are not good to immerse yourself in constantly, but I wouldn't call them bad. (Thayler interview)

Popular musics, such as rock and roll, as well as Western classical musics, especially pieces by baroque composers and Beethoven, are viewed by many ba'alei teshuvah as opposite ends of a spectrum defined by text: popular music is (mostly) texted and therefore an obvious problem; classical music is (mostly) instrumental and thus more open to interpretation. Although both are seen as potentially harmful, classical music is regarded as more subtly so:

> A lot of girls take piano lessons. They'll get into classical music, and the more years they play, the more they're floating around with Beethoven and Bach, and I'm very strong on the concept that the girls should know that music has a definite effect on them. A lot of girls now listen to the radio. It's not a good

thing, not a positive thing, certainly not on the radio. It doesn't make too many contributions to what Hasidic girls should be. I told them that in my days, things were censored on radio. I remember there was a song that came out, that it was banned because of the words. Now that's an unheard of thing. I said, "You know, girls, the Torah tells us that music takes you from where you are and puts you where you want to be, and it connects you with the composer, and certainly as an author wants you to be connected with his characters and feel, certainly a good composer wants the same thing to happen." But who wants to be connected with the Rolling Stones when they were on some trip?

Now classical music is much more subtle. It definitely could have a negative effect on a person, just it's much, much, much more subtle. . . . [When you listen to popular music,] how many times do you find your toes tapping, and it really pulls on your animal soul. It really does. Classical music is much, much, much more subtle. I very rarely listen to that. None of the records that I have are such music. Why? The example that I give to myself is that it's like an elevator. Some stores, it's written inside the elevator, "fourth floor, lingerie; sixth floor, shoes," and you know specifically where you're going should you push the fifth button, and you travel there. Classical music is so subtle, if you're in transit, it takes you somewhere. But where? Why don't you know? Because you haven't stepped out of the elevator. Should the door open, and I walk out as a result of this music, I don't know where I would be. (Teldon interview)

Most ba'alei teshuvah, however, simply give up listening to or performing music that is connected in any way to their former lives, at least initially:

When I first became religious, I stopped listening to rock and roll and classical music. Rock and roll is heavily emotional. I had to end a relationship with somebody that I was in love with, and listening to rock and roll kept reminding me of this person. And also because I didn't want the words of the rock and roll to fill my head, because all that "I love you, but I can't have you," or "I love you, and isn't it great?" wasn't happening in my life right then, and I just didn't want to fill up my mind with that kind of stuff anymore. I wanted to clean my mind out of that kind of stuff. When I first became frumm [religious], I tried to control my environment as much as I could. I tried to just expose myself to positive influences, because I knew that anything heavily secular was just going to pull me apart, and I wanted to minimize the conflict. I mean, I knew it. And as I became more and more religious, so I've become more and more relaxed about it. I love baroque music. Although it's hard for me to put together the fact that this same baroque music was all mostly religious in nature. I mean, I loved Handel's *Messiah*, and I love Bach, and I know that these are not what you would call pro-Jewish souls. (Hankin interview)

But when children arrive, the prohibition against music's harmful influences becomes even stronger, especially for women:

> You have to be very careful what you surround yourself with. They say that the body doesn't have, like, a choice of its own. It's attracted to its surrounding. It has neutral value, so if you put it in a gross setting, it becomes gross, so that you want to provide for it—in your sober moments!—you want to provide. So, I've done things—like, I've given away records—because I knew that they were a temptation to me from my past. I would be bound to listen to them, and I don't want to. I spent enough years on that, twenty-seven years; I don't need it anymore. If you want to reconstruct your life, then you do it in the best manner, and you make sure that you provide yourself with the best—and even more so, when you have children. Every nook and cranny of my house should be the way it has to be, because my son is that sensitive. You know, he could become a different person in a minute, and who am I to think I am any more of a grown-up? I, also, could become caught by things. That's our nature. (Thayler interview)

Ba'alot teshuvah also must deal with the limitations of kol isha. While males are encouraged to sing and to participate in musical activities, women must always be aware of their surroundings. And although kol isha is ostensibly a limitation for men (they may not hear women singing), women simply will not sing if they are in a mixed-gender group, nor do they usually assert themselves and ask the men to leave. Instead, women are far more likely not to sing or to leave the room if they must sing. For lifetime Lubavitcher women, this is not a problem—it is simply the way they have been raised. But for ba'alot teshuvah, giving up the freedom to sing unself-consciously is often extremely difficult, even painful, as Thayler stated when I interviewed her:

> This was a very, very difficult thing for me. Even with my husband, I can only participate in music at certain times, not other times. So it means that I always have to be conscious, what state of being I'm in, but it's very difficult restraining yourself. I mean, especially for people who are not accustomed to restraining themselves, and if they've done everything they've ever wanted all their lives, it's particularly a challenge. I knew this was right. I knew I had to do it, but I knew it was very difficult. I knew I wasn't going to like it. I didn't have to pretend I was going to like it. I suffered. For a while, I really suffered, until I could, you know, recondition myself, so that now, in fact, it's

a joy. I never . . . well, I'm just an outgoing personality. I never really became *passive* to appreciate things. I mean, even when I was in nature, I was busy talking about how beautiful the tree was, but I never really *received* the tree. And I never really learned about music in my life. I never was able to appreciate it until I was forced not to participate. This is very interesting. I can really close my eyes and really feel it like I never felt it before, and I can really sing when I want to sing, and the singing itself is more meaningful. When you have to refrain from something, when you [finally] can express it, it has that much more impact.

Note

1. Carl Orff (1895–1982), a German composer, was also a music educator who created his own musical instruments based on the idiophones of traditional African and Indonesian musical cultures. He would use them to teach basic musical concepts (such as improvisation) through his own music or arrangements of classical pieces. Many school music programs in the United States and Europe today use Orff instruments and arrangements in pedagogical settings.

10

Performing the Modern in Music

Both the greatest threat to—and the greatest opportunity for—the contemporary Lubavitcher community lies in its negotiation with the modern; sorting the neutral and usable aspects of American culture from the potentially damaging and contaminating ones is a daily, ongoing process. This chapter discusses a number of different musical contexts, each of which offers a rich setting for examining how different negotiating strategies intertwine in daily contemporary Lubavitcher musical life.

Traditional Compositional Practices

If contemporary musical sounds and performances must somehow be linked to the past, do new, modern nigunim ever enter the repertoire? In a sense they do, as contemporary Lubavitcher musicians create them in the present generation. However, in another sense they do not, as new nigunim (discussed in chapter 7) are virtually indistinguishable from those of the past. Today, by far the most common form of composition is still the same as that practiced in the eighteenth century: borrowing and adapting older nigunim for use in new, modern contexts.

Such a compositional technique was used each year, while the Rebbe was alive, to generate a new nigun for his birthday. This practice, begun in 1971, when the Rebbe turned seventy, was initiated by Cantor Moshe Teleshevsky, a well-respected Lubavitcher musician whose song "B'cho Hashem Choosee-see"[1] was constructed from an older nigun and a new text taken from Psalm 71. Example 20 is the original transcription of the piece taken from a 1972 Lubavitcher publication (Lubavitch-Chabad 1972).

Songs of '71'
Arranged by Jerry Rosen

B'CHO HASHEM CHOSEESEE
Adapted by Cantor Rabbi Moshe Teleshevsky

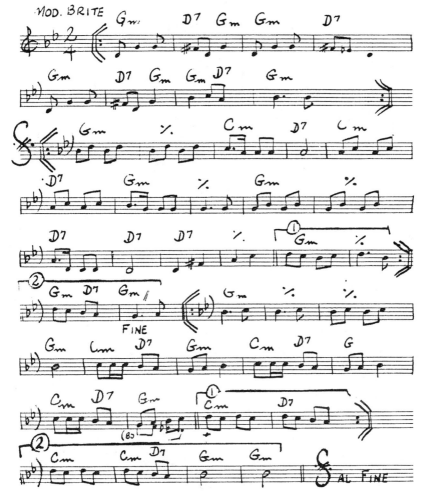

Example 20. "B'cho Hashem Choseesee" (reprinted from Lubavitch 1972:127)

Teleshevsky describes how he came to compose this piece and its resulting instant popularity within the community:

> Well, I started the tradition [of giving the Rebbe a song for his birthday] in
> 1971, and then it went on from there. Three days, three days in a row, twenty-
> four hours a day, they sang this nigun, before the Rebbe's birthday party. I
> took a group of boys, and I sang it twice or three times, and they picked it
> up, and then it went just like [he snaps his fingers]. They learned it by ear. It
> didn't take long. In one minute, the whole congregation. . . . I will never for-
> get this picture, before the Rebbe came out at this gathering for his seventi-
> eth birthday. They were singing. The whole world was this song. It was so
> beautiful. Even the Rebbe was singing it. He was overjoyed; he thanked me
> for this nigun. (Teleshevsky interview, 1974)

Rabbi Ephraim Rosenblum is also a composer of new nigunim. Unlike
Teleshevsky, who composes by adapting, Rosenblum actually composes new
songs that sound old, songs closely resembling the older nigunim attributed to the early heads of Habad. Rosenblum states that he composes them to
express his own innermost feelings and that they were created, as were the
older traditional songs, in moments of quiet and solitary contemplation.
Example 21 shows that his basic compositional style exactly mirrors those
musical norms established by the early Lubavitcher composers (discussed in
chapter 6 and elsewhere).

Example 21. First section of "Rosenblum's Nigun," *devekut* style, composed and
performed by Ephraim Rosenblum, 1975 (transcribed by the author)

Rosenblum describes another composition that he created as a present for his neighbor's son, who had become a hazzan (example 22), and then shows how he made another version of it that was truly Hasidic (example 23):

So, something came to my mind, but I had to work on it all Shabbos without a tape recorder. By the time Saturday night was around, I had more or less completed it. Again, as I said, the only thing is, I think that all of us are guilty of making a song, of taking parts of one or the other, but if I did it, it was subconsciously, and I haven't found any similarities between what I wrote [and anything else]. This is the only thing which makes me a little bit wary of saying something is my own, because when you make something, it's always part of what you heard somewhere or other, but I haven't found any exact similarities. This, by the way, I had someone notate. It was played already by some weddings.

Now, let me show you what I did with this tune. I slowed it down, and I made it a Hasidic song. You know, I took the exact same music and changed the—how should I say?—the expressions and the tone. And when I sang it— in fact, I sang it to my niece, and she didn't even recognize that it was the same song. I had to prove to her that it was the same song. Of course, musi-

Jeremiah 33:10-11

Yet again, these shall be heard [. . .] in the cities of Jehudah
And in the streets of Jerusalem [. . .] the voice of joy
And the voice of gladness, the voice of the bridegroom
And the voice of the bride   (Jewish Publication Society 1955:1214).

Example 22. "Oyd Yeshama," *lebedig* style, composed and performed by Ephraim Rosenblum, 1975 (transcribed by the author)

Example 23. "Oyd Yeshama," Hasidic style, composed and performed by Ephraim Rosenblum, 1975 (transcribed by the author)

cally you'll hear right away that it's not. But the notes are the same; the notes are identical, but it's a different kind of feeling. (Rosenblum interview, Aug. 1975)

And, finally, using a traditional compositional device, that of borrowing, Rosenblum describes how he adapted a previously composed nigun, "Ashreinu," to his own aesthetic principles: "Then I have one that I plagiarized from. . . . I took a lebedig [happy] nigun [example 24] and made it slow [example 25], but the nigun wasn't mine completely. I went, and I simply stole it, and I made a slow nigun from it. In fact, unless I told anyone where I took it from, no one would know" (Rosenblum interview, Aug. 1975).

In effect, Rosenblum has both originally composed new songs that sound

Example 24. Beginning of "Ashreinu," performed by Ephraim Rosenblum, 1975 (transcribed by the author)

mi-yam---- mam mam   me - -m- a--------------- yoi   nam,   ah   ma - - ma - - - - - - i

ye-oh   mam,   a   mai   ye-oi   ye-mam mam   a - i   na   ya   na   nam

o - i   na   ya------ na nam a--- oi   na - - - m - - me - am.

Example 25. "Ashreinu, Made More Hasidic," recorded by Ephraim Rosenblem (transcribed by the author)

old and has adapted old songs to sound even older (i.e., Hasidic). In this way, he is completely in keeping with the basic Hasidic belief in the heightened spirituality of the past. And, in much the same way as his spiritual ancestors, the former Rebbes and heads of Habad, he is contributing to the enrichment and growth of the nigun repertoire in contemporary times. It would be a mistake, however, to see his compositions as nostalgic throwbacks to the old days; rather, one should see them as Rosenblum does, as "pulling-forwards," re-creations of the past in the present. But, are they nigunim? In the following interview, Rabbi Rosenblum comes as close as he can to answering this question:

EK: Would you call the songs that you compose nigunim?
ER: The songs I compose [almost laughing]? Whatever. . . . I don't know what to call them. I just sat down and composed them.
EK: Are they in the style of old nigunim? Would they be called nigunim by somebody else listening to them?
ER: You better ask somebody else [laughing]. I don't know.
EK: I would call them nigunim.
ER: Okay, possibly.
EK: Because they are composed in the style of what I think of as a nigun.
ER: The trick is to take this and play it for someone and don't tell him who you heard it from. Tell him it's supposed to be an old nigun, and can he pass judgment on it?
EK: Let's go back to the Pepsi commercial that was taken, and I heard it sung. You know, "We're in the Rebbe's Generation" and all that. Now, is that a nigun?

ER: No.

EK: Why?

ER: It wasn't meant to be a nigun.

EK: Why not? What is it that makes it not a nigun—that it wasn't written in the style of what we call a nigun?

ER: Yes, perhaps.

EK: Okay, now, let's say that the Rebbe went out, and he took the Pepsi commercial and sang it. Would that be a nigun?

ER: If the Rebbe made it into something, I guess it would be a nigun.

EK: No, but what if he did exactly what the other person did and, say, just changed a couple of words here and there. Would it be called a nigun because it was his, or would it be called a nigun only if it was composed or sung in the old style of what we call nigun?

ER: Could I ask you something?

EK: Sure.

ER: What makes a Rembrandt a Rembrandt?

EK: He painted it.

ER: Okay, now if I paint something in the style of a Rembrandt, will that be a Rembrandt? In other words, it would take the connoisseur to know the difference. Someone who isn't a connoisseur will say, "Well, it looks like it's pretty close. It's a Rembrandt style or something." Okay, "It's a Picasso style." There's imitation and there's the real thing. Let's leave nigun for a second. What makes a Rembrandt a Rembrandt?

EK: The fact that he painted it.

ER: So what makes it so fantastic? I mean let's say that you had lots of money to spend on art, and you wanted to buy the kind of pictures which are really the outstanding ones. And someone would tell you—you didn't know too much, let's say—they say, "Well, this is a Rembrandt. It's worth two hundred thousand dollars," and you'd shell out two hundred thousand dollars to have a Rembrandt. To you, what would be a Rembrandt?

EK: Well, probably nothing in that circumstance, because I wouldn't know anything anyway. I mean I would have to take somebody else's word for it, somebody that knew something.

ER: In Rembrandt's time, what made a Rembrandt a Rembrandt? His feeling, his spirit.

EK: What makes a nigun a nigun? Its spirit?

ER: What went into the one who composes the nigun? What kind of feelings did he have? What was his experience composing the nigun?

EK: Oh, are you saying his intention had to be right?

ER: Either his intention or just whoever he was at that moment. Maybe his kavvanah was experiencing a type of feeling which was so high that it brought about a nigun. I don't exist at that level—so what I compose, is it nigun? (Rosenblum interview, 1975)

Another form of re-creating the past in modern times has been, especially lately, the musical phenomenon known as "We Want Moshiach, Now!" After the Rebbe suffered a stroke and underwent surgery in 1991, the messianic fever began to rise, primarily in the Crown Heights community and in Israel. As Lis Harris noted:

> Without putting too fine a point on it, the Lubavitchers are not too reluctant to say that it just so happens that Rabbi Schneerson meets admirably the scripturally ordained requirements Maimonides codified in his Book of Judges for the Messianic role. . . . With their "We want Moshiach (the Messiah) Now" posters and bumper stickers, outreach programs, "Call-a-Hasidic-Lecture" hotline, and impassioned street proselytizing, the Lubavitchers sometimes seem like a team of Messianic advance men. If the present generation does not live to see the paradisiacal era, they appear to be saying, it won't be because they didn't work the precincts. (Harris 1985:109)

In addition to the T-shirts, flags, and banners proclaiming the Rebbe as the Messiah that flooded Hasidic communities in the early 1990s, a number of songs with the title "We Want Moshiach, Now!" were adapted to encourage the messianic age to come quickly. One of these, originally a traditional Lubavitcher nigun, was borrowed and reset with an English text (example 26). This, of course, is not the first instance of this kind of borrowing. What is unique, however, is that the Rebbe learned this song and called for it at his farbrengen, marking it as perhaps the first song in English to be incorporated into the Lubavitcher nigun repertoire. In this way, an old song (a tradi-

Example 26. "We Want Moshiach, Now!" performed by Rus Dvorah Shatkin, 1990 (transcribed by the author)

tional nigun) became new ("We Want Moshiach, Now!") but was immediately made old again (Hasidic) in the context of its performance. Rus Dvorah Shatkin explains how this song came to be: "The Rebbe popularized 'We Want Moshiach, Now!' He said it in English. He said 'want' is so strong in English, you really can't compare it [to any other language]. I guess he sees that Americans are so spoiled that when they *want* something, they get it! It's sung at every gathering now. That's definitely a nigun" (Shatkin interview, Dec. 1990).

Old and New Together

With the popular media all around them, Lubavitchers, like most Americans, cannot totally escape their influence. Most Lubavitcher homes have radios, televisions, computers, and VCRs. Of course, programming is strictly monitored, and children especially are directed to listen to and to watch Jewish-oriented tapes and videos, such as the music cassettes recorded by Eli Lipsker and His Little Soldiers.

Chapter 5 of this study discussed the Lubavitcher conceptualization of music, noting that the large category of "potential nigunim" could be subdivided into smaller categories of musics that were regarded as closer or farther from the divine source. Musics in the middle of this continuum—such as some Western classical examples, so-called soft-rock or folk-rock pieces, and songs from Yiddish theater—are regarded as more or less neutral within the larger category of "potential nigunim," and they are frequently adopted by the Lubavitcher community and adapted to fit specific social and religious contexts. Menachem Mendel Schneerson (not the Rebbe) discusses which kinds of popular, contemporary, non-Jewish musics are best suited for borrowing and incorporation into the Lubavitcher musical repertoire, beginning with a musical trick he once played on his yeshivah teacher:

> I studied in France for a year. And the dean of the school had been living behind Hasidic walls for years and didn't know what was going on in the rest of the world. He lived in France thirty or forty years. Whenever there was a get-together, I would be the one who starts the songs. And one day we decided to play a trick on the dean. It was a nasty trick. He was a holy person. I sang some songs I heard on the radio. I dressed them up a little bit, you know. He bought it.
>
> There are some songs, such as country music, that you can adapt easily. Most rock and jazz you can't. Simon and Garfunkel songs—those you can

adapt. It's in the beat or rhythm. It's not the same as a Hasidic tune, it doesn't have the depth. I can tell even when I buy some Jewish records today. You can tell—they're pasted together. Songs you hear on the radio don't have the depth. (Schneerson interview)

This listing illustrates, as did the organization of the *Sefer Ha-Nigunim* in midcentury (found in chapter 5), the social ranking of today's contemporary musics vis-à-vis the Lubavitcher community. Easily adaptable songs—including country and western and folk-rock tunes, such as those recorded by Simon and Garfunkel—are taken from social groups that are regarded by today's late-twentieth-century American Lubavitchers as friendly or, at least, nonthreatening. That Simon and Garfunkel and Bob Dylan, another frequent Lubavitcher choice, are Jewish only helps here. They may not be Hasidic, but they and their music are all part of the same Jewish body. Songs that cannot be adopted, such as heavy-metal rock music and jazz, are associated in the Lubavitcher mind with openly explicit sexual practices, drug use, and with African American and neo-Nazi cultures, sources felt to be irrelevant or threatening to Lubavitcher values.

Musically, these soft-rock and folk-rock examples also fit the Lubavitcher aesthetic philosophy. Many of the musics cited above are performed by solo singers, are in minor keys, or use a blue-note or neutral third reminiscent of the harmonic, minor scalar-melodic patterns found in the melody-types common to Lubavitcher nigunim and Yiddish folk music generally. Often, such songs are harmonized simply and are accompanied by an acoustic guitar; thus, they have not been electronically manipulated. More importantly, the driving, sexually explicit texts and rhythms of hard rock are absent.

Probably no other example of recently composed popular music has captured the imagination of the Lubavitcher population—and, indeed, of the entire Jewish community—better than the Broadway musical *Fiddler on the Roof.* Based on the stories of the great Jewish writer Sholom Aleichem, this musical beautifully captures and embroiders on the central cultural, social, and religious themes facing the Jewish community in America today: adherence to tradition in the face of change; the situation of Eastern Europe and Russia as the loci of past spiritual values and of institutionalized bigotry; the changing roles of women in Judaism; and modernization. From the time of its composition in the early 1960s to the present, *Fiddler on the Roof* has become a Jewish cultural icon. As such, it often figures in modern Lubavitcher settings, such as the following skit.

The Women's Convention Skit

It is spring 1995, and I am in Crown Heights to attend the yearly International Lubavitcher Women's Convention, during which thousands of women from all over the world come together to celebrate Jewish womanhood. The conventions, begun in 1955 at the request of the Rebbe, were formed to celebrate the perceived natural and superior qualities of Jewish women.[2] The Rebbe, in his initial 1955 opening speech, cited many reasons for this superiority and predicted that in the generation just prior to the coming of the Messiah, Torah scholars would come to follow the advice of their wives. He concluded: "If you want to accomplish [something] with the men, you must first accomplish with the women" (Lubavitch Women's Organization 1984:13).

The four-day program is crammed with activities: talks, stories, prayers, field trips to the Rebbe's library, and, on the last day, a visit to the men's synagogue at 770, where the Rebbe would traditionally give his closing remarks. All through the weekend, books, recordings, videos, and other convention ephemera "for women only" are sold, borrowed, and exchanged. Saturday afternoon marks the high point of the convention: an inspiring talk by a visiting Rabbi and a skit presented for the entertainment and enrichment of the conferees.

The Saturday afternoon program and skit are not held at 770 this year; instead, they take place at Oholei Torah, a synagogue located at 667 Eastern Parkway, to accommodate the large crowds. This synagogue is a far cry from the ramshackle one normally used by Lubavitchers. Framed by beautiful, stained-glass windows, each identified at the bottom by a rendering of the donor's name, the sanctuary holds long, curving pews of dark mahogany stretched over plush carpets. Rumor has it that, every now and then, someone will propose moving to this synagogue. It is larger, more comfortable, and much grander than 770. "No, 770 is the place where the Rebbe davened (prayed). We cannot move," is the inevitable reply.

The program is introduced by a woman in her late fifties who could easily have developed a career as a stand-up comic. There are over two thousand women of all ages and nationalities in the audience, all laughing uproariously at her jokes, which are delivered fluently in English, Yiddish, and Russian. She is followed by a handsome young Rabbi from Italy, who is in the process of codifying and publishing the Rebbe's talks.

It is soon time for the skit, entitled "Now We're in *Geulah.*" Geulah refers to the future, the time immediately following the coming of the Messiah and the ending of the *golus* (wandering), when Jews will be restored to their homeland, and all will be well. The skit is written, directed, and performed by a group of Lubavitcher women from Toronto.

There is nothing truly special or unusual about this particular skit; it is like many others performed for a variety of Jewish audiences for a variety of occasions. Such skits, in fact, have long been a staple of Jewish culture, both in Eastern Europe and America. Often quite witty and at times pointedly political, they capitalize on common stereotypes of both the secular and the Jewish world. They are, of course, meant to be instructive, but lightly so, with more than a heaping touch of obvious humor. "Now We're in *Geulah*" was performed in English.

Skit: "Now We're in *Geulah*"

The skit of five scenes has seven characters (played by six women): a Russian Lubavitcher woman; a Lubavitcher woman from America; a young ba'alat teshuvah; a rabbi (the husband of the Russian woman); a hypnotist; a young student ba'alat teshuvah; and a Russian soldier. A doll was used for the eighth character, a baby boy. The action takes place somewhere in Russia, probably in the late nineteenth century.[3] Throughout, the action is punctuated by tunes adapted for this play from *Fiddler on the Roof;* its lyrics have been changed to fit the story line.

Scene 1: A Park Bench in Russia

The first three characters enter. They talk about their lives as Hasidic women, each speaking from her own different perspective. The first, a simple Russian woman, complains about her husband, the rabbi—how he never says anything nice and never helps her in the house. The second, a well-dressed, well-spoken woman visiting from America, talks about how her husband is always out, how many children she has, and how sad she is still to be in golus. The third is portrayed as a bimbo ba'alat teshuvah, acting with wild, "dumb blonde" gestures and asking silly questions.

Scene 2: The Home of the Russian Lubavitcher Woman and Her Husband, the Rabbi

The woman is cooking dinner over a small stove while her husband is reading the paper and complaining about everything: she does not look pretty enough, the food is not cooked properly, the house is a mess, and so forth.

They have a bit of an argument, and he leaves to go to the synagogue, where a program is about to be presented in the meeting room.

Scene 3: The Meeting Room at the Synagogue

A hypnotist has arrived to put on a show. Also in the room is a young, serious ba'alat teshuvah. The rabbi arrives and takes a seat. Through various tricks, the hypnotist convinces the other two that they are in geulah, and they leave happily.

Scene 4: On the Way Home

The rabbi is walking home, singing and dancing in the street. He meets a Russian soldier who threatens to take him away. The soldier is carrying something under his coat. The rabbi rips the coat away and discovers that the soldier is holding a male baby. The guard is overwhelmed by the spirit of the rabbi and tells him that he (the soldier) is really Jewish and needs to find a *mohel* (ritual specialist) so that his baby can be circumcised properly. The two hug wildly and go off together.

Scene 5: Back Home

The Rabbi returns home all cheery and excited. He begins to compliment his wife's appearance and cooking. She is surprised but happy. She does not understand what has happened, but she is not questioning too closely. Geulah is surely here.

Finishing Number

All characters come onstage and sing songs adapted from *Fiddler on the Roof.*

~

Although a mere skit, this story is rich in spiritual, social, and gender symbolism. It seems to capture many of the themes so much a part of modern Lubavitcher life: the story takes place in the Russia of the past; the characters cover the gamut of Lubavitcher actors in the modern world, from the rabbi to the bimbo ba'alat teshuvah, including, perhaps, some divine intervention in the character of the hypnotist. Lubavitcher class differences are represented by the Russian woman (simple, pious) and her American counterpart (well-dressed, affluent). The theme of redemption and transformation through adherence to Jewish law is there, beautifully illustrated in the scene between the rabbi and the Russian soldier who, despite all odds, are united in the process of accomplishing the most important ritual procedure of Jewish law, male circumcision. And, while each of the characters has his or her own agenda, all share a common sadness in the persistence of the golus and the joy of reaching geulah.

At a deeper level, the skit illustrates some of the tensions within the modern Hasidic community between men and women, between lifetime Lubavitchers and ba'alei teshuvah, and between the contemporary, perhaps corrupted, American and the simpler, perhaps more pious, Russian Lubavitcher communities. The men and women in the story are presented as contrasting: the men are seen as generally ineffective or as tricksters, while the women appear as pious and hardworking; the ba'alot teshuvah are seen as either students (i.e., not yet really Hasidic) or inconsequential to the community; and the American Lubavitcher is portrayed as wealthier and more educated than her Russian counterpart, thus being more in contact with the modern, Western, and corrupted secular world.

It is the tension between men and women, however, that seems to be most prominent here, both in the story line of the skit and in its performance. In the first scene, for example, the women complain mainly about their husbands' lack of attention to them and their children. Although class and lineage differences are present in the two married female characters, they share a common view of their husbands and, perhaps by extension, all men. After all, the rabbi, supposedly a holy, learned figure, is presented here as crabby and a bit stupid; the Russian soldier, first seen as an outsider and a possible threat to the rabbi, is only redeemed when he produces a young (still malleable)[4] male child needing circumcision, the quintessential symbol of God's special connection to Jews. And, what about the character of the hypnotist? Is this story really meant to be a joke? Is the hypnotist just that: has he simply fooled the rabbi and young student into thinking that the geula has arrived? If so, then how to explain the soldier's sudden redemption and the rabbi's good mood? If God, in the form of a trickster, has not intervened, how can this have happened?

It is also significant that this skit is being acted by an all-female cast for an all-female audience, all of whom are insiders to the various gender codes that abound. Much as in the drag shows analyzed by Judith Butler in her work,[5] gender is enacted here in exaggerated costuming, bodily gestures, and voice types. The three male characters wear clothes that are far too large, indulge in wild, rambling gestures, show their anger and joy openly, sit and stand crudely, speak and shout loudly, and generally seem uncouth, un-learned, and unholy. The women, by contrast, move and speak modestly, seem to take pride in (while constantly complaining about) their husbands and children, and are generally pictured as stoic in the face of male silliness. Only the young bimbo ba'alat teshuvah, the female character closest spiri-tually to the secular world, is characterized by the vacant looks and gestures most lifetime Lubavitchers associate with marginal hangers-on, especially females. In this way, the skit, like any good comedy routine, functions at many levels to entertain, instruct, and perhaps expose or protest existing power relations. And while I am not suggesting that this performance is truly a drag show—with blatant sexual and power dynamics openly on display—it does serve, like drag shows in secular society, to reinforce commonly held gender and class stereotypes within the framework or template of contemporary Lubavitcher cultural and social norms.

The stereotyping seems to work, much to the amusement of the audience, partly because it is periodically punctuated by the friendly, familiar musical icon *Fiddler on the Roof.* The skit cannot go too far afield with its uncouth rabbi, unworldly hypnotist, and vacuous ba'alat teshuvah without returning to the somehow reassuring melodies of this universally respected musical work, even if the words have been altered to fit this particular context. When audiences hear the familiar contours and harmonies of "Tradition" and "If I Were a Rich Man" being belted out by the female cast, they know that the story will end well. The Russian soldier will be redeemed, the baby will be circum-cised, the rabbi will return to his wife with a better appreciation for her, the hypnotist will disappear without too much scrutiny, and the silly ba'alat te-shuvah will somehow learn the answers to her pointless questions or will stop asking them altogether. The music, as a character in its own right, thus takes on a separate role as the familiar friend providing a safe and orderly musical context or environment for enacting a story that is potentially out of control.

In borrowing and adapting songs from the popular (secular) culture, the Lubavitcher community is practicing a form of limited assimilation. Hear-ing, learning, and passing on these songs through performance contexts such as the one described above involve actual interaction and negotiation with the secular world from which these tunes originate. Changing their words and performing them in an informally religious context are traditional Lubavitcher strategies practiced today that make these tunes usable by elim-inating their contaminating influences; but, incorporating such music into the Lubavitcher world has also involved opening the fence, if only for a moment, to allow a musical flow to take place. In this way, both the outside and the inside adjust to one another.

Contexts for Recruitment: Outreach Strategies

Since the Six-Day War of 1967, the Rebbe has made it his personal responsibility to develop a network of emissaries throughout the world. As the saying within the community goes, "Where there's Coke, there's Habad." Recruitment, in the form of Habad Houses, mitzvah tanks, university programs, grocery-store displays, classes, camps, and coffee klatches, has been quite successful in drawing all sorts of people, both Jews and some non-Jews, into the community. How long such people stay is often a matter of debate; but clearly, the community has grown worldwide over the past thirty years as a result of these efforts.

Music Class in Manhattan

Chaim Burston, first introduced in chapter 9, has started a music class in Manhattan for anyone interested in learning about hasides through music. Examining this context can be instructive, because it highlights many important modern Lubavitcher values. After all, the purpose of this class is to instruct those unfamiliar with Hasidic life and philosophy through music. Thus, essential ideas concerning music and its power to communicate, as well as ideas about the substance of such communication, will be evident here.[6]

As a professional musician before becoming a Lubavitcher, Burston is aware of the power of music to communicate deep feelings and has used his expertise to develop this strategy for recruitment. Every so often, he travels with his synthesizer to Manhattan, the Bronx, and elsewhere to present an evening of Lubavitcher music in the context of an informal gathering of mostly nonobservant Jews who are curious about Hasidic life (fig. 12). Usually, these meetings of about eight to twelve people take place in someone's home, so they have the feeling of a private, salon-type performance. Burston wants the evening to be interactive, though—that is, he encourages questions from his audience and asks questions of them. He is hoping that by discussing music, the songs on their own will bring people closer to hasides.

This evening, Burston starts by recounting what happened to him in his car on the way to this meeting:

Figure 12. Chaim Burston at a Manahattan music class (photograph by the author, 1991)

I got in the car and, you know, just by habit, I pressed the button on the radio, and for about ten seconds I had this music that was such a total bringdown. The lyrics! After ten seconds I said, Forget it! I'm closing the radio. I couldn't listen to it. The concept of music is that it takes you somewhere, you travel somewhere through music. It's a great vehicle for transporting a person. But as [with] anything, [you] can travel either up or down. Hopefully, a nigun is where a person is transported up, is elevated to a higher plane, to a connection with Hashem. . . . In Hebrew, each letter has a numerical value, and the numerical value of *sulam*, which is "ladder," is the same as that for "kol," which is "sound" or "voice." Voice is like a ladder. It just transports a person from one plane to another. . . . On the other hand, if you take music, and it transports a person into the wrong place—like those lyrics, they obviously wanted to transport a person into a certain place, a certain place that was absolutely a non-Jewish feeling, a non-Jewish concept. And it was very powerful. (Burston interview)

In this way, Burston has set the stage for the entire evening's performance. Beginning with a story about his habit of turning on the radio in the car, he quickly minimizes the difference between himself and his audience. He is aware that the people listening to him are mainly secular Jews, who may have a rather stereotyped view of his attitude toward modern technology. "You see," he is in effect saying, "I listen to the radio just like you do. We have all had this experience; we all know from our own lives how powerful music is to take us away."

Burston announces that he will devote tonight's class to nigunim composed by, or attributed to, Schneur Zalman, the founder of Habad Hasidism—in short, those nigunim held in the highest spiritual and musical regard by the Lubavitcher community. One might ask: Why these particular songs? Burston recognizes the enormous gap between the spiritual level of these compositions and the people in the room. Only the most powerful, inspirational nigunim can fight the spiritual inertia that he perceives there.

A main theme of the evening is the notion of expansion and contraction, running toward and returning to. This idea, related to the Hasidic explanation of the Creation (see chapter 3), is one of the most basic in Hasidic philosophy. Burston introduces the second nigun attributed to Schneur Zalman, "Kaayal Taarog" ("Like a Lamb Yearning"), with the following explanation of the text:

Just as the lamb wishes to drink from the river water, so does the soul long for God. And then, the next verse is about tefillin. A man should have tefillin between his eyes. There are two movements in life, running and returning. Everything in the world is in a state of running or returning. For example, the heartbeat, pumping and quiet; breathing, taking in and giving out; the ocean, the waves; you sleep, and you're awake, then you have to retract again, and you're asleep, and you're awake. Everything is in the process of expansion and contraction.

Spiritually, one application for this is running towards God, leaving the practical and going up into a very high spiritual level, whether it be in Kabbalah, a person has a mystical experience, or in praying, learning Torah, Shabbos, leaving the world, not being involved with the world—these are all movements of running. Then there has to be returning. The main purpose of the running is for the returning. The returning means come back into the world, come back to practical life, come back to your family, come back to your job, come back to everyday relationships with people. And because of the running, the returning is much better. You're able to act properly, to do what you should be doing, have the powers to do it, to take care of the things you have to do but not be brought down by them. . . .

Let's say there was no running, no reaching a higher level; then if the person is just on the level of returning, all the time could he be brought down. And, again, if a person is too aloof, not returning, this is also against God's will. God's will is not that a person should just be up in the sky and not in the world. God wants a dwelling place in both worlds. . . . and not just being secluded—that's a very non-Jewish concept. It's very Jewish in terms of temporarily being secluded, temporarily cutting ourselves off, for the purpose of the return but not as a thing for itself. (Burston interview)

In this explanation, Burston has not only beautifully illustrated the tension between the spiritual and the mundane in everyday life; he has attempted to dispel yet another commonly held stereotype: that Hasidim are insular, cliquish, choosing to close themselves off from the secular world.

Musically, Burston's arrangement of "Kaayal Taarog" (example 27) is an

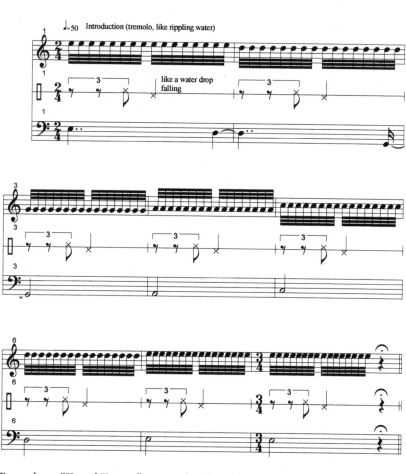

Example 27. "Kaayal Taarog," arranged and performed by Chaim Burston, 1991 (transcribed by the author)

Example 27. (continued)

interesting blend of old and new. Although performing an old and spiritually elevated song associated with Schneur Zalman, he is performing it instrumentally, using a modern synthesizer and New Age harmonies, which appeal to him as the appropriate sounds for modern nigun performance. When I interviewed Burston, he described working with a multitrack recording device in his own electronic studio and how his dream to marry popular, modern music with nigunim came to be: "Traditionally, [nigunim] are sung with voice, but I always imagined them with some kind of arrangements behind them, instrumental. There was always a dream in the back of my mind to do something with them, with these pure beautiful nigunim. Then, when the sort of New Age, meditative sounds came in, I could more readily envision this, because these sounds are very meditative, very simple, very beautiful, these very deep sounds that could be done with synthesizers."

Finally, his use of New Age sounds, such as flutes that "float" and harmonies that move in streams (not in the usual functional fashion of tonal music), mark this arrangement as new and yet somehow aesthetically appropriate. Burston feels that he has preserved, even heightened, the spiritual level of this song in his arrangement because the instrumentation and harmonies of New Age music seem to fit the dreamy, drifting sensation of floating both on water and on music. When asked why he used the flute sound in these arrangements so prominently, Burston responded with aesthetic and practical answers:

I gravitate toward the natural sounds. I use flutes, violins, the more natural kinds of sounds. If I'm doing more lebedig [happier] kinds of music, I'll use funkier sounds, more experimental sounds; but for these nigunim, it doesn't go. I love that floating sound. This is called "floating pan," panflute. There are 185, what you would call "multisounds," in the internal structure of this synthesizer. I came to this one by taking another sound and opening up the basic component and going through a bunch of other sounds and sort of plying that basic wave form to the other. This was not a sound that came in stock, in the memory. I had to do a little exploring.

Burston continued with a story, fairly typical of all who use computers but also relevant to the night's spiritual theme of restoration, and described a special notational device that he had invented to program the beginnings of over two hundred nigunim:

I keep losing [my songs,] so I made a backup this week [chuckling]. I was talking to someone, trying to get some work done. . . . I got involved, and I put in the wrong disk. I saved it to memory on the wrong disk, and I wiped out five hours of work! Thank God I restored it! I'm glad I restored it. I'm glad it was wiped out, because I restored it in a way I like better . . . than before. And then this week, I wiped out twenty hours of work, but I had a backup. It was cool—I just brought it up. . . . I also program the first ten notes of songs that don't have any name, so at least it can remind me to have some way to tune into . . . . You know, 'cause some nigunim don't have any name, so how am I going to remember that's what I want to play out of, let's say I listen to 200 nigunim. So, I program the first ten notes, and for, let's say, for a quarter note, I use a small-case letter, for a half note or whole note, a large-case letter, so at least I have some connection with what I'm going to do. It's very exciting to actually have it there instead of having to look at my papers, a book, and think, What's it called?

Burston's work outside the Crown Heights community is both a pleasure for him and a task he is encouraged to perform. His music represents a skillful merging of traditional and modern sounds and presentation. Unlike Ephraim Rosenblum, who creates new music that sounds old, Burston re-creates old music that sounds new. In borrowing aspects of the modern world to accomplish this task, though, he is creating a path through the fence. Burston feels the path is neutral in and of itself; if the person journeying on the path has the proper intention and training (he has been a ba'al teshuvah for over twenty years) and is performing a righteous mitzvah (bringing someone closer to hasides), then the break in the fence is ultimately a good one.

Zehava Sachs, a ba'alat teshuvah, had been living within the Crown Heights community for six years when I first met her. She was, and still considers herself to be, primarily a musician. She has composed a number of songs that she frequently performs at women's gatherings. Unlike Chaim Burston, though, she does not perform her music, or traditional Lubavitcher nigunim, in the context of mixed-gender secular groups. Her music is a mixture of contemporary soft rock, using guitar with standard harmonies as accompaniment. Example 28 is "Sabbath Song," a song for women and girls only, which captures in both its words and tuneful melody the sensibility and sensitivity of contemporary Lubavitcher women's music.[7]

Camp

Throughout the United States each summer, Lubavitchers run a network of day camps for religious and nonreligious children. Some studying takes place, but mostly the children take part in summertime activities that would be found at any other camp in America: swimming, baseball, hiking, and boat-

Example 28. "Sabbath Song," composed and performed by Zehava Sachs, 1975 (transcribed by the author)

Example 28. (continued)

ing. Some of the time, though, is spent around the campfire learning old songs with new words. The songs that are chosen are usually familiar commercial or children's nursery-rhyme tunes heard every day by the children on television and radio. Below are the words to three of them.[8] Seen essentially as silly, such songs are used, nonetheless, to "drill Hasidic concepts into the children" (Teldon interview).

> "Mazuza" sung to the tune of the theme from the television series *Batman:*
> Ma-zuma-zuma-zuma-zuma-zuma-zuma-zuma-zuma-zuza!

> "I'm Popeye, the Sailor *Mensch*" (man, human):
> I'm "Popeye, the Sailor Mensch;
> After I eat, I *bensch* [pray].
> And I make kiddish because I am Yiddish.
> I'm Popeye, the sailor Mensch.
> I'm Olive Oyl, the sailoress.
> Before I eat, I bless.
> Each Friday night, the candles I light.
> I'm Olive Oyl, the sailoress.

> "Music, Music, Music":
> Put another nickel in
> In the metal tzeddakah [charity] tin.
> That's the Jewish thing to do,
> Give tzeddakah, tzeddakah, tzeddakah.

In the examples presented above, making these songs Hasidic textually is a rather easy process: simply remove the secularized words and substitute words conforming to Hasidic concepts, a common practice found within many cultures, especially in children's repertoires. Making it Hasidic musically, however, is a process that involves slightly more creativity. Rus Dvorah Shatkin illustrates how a simple American folk tune became a nigun:

> There's a story about a young Hasid in Israel who was playing a joke on an older rabbi. This older one was very holy—he was imprisoned in Russia, is very close to the Rebbe, he lives in Israel—Kfar Habad. The young one once sang him this nigun. I made up a story to it. I do this sometimes for nonreligious audiences. I say like this, "There was once a farmer who was upset because there was a drought, and he wanted it to rain, so he sang this nigun so it should rain." This young Hasid sang it for the older one, and he said, "Oh, what a pretty nigun!" The nigun goes like this [example 29]. (Shatkin interview, Dec. 1990)

+ = hand clap

Example 29. "Young Hasid's Nigun," performed by Russ Dvorah Shatkin (transcribed by the author)

Here, just as in the case of Ephraim Rosenblum's nigunim, making this tune Hasidic involved a two-step process of narrative and musical recontextualization. First, the song had to be recontextualized with a story, preferably one that would attest to the miraculous properties of the song when performed in its new guise. Second, the most salient musical characteristics of the nigun repertoire had to be added: the tempo slowed, ornaments added, and the whole tune reset in a minor key. A final touch here was that the story of how this composition came to be was framed as a joke or trick, similar to the ones that Menachem Mendel Schneerson played on his dean, that the hypnotist played on the foolish Rabbi and young student in the skit "Now We're in *Geulah*," and that Ephraim Rosenblum played on his niece. This touch, adding elements of mystery and humor, is one of the keys to the tune's success.

These songs, and many others taught at camp, borrow freely from the popular or commercial music repertoires of the United States and Israel. One particular tune, "Dvorah Leah's Song," is taught year after year to all of the girls who attend camp and has become something of a musical marker of Lubavitcher women's gender identity. The song is based on an Israeli tune, "Har Ha-Gilboa"; the text was composed by Miriam Bela Nadoff,[9] and it tells the story of Dvorah Leah, the daughter of Schneur Zalman, who is said to have sacrificed herself for her father. One woman describes her own personal connection to this song:

> I can only tell you what has been important to me, having known what she did for Hasidism. Without even focusing on the facts of her life, Dvorah Leah

is very much a part of who the women of Habad are. It's a song that every generation of girls sings, they pick it up in camp or in school, and they sing it over, and over, and over again, and I think the story of Dvorah Leah is very much a part of who we are. What was important for me, in that song, I can tell you, was the fact that she left behind a little boy who grew up in the way of hasides. And what she ingrained in him was what made him the man he became, is what made him the person he was. Her first steps of education of this child—that is what enabled him to be the person he was. (Teifenbrun interview)

There are many versions of Dvorah Leah's story and almost no explanations for her death other than that she was compelled to make an extreme sacrifice. (This action is never referred to as a suicide.) The popularity of this song, though, seems to attest to its salient and idealized message of female sacrificial love. Below are a version of this story and also of the song composed in Dvorah Leah's honor, as they were told and sung to me by Leah Namdar, a lifetime Lubavitcher from England, now living in Crown Heights (example 30):

The Alter Rebbe called his daughter Dvorah Leah into his room, and he told her a story about a tree which has to be guarded for thirty years and to be tended. Then he said something about the tree being in danger. She knew that somehow hasides was in danger. She realized that her father was going to tell her that he was about to pass away. For him to pass away at the beginning, at the dawn of the Hasidic movement, she realized that if that would happen, it wouldn't be good. She was a young woman, just married with a little baby two years old. And she called three prominent Hasidim together, and she said, "Before I tell you anything, you have to agree to do what I say," so hesitantly, they agreed. And she told them that she wanted them to be her *bait din* [court]. She wanted them to be the judges and to rule that "My life be given instead of the Rebbe's life, my father's life." And, obviously, they were very frightened to make such a rule, but they did because they promised. And that year at Rosh Hashanah, she came in to her father; and before he could give her the blessing for the new year, she interrupted him and gave him the ruling, and he realized what she had done. And the day after Rosh Hashanah, she passed away. She asked her father to take care of her child, who grew up to be the Tzemach Tzeddick. (Namdar interview)

Media

Electronic media provide perhaps the most extensive form of outreach for the Lubavitcher community and can be seen as a context for negotiating with

Words: Miriam Bela Nadoff

Music: "Har Ha-Gilboa"

1. The song we sing be - gins with tears, but tears are not al------------ways
2. My fa - ther called me in one day, and told me a - bout-------- a

sad. Some times we give and then we find we've gained more than all------ we
tree. "You have to guard it thir - ty years and tend to it care------ful--

had. D - vor----------ah Le-----ah's song---------. The song on----ly wo -men can
ly. And then the tree stands firm its bran -ches spread out to the

sing. Who know the pain that part-ing brings but still in Ha-Shem they
sun. And all the peo - ple far and near can ga - ther its fruit so

trust. Who know the joy that lov - ing brings, but still they do what they must.
sweet. And all the peo - ple far and near can ga-ther its fruit to eat."

3. "Hasides is just like a tree
Growing up strong and true.
Until the time Moshiach comes
We need it for every Jew.
The Ba'al Shem Tov sowed the seeds
It grew to a tall tree of life.
Now thirty years have passed," he said.
"With my life I'll guard that tree."
"Now thirty years have passed," he said.
"There's fruit here for all to see."

4. My father's eyes filled up with pain,
Told me more that he meant to say.
Our precious tree might come to harm,
Wither and die away.
I saw as he could see
How evil had gathered around.
There was danger to his very life
From someone we hardly know.
There was danger to his very life
From someone we hardly know.

5. "My father, we can't risk your life.
We need you to lead us on.
You know the way through dark and gray
Until a new day must dawn.
I know what must be done
The tree I will guard with my life.
Only take my little boy
And keep him so close to you.
Only take my little boy
And teach him to be a Jew."

Example 30. "Dvorah Leah's Song," performed by Leah Namdar, 1991 (transcribed by the author)

the modern. The production of audio- and videocassettes, movies, a Web site, and a computer listserve have taken the Lubavitcher brand of Hasidism far beyond the confines of Crown Heights. Produced ostensibly for the Orthodox market, these media are easily obtained at Drimmer's (or any other of the many stores in Brooklyn selling Jewish products) or on the Internet. Such media include collections of nigunim arranged for Western classical orchestras, such as Yisroel Lamm's "Philharmonic Experience," old and newly composed songs for children, such as those learned in school or at camp, many tapes of songs for women that include newly written music for lighting candles, raising children, and promoting individual spiritual fulfillment.

What has been more difficult to accept, especially for older members of the community at large, however, is the growing media borrowed from heavy rock and rap sources. These include an album recorded in Florida by a group calling itself Two Live Jews; another group performing what it called "schlock rock"; and a group whose CD *Radical Rappin' Rebbies,* was arranged by a ba'al teshuvah, Moshe Antelis, and performed by three skilled Lubavitcher rock musicians. One of the songs on this tape is "Shabbos Thing," a rap-style version of the classic rock song "Wild Thing." Example 31 is the chorus and first verse.

Example 31. "Shabbos Thing," Antelis, 1990 (transcribed by the author)

Many of the older Lubavitchers and most of the lifetimers regard these types of borrowings as highly suspect, a little too close to the sexualized secular world outside the fence; but they will admit that these songs are effective in attracting otherwise unapproachable Jews to Hasidic life. Indeed, it was in the house of the Lubavitcher musician Eli Lipsker that I first heard about *Radical Rappin' Rebbes*. Lipsker's son, who was sitting with his father during our conversation, confessed that he had recently purchased the tape, more or less as a joke. His father shrugged this off, reassuring me that this was definitely *not* Lubavitcher music—although it if reached a Jewish soul and brought someone closer to hasides, it would have accomplished its purpose (Lipsker interview). And then he went on, referring to our meetings over the years with considerable ironic amusement: "After all, what else would have ever brought *us* together but music?"

Notes

1. This and other song titles use Lubavitcher spelling.

2. For an excellent discussion of the history of this event, see Morris (1998).

3. I reconstructed this skit from memory as it was presented on Saturday afternoon, so no recording or writing was allowed.

4. Turner (1969) might label this state a "liminal" one, in that the male infant is on a threshold between nonexistence and existence (from the Jewish point of view) and is thus vulnerable.

5. See also Robertson (1989) for a discussion of drag shows.

6. See Davidman (1992) for a similar scene of teaching and learning, an excellent context for the ethnographer clearly to see important cultural values.

7. See appendix 2 for more texts of women's songs.

8. Another such appropriation, "You're in the Rebbe's Generation," sung to the tune of the 1970s Pepsi commercial, can be found in Koskoff (1976).

9. Nadoff, a resident of Pittsburgh, Pennsylvania, has taught a variety of subjects in a Lubavitcher-run school there for many years, although she is not herself a Lubavitcher.

PART 4: CLOSING

The last two chapters, chapter 11, "Music and the Performance of Lubavitcher Identity," and chapter 12, "Closing Scene," present summaries of the major ideas discussed in this book and some attempts to answer the basic question of this research: why is music so central to Lubavitcher life? The book ends with the death of the Rebbe and the hope that the Lubavitcher community will not fall into despair at this great loss.

11

Music and the Performance of Lubavitcher Identity

In examining music in Lubavitcher life, this study has attempted to articulate a rich system of beliefs and practices that define Lubavitcher identity within the context of late-twentieth-century America, while at the same time presenting real Lubavitchers, who are coping, like all Americans, with the joys and vicissitudes of contemporary life. And while it is clear that Lubavitcher culture has flourished in this context (despite earlier predictions), it has done so not only because it has held on to its Old World ideas and strict observances but because it has also transformed those beliefs and practices to fit new contexts. That it has done so without destroying their spirit attests to the flexibility and creativity of individual Lubavitchers as they navigate their, and our, worlds.

One of the things I was interested in exploring in this work initially was the tension between change and continuity within Lubavitcher musical life over the past two decades, a time that has seen rapid technological, political, and economic change within the larger social framework of the United States and the Lubavitcher community itself. I was interested in seeing precisely what would change musically over this twenty-year period and what would remain the same. The three areas I focused on here were the rise of technology, the growth of revitalizing religious movements, and the women's movement, three powerful forces that affected the society at large. Lubavitchers dealt with these changes as well; but they did so in characteristically Lubavitcher-creative ways: by using technology to set up web sites and cable television networks to broadcast the Rebbe's farbrengens, Hanukkah celebrations, and other events; by opening up their communities to all Jews wishing to return to Orthodoxy, regardless of their current spiritual status; by encouraging the musically inclined to continue their cultural work with new musical sounds and performance contexts; and by developing safe contexts for women to become more politically and musically active.

But there were also things that remained the same: a basic conceptualization of music, a stable hierarchy of musical genres, a strict adherence to correct performance contexts and behaviors, and a solid bedrock of religious and social structures on which to hang the flexible and always changing musical choices made in real life. It is precisely this tension, or dialectic, between the solid, Old World core of Jewish identity (the divine head) and the New World reality of life in America (the calloused heel)—a tension that constantly calls one's identity into question—that allows Lubavitcher musical culture (the heart) to thrive here. The constant pull to the "other side" creates an even stronger pull toward the divine. In a way, the divine cannot exist without the other side; the more compelling the call to immoral behavior, the stronger the need to adhere to the solid core.

Certainly, the death of the Rebbe has dampened this vitality for the moment. Farbrengens are somewhat dispirited now, and there are fewer informal musical gatherings. It may be some time before the community recovers its joy and enthusiasm for life. However, Rebbes have died before, and the death of one Rebbe, even a much-loved and powerful one, will not extinguish the spark, because there is so much resiliency built into the Lubavitcher social and religious system as a whole.

Lubavitchers have been able to maintain their core identity in the context of their often chaotic, everyday modern lives because they have creatively structured and manipulated boundaries between notions of order (represented by Jewish law, observant practice, the past, and hard spiritual work) and disorder (represented by contemporary secularism, base animal urges, and out-of-control behaviors). Manifest at all levels of Lubavitcher life, these binary contrasts have created, in theory, a secure environment within which sometimes difficult issues of Lubavitcher identity—such as gender, spirituality, and lineage—are continuously and safely acted out and negotiated in the context of everyday life. Not regarded as confining or restrictive by Lubavitchers, this environment is seen rather as an open and free space within which to negotiate and mediate all forms of tension, both within the group and in interaction with the outside. Lubavitcher music, in its role as an agent for either good or evil, thus becomes, in the proper, Lubavitcher-sanctioned contexts, a powerful ally in the face of threatening, or potentially chaotic forces.

Throughout this book, three metaphors have appeared repeatedly as coded symbols of the space created by these binary contrasts. The first, that of the fence—seen in the message from Chabad-Lubavitch in cyberspace and in the description of male-female relations given by Esther Sternberg, among other places—is cited as evidence for the two primary conceptual social spaces defined as "within" and "without." Obviously, the basic human distinction between within and without helps define the individual or collective self in relation to an other.

Although conceptualized as solid, the fence is, in the reality of everyday living, filled with gates and paths that enable passage to the other side. In the course of real life, when appropriate, the fence can be opened from the inside to accept people, musics, and anything else that is usable; or the fence can be opened from the outside to gain access to the protected space within. Furthermore, the fence that separates in from out is hierarchic, containing various spaces (or stages) of separation. That is, there is an ordering of levels that, depending on one's perspective, either protects one on the inside with many layers or allows one on the outside access inward only through a series of hard-earned stages. This provides a number of real-life choices for individuals either wishing to enter or momentarily leave the community. For example, seen from the perspective of out-to-inward movement, one sees that ba'alei teshuvah wishing to enter the community cannot do so all at once; instead, they must go through a series of stages (including study at a Lubavitcher-run school and marriage within the group) that integrate their old lives with the new. Similarly, popular or other non-Lubavitcher musics cannot become nigunim without undergoing various textual, musical, and performance changes, and so on.

Seen from the perspective of in-to-outward movement, one sees, for example, that the law that prohibits men and women from engaging in unsanctioned sexual relations, considered one of the gravest and strictest of all Jewish laws, is protected by many layers of other, lesser laws (i.e., many fences), such as the ones that prohibit men and women from being alone in a room together with the door closed or proscribe warm greetings between men and women. The more outside one is, the harder it is to get inside; the more inside one is, the more protection is needed. But, at each step of the way, a conscious, individual choice must be made, and a medium to realize that choice must be available.

The second metaphor used frequently by Lubavitchers, that of the ladder (or elevator), is often invoked to describe a spiritual space. Here, the directional movement is conceived as more up/down than in/out. Referred to in discussions of the four-stage process of devekut and its corresponding materialization in musical structure and performance, in relation to the spiritual journey of the ba'al teshuvah, and in the theorization of specific genres of music that can take one up or down, the ladder, like the fence, is also hierarchic: it has rungs (or floors), contains spaces in between its levels, and requires either real work to climb upward (if one starts at the bottom) or an easy walk (if one starts high).

The third important metaphor, that of the human body, provides the dimension of distance, the nearness or farness that, together with the in-and-out nature of the fence and the up-and-down structure of the ladder, creates a three-dimensional, living context for the enactment of Lubavitcher identity. The human body, referred to in many contexts, is both a literal and symbolic body containing three essential metaphorical parts: the head at the top, symbolic of the divine soul, the intellect, the height of spirituality; the heel at the bottom, representing the current generation, of those closest to the ground (itself symbolic of the contemporary, secular social context); and the heart, located inside the body at a distance (both an up/down and in/out distance) from the head and the heel, containing the two animal souls that direct human behavior. As the souls are in constant communication through the blood that travels on a circular route upward, downward, and inward through the heart's two ventricles and then outward and far away to the extremities, the body provides the metaphorical context within which all three of the directional metaphors central to Lubavitcher thinking are united.

Where, though, is music in all of this? Again, certain metaphors arise when Lubavitchers speak of music and its power. First, as Schneur Zalman writes, music is "the pen of the soul"—that is, music is conceptualized as an agent of the passionate and vital animal soul, existing neutrally in between the heart's right and left ventricle, able to express both the highest or coarsest feelings and values. Second, music is referred to as a vehicle, much like the ladder, a means to take one somewhere, either up or down. However, though certain musics will always bring one down and others will always elevate, it is ultimately the spiritual status, intention, and choice of the individual user, hearer, performer, or composer of the music that directs its course within a specific, real-life context. It is up to the individual, located in his or her own space on the ladder or the fence, to decide how the potential power of music will be used; but it is the music itself that contains the means to express the inner workings of the individual soul.

Thus, the metaphors of the fence, ladder, and body may provide the symbolic social and spiritual context for the enactment of Lubavitcher identity; but music is the medium through which such identity is expressed and nurtured. Like the blood that circulates through the literal body, enabling interaction between the two souls, music has the potential to circulate core Lubavitcher social and religious values through the larger, metaphoric Jewish body and outward to all of humanity. Music, its creation, and performance thus allow spiritual and social movement to take place effortlessly through both space and time: in and out through the fence separating the self from the other; up or down the spiritual ladder leading to the divine realm or to the other side; or back and forth from the spiritually idealized past to the weakened present.

Because of the power inherent in music, one of its most important uses for Lubavitchers is as a protective shield. That is, while creating or performing Lubavitcher-sanctioned music, one is protected against potential dangers from the other side. And if one is sufficiently protected, it is far easier to allow other forms of potentially harmful or difficult mediations and adjustments, those that really occur in everyday life, to take place. For example, one finds Lubavitcher music used in service against the Napoleonic Army, against a Russian nobleman, against the Satmarer community in Brooklyn; one sees nigunim performed in potentially contaminating contexts, such as non-Lubavitcher get-togethers in Manhattan or for new ba'alei teshuvah in Ukraine; one sees women performing their own music at their own farbrengens and, even more publicly, through recordings and videos. Even contemporary musics that are normally not associated with Lubavitchers but that have been adjusted to fit Lubavitcher aesthetic and religious principles and contexts, such as "Dvorah Leah's Song" or "Shabbos Thing," protect their users, thus enabling them to open the space through the fence for a moment to let the outside and inside become one. In this way, Lubavitcher music, its creation, and—most important—its performance provide a way for the individual, coping with real life in contemporary times, to pass unharmed between the boundaries, enabling social and religious mediation to take place.

12
Closing Scene:
"The Rebbe Dies"

June 12, 1994

I have been to visit a friend for the weekend, and on my way home, I have
tuned in to National Public Radio's "All Things Considered." Someone has
just announced that the Rebbe, Menachem Mendel Schneerson, has died after
a long illness. He was ninety-two.

I am remembering the two times I saw him face-to-face. The first was long
ago, in 1975, during the fall holidays. It was Simhat Torah; and as was the
custom, the Rebbe passed out pieces of honeycake to the women and children. I was there to receive this gift. I had been waiting in the woman's gallery since early morning. It was very hot. All the synagogue and gallery doors
were open on this bright September day, and bees and wasps, attracted to the
honey, were flying freely in the room.

It was getting more and more crowded; still, the Rebbe had not arrived.
I was being jostled around some, and as the room filled up, more and more
women were pressing dangerously against the tinted plastic sheets that shielded the gallery. There was no chance of forming an orderly a line. Finally, about
4 P.M., the Rebbe arrived, and it was time to proceed through the open door
to the foyer outside his study to receive the cake. I waited another hour or so
for my turn. It was unbearably hot, and the sticky-sweet smell of honey per-
meated the room. I was getting lightheaded and a little sick.

Suddenly, it was my turn. I looked at the Rebbe, straight into his eyes. He
looked back into mine and said a low prayer to me, under his breath, as I
quickly moved on. Just as I passed him, still staring at his head, a bee landed

on my right arm and stung me with such force that I dropped my cake. Later, when I told this to my Lubavitcher friends, they laughed and said that it was obvious that I had been stung with the force of Torah! This story quickly passed through the neighborhood, and I became something of a minor celebrity for a few days.

The second time I saw the Rebbe was in January 1992. I was in Crown Heights on a cloudy, damp Sunday. Most Sundays, the Rebbe hands out dollars to the women of the community to encourage charity. I had just ascended the stairs from the Kingston Avenue subway and had stepped into a shop for a newspaper. Suddenly, I became aware of sirens, squad cars careening down the street, and police running everywhere, with very large weapons. I moved into the street. Police helicopters were flying overhead.

"What happened?" I called out.

"Someone just got shot in the subway," a young, bearded man answered.

In my subway? I thought. The one I was just in? Someone got shot? People were racing everywhere. I started talking to a man passing by.

"What's going on? Who was shot?"

"A policeman," he answered. "That's the second one this week!" The second one this week! I looked over at the entrance to 770. A long line of women and young girls stretched down the steps. They paused for a brief instant to look at the street. The Rebbe was there, in the middle of all this commotion, handing out dollars. I joined the line, camera ready, just in case I saw a fleeting movement of the shooter.

About an hour passed. Police were still around, interviewing people, but the helicopters were gone. It seems that a man had been holding up passengers on the subway when an off-duty policeman had tried to stop him. The man shot the policeman, hopped off the train at Kingston Avenue, and vanished into the Crown Heights neighborhood. The fuss was over. People were used to this. Shootings are still a common occurrence in Crown Heights. The line continued to stretch from the Rebbe's study door.

I covered my head as I approached the Rebbe. I was married now and had no wig. He looked very old and tired, but his eyes were still piercing. He handed me a dollar with a little smile and a prayer. No bees this time, I thought. I moved on.

As I left, I was approached by an old woman carrying a bucket. "Tzeddakah, tzeddakah" (charity, charity), she pleaded. The Rebbe gives dollars away to encourage the recipients to give to the poor—but today, I was not going to give her this one. I was going to get it laminated with a special prayer written on it for my son, David, at a nearby Lubavitcher dollar-laminating stand.

July 11, 1994

Today marks the thirtieth day since the death of the Rebbe; and tonight there is a memorial service for him at the St. Regis synagogue here in Rochester, New York. I decided to go as soon as I got the notice.

I have never been inside this synagogue (which used to be a church). It is quite beautiful. It is an Orthodox synagogue with men's and women's sections. As I enter, I see about fifty people here. The service starts, and it is very loving and joyous in its way. A few rabbis, including Rabbi Vogel, the Rochester shaliach, get up, one after the other, to speak of their memories of the Rebbe and to tell some wonderful stories about his "miraculous" wisdom and sensitivity. One of the speakers actually brings me to tears when he describes his meetings with the Rebbe. It is true—the Rebbe had those incredible piercing eyes, and he really did look through one and into the soul.

There is a wonderful spirit about these people: even in sadness, there is joy. When the service is almost over, someone gets up and tells a story about Rabbi Akivah returning home after a long while only to find foxes running in and out of his synagogue. All of his followers begin to weep at the desecration, but Rabbi Akivah begins to smile. When they ask him why he is smiling, he says, "Even in destruction there is hope, because one can only rise."

Glossary

Below is a list of Hebrew and Yiddish terms that appear in the text. Occasionally, I have indicated an alternate spelling that reflects the different pronunciation between the Ashkenazic and Sephardic forms of Hebrew. The first version is the one I have adopted in this book.

ahavah rabbah: one of the best-known musical modes used in Jewish prayer
avodah: work, divine service
ba'al teshuvah (*ba'alei teshuvah,* masc. and mixed pl.; *ba'alat teshuvah,* fem. sing.; *ba'alot teshuvah,* fem. pl.): penitent, a title given to a person who returns to orthodoxy
benoni: the average, "intermediate" person
binah: understanding
daat: knowledge
daven: pray
devekut (deveikus): devotion; adherence to, or oneness with, God
En-Sof (Ein-Sof): limitless, infinite, the nothingness of God
ervah: sexual stimulation or incitement
eruv: border, fence, especially a boundary around a Jewish community that creates a space for some relaxation of laws, such as carrying objects on the Sabbath
farbrengen: Hasidic gathering
Fonke: from Fonye, a non-Jewish Russian
forshpil: literally, foreplay; a celebration given to a young woman on the Sabbath before her wedding
frumm: pious; observant
Gemara: commentary on the Mishna; the Gemara and the Mishna together constitute the Talmud
geulah: redemption; a period after the arrival of the Messiah and the restoration of Israel
golus: wandering; diaspora

Habad: religious philosophy developed by Rabbi Schneur Zalman; acronym formed from three Hebrew words: hochma, binah, daat

halakhah (halakhah, halakhic): law, legal

hallah: a braided loaf of bread served on the Sabbath

Ha-Shem: literally, "The Name," another name for God

Hasid (pl. Hasidim): pious or righteous one

hasides (hasidut): religious way of life

Hasidism: a religious movement that grew out of the teachings and philosophy of Israel ben Eliezar (1698–1750), the Ba'al Shem Tov

hazan: cantor

heder: Jewish day-school

hitlahavut (hitlahavus): enthusiasm

hochma: wisdom

kabbalah: mystical literature and teachings

kavvanah: intention

kelippah (pl. *kelippot*): husk, shell, casing

kelippot nogah: neutral husks

keter: crown; the first of the ten emanations of God according to Jewish mystical tradition

Kiddush: the blessing over the wine, spoken or chanted at the beginning of the Sabbath and other holy days

kol isha: a woman's voice

lebedig: happy

Lubavitcher: a member of the Lubavitch Hasidic court

maqam (makam): general term for a Turkish musical mode

malkhut: kingdom, one of the ten emanations of God according to Jewish mystical tradition

mechitzah: partition or screen separating men's and women's areas

mikvah: ritual bath

Mishnah: codification of oral law; together with the Gemara constitutes the Talmud

mitnaggedim: early opponents of Hasidism

mitzvah: religious obligation, good deed, blessing

mohel: ritual specialist who performs circumcisions

Moshiach: Messiah

nefesh: soul

neshamah: soul

niddah: an excluded or ritually unclean person

nigun (pl. *nigunim*): Hasidic song, tune

peyot (peyes): earlocks

rasha: an evil person

rasha gamur: a totally evil person

rasha she-enu gamur: a partially evil person

Rebbe: Hasidic leader

rikkud: dance

Sefer Ha-Nigunim: three-volume *Book of Songs*

sefirah (pl. *sefirot*): beam, ray

shabbat (shabbos): Sabbath
shaliach (pl. *shelichim*): emissary
sheitle: head covering, wig
shekkinah: indwelling of God
shul: school; synagogue
Shulhan Arukh: the set table; a book of Jewish laws
simhah: happiness, joy
sitra ahra: the other side, evil
tallit (tallis): prayer shawl worn by men in the synagogue
Talmud: the codification of Jewish oral law and its commentaries; a compendium of
    teachings
Tanya (literally, "It has been taught"): book by Rabbi Schneur Zalman that outlines his
    religious philosophy, Habad
tefillin: phylacteries
teshuvah: repentance
tikkun: restoration of order
Torah: teachings; all of Jewish literature
tzeddakah: charity
tzniut (tsnius): modesty
yeshivah: religious school
yiddishkeit: Jewishness
zaddik: holy person, saint
zaddik gamur: a completely perfect saint
zaddik she-enu-gamur: an imperfect saint
zemirot: table songs
Zohar: Book of Splendor, the major book of Jewish mysticism

Appendix 1:
Partial List of Lubavitcher Recordings Made in the United States

Lubavitcher Nigunim

Chabad Melodies, Vol. 1. Rabbi Samuel Zalmanoff, dir. Collectors Guild CGL 615, 1960.

Chabad Nigunim, Vol. 2. Rabbi Samuel Zalmanoff, dir. Nichoach-Lubavitch, N-5721, 1961.

Chabad Nigunim, Vol. 3. Rabbi Samuel Zalmanoff, dir. Nichoach-Lubavitch, N-5722, 1962.

Chabad Nigunim, Vol. 4. Rabbi Samuel Zalmanoff, dir. Nichoach-Lubavitch, N-5723, 1963.

Chabad Nigunim, Vol. 5. Rabbi Samuel Zalmanoff, dir. Chabad-Nichoach N-5725, 1966.

Chabad Nigunim, Vol. 6. Seymour Silbermintz, music dir. Nichoach-Lubavitch, N-5724, 1969.

Chabad Nigunim, Vol. 7. Rabbi Samuel Zalmanoff, dir. Nichoach-Chabad-Lubavitch, N-5726, 1969.

Chabad Nigunim, Vol. 8. Seymour Silbermintz, music dir. N-5727, Nichoach-Lubavitch, 1976.

Chabad Nigunim. Seymour Silbermintz, music dir. Kehot Publication Society, NC-101, 1973.

Chabad Nigunim, Vol. 9. Seymour Silbermintz, music dir. Kehot Publication Society, NC-102, 1977.

Chabad Nigunim, Vol. 13. Seymour Silbermintz, music dir. Kehot Publication Society, NC-103, 1981.

Chabad Nigunim, Vol. 14. Seymour Silbermintz, music dir. Kehot Publication Society, NC-104, 1982.

Chabad Nigunim, Vol. 15. Seymour Silbermintz, music dir. Kehot Publication Society, NC-105, 1983.

Chabad Nigunim, Vol. 16. Seymour Silbermintz, music dir. Kehot Publication Society, NC-106, 1984.

Note: Volumes 10–12 of *Chabad Nigunim* are no longer available.

Other Lubavitcher Recordings

Eli Lipsker Sings "Lift My Eyes to the Mountains." EL 114, 1987.

Farbrengen Nigunim, Vols. 1–6. Recorded live at 770 Eastern Parkway. Compiled and distributed by WLCC, 313 Kingston Ave., Brooklyn, NY 11213.

Nigunei Sholom: Songs of Chabad from the Renowned Chosid and Composer, Rabbi Sholom Charitonow. SN-422, J.S.S.A. Productions, 1973.

Sound-Documentation of the Chabad-Lubavitch Books of Chasidic Songs (Sefer Ha-Nigunim), Sung and Accompanied by Eli Lipsker. Levi Yitzchok Library of L.Y.O. All 347 nigunim in the collection are recorded on sixteen cassette tapes. N.d.

Other Popular Recordings

Cantor Moshe Teleshevsky, with Abraham Nadel and His Choir. Cantorphone, FRS-113, n.d.

Eli Lipsker and His Little Soldiers Singing "We Want Moshiach, Now!" EL 113, n.d.

Levin, Shoshana. *Listen to the Light.* For women only. 1994.

Maise, Dana. *Diary.* For women only. Jeffrey Lesser and Steve Gaboury, arr. DMC 7960, 1994.

Navon, Ruthi. *Lead Me to Your Way.* For women only. Yaron Gershovsky, arr. and prod. 7/70 Productions, 1988.

Radical Rappin' Rebbes: Not Too Religious to Rap. R Productions, Mantelis Records Studio, 1990.

Schlock Rock. *Learning Is Good!* WW 358, n.d.

———. *Purim Torah.* WW 764, 1987.

Sheya Mendlowitz Presents Music of the Lubavitcher Chasidim. Moshe Laufer, arr. Holyland Records and Tapes, HLC-770, n.d.

Werdyger, Mendy. *Sheya Mendlowitz Sings "Chaverim," Vol. 2.* For women only. Moshe Laufer, arr. Aderet Music Corp., 1991.

Yisroel Lamm and the Philharmonic Experience. Holyland Records and Tapes, HASC-03, 1988.

Appendix 2:
Song Texts for Bais Channa Girls and Young Women

1. "To Love a Fellow Jew"
   To love a fellow Jew
   Just the same as you
   Is the basis of our holy Torah
   He may be far from me
   Across the widest sea
   Still, I'll always love him
       just the same.
   For seventy, eighty years
   A *neshema* [soul] wears and tears
   Just to do a favor for another
   Love him with all your heart
   The heavens spread apart
   For every Jew is really our brother.

2. "Every Jew Possesses"
   Every Jew possesses a neshema from above
   It's clear and it's pure and it's brighter even than the sun.
   And his *goof* [body] is low. Within him burns a neshema
   Though it may not show.
   With this thought in mind, we must set our goal:
   To love every Jew with our heart and soul.
   Through *Ahavas Yisroel* [the love of Israel] we come to love *Ha-Shem* [God]
   And honor his Torah like a precious gem.
   As soon as we arise, our *nefesh* [soul] weeps and cries,
   "When will we return to Thee, Ha-Shem?
   Grant us your mercy and redeem us all from *golus*."

3. "The Little Bird Is Calling"
   The little bird is calling; it wishes to return.
   The little bird is calling, it does not cry, but yearns.
   It's captured by the vultures, it's crying bitterly
   Oh, to see my nest, again—Oh, to be free!
   The little bird of silver, so delicate and rare
   It chirps among the vultures, outshining all that's there.
   How long, how long it suffers, how long will it be?
   When will come the eagle to set the little bird free?
   The little bird is Yisroel, the vultures are our foes
   The painful wound is *golus,* which we all fear and know.
   The nest is *Yerushalayim* [Jerusalem], where we hope to be once more
   The eagle is *Moshiach,* whom we are waiting for.

4. "My Mother's *Shabbos* Lights"
   Amongst the smiles, amongst the tears
   Of my childhood sweet and bitter years
   There's a picture that my memory fondly frames:
   My mother's Shabbos candles, which made our home so bright
   Which faithfully she lighted with a prayer on Friday night.
   And then around the table, we gathered and we heard
   My father chant the *Kiddush* [Sabbath prayer], his heart in every word.
   Our humble home became a mansion in this mystic glow.
   Our hearts were filled with hopes and dreams, and thoughts of long ago.
   And still the tragic story of Israel's darkest nights
   Have never dimmed the glory of my mother's Shabbos lights.

5. "We've Existed"
   We've existed so long
   'Cause the Torah kept us strong
   And the Torah will never disappear
   Through the ages it was brought
   By the children who were taught
   To follow it, and constantly declare:
   "I'm a Jew, and I'm proud
   And I'll sing it out loud
   'Cause forever that's what I'll be.
   I'm a Jew and I'm proud
   And it's without a doubt
   That Ha-Shem is watching over me.

6. "The Crown of Creation"
   The crown of creation lay broken and bent
   We shattered our dreams in the dust
   Darkness replacing the once holy light.
   Who can renew the last trust?

The crown of creation lay broken and bent
What once could have been is all gone
But it's in our power to build and carry on.
Oh, mother of royalty, woman of strength
The message alive in your home.
Reveal the dimension so hidden within
Replacing the crown of women again.
Mother of royalty, woman of strength,
You carry the promise, the name that you bore
Will yet shine evermore
Restoring the crown to us again.

Note: These were given to me by Miriam Bela Nadoff, Pittsburgh, Pennsylvania, March 1991.

References Cited

Interviews by the Author

Burston, Chaim. Manhattan, N.Y., January 1991
Gansbourg, Henches. Brooklyn, N.Y., January 1995
Gansbourg, Hirshel. Brooklyn, N.Y., January 1991
Gurwitz, Hanna. Brooklyn, N.Y., April 1977
Hankin, Sarah Ellen. Brooklyn, N.Y., April 1976
Lipsker, Eli. Brooklyn, N.Y., August 1990 (2 interviews)
Nadoff, Miriam Bela. Pittsburgh, Pa., March 1991
Namdar, Leah. Brooklyn, N.Y., January 1991
Rosenberger, Mirala. Brooklyn, N.Y., January 1991
Rosenblum, Ephraim. Pittsburgh, Pa., November 1974, August 1975, April 1976, December 1990
Rosenblum, Miriam. Pittsburgh, Pa., November 1974
Sachs, Zehava. Brooklyn, N.Y., November 1976
Schneerson, Menachem Mendel. Brooklyn, N.Y., January 1991
Shatkin, Rus Dvorah. Buffalo, N.Y., September 1990, December 1990
Sternberg, Esther. Brooklyn, N.Y., August 1990
Tampkin, Rifka. Brooklyn, N.Y., January 1991
Teldon, Chaya. Brooklyn, N.Y., April 1977 (2 interviews)
Teleshevsky, Moshe. Brooklyn, N.Y., November 1974, December 1975
Teleshevsky, Mrs. Moshe. Brooklyn, N.Y., December 1975
Thayler, Rochel Blima. Brooklyn, N.Y., November 1976
Teifenbrun, Freidi. Brooklyn, N.Y., January 1991
Vogel, Masha. Rochester, N.Y., March 1988
Vogel, Nechemia. Rochester, N.Y., March 1988, August 1996

Articles, Books, Dissertations, and Recordings

Ardener, Sherry, ed. 1975. *Perceiving Women.* London: Malaby Press.

Avenary, Hanoch. 1964. "The Hassidic Nigun: Ethos and Melos of a Folk Liturgy." *Journal of the International Folk Music Council* 16:60–63.

Barz, Gregory, and Timothy Cooley. 1997. *Shadows in the Field.* New York: Oxford University Press.

Baum, Charlotte, et al. 1975. *The Jewish Woman in America.* New York: New American Library.

Beck, M. 1991. "Bonfire in Crown Heights: Blacks and Jews Clash Violently in Brooklyn." *Newsweek,* September 9, 48.

Behague, Gerard. 1984. *Performance Practice: Ethnomusicological Perspectives.* Westport, Conn.: Greenwood Press.

Belcove-Shalin, Janet. 1988. "The Hasidim of North America: A Review of the Literature." In *Persistence and Flexibility: Anthropological Perspectives on the American Jewish Experience.* Ed. Walter P. Zenner. 183–207. Albany: SUNY Press.

———. 1995. "Home in Exile: Hasidim in the New World." In *New World Hasidim: Ethnographic Studies of Hasidic Jews in America.* Ed. Janet Belcove-Shalin. 205–36. Albany: SUNY Press.

Berger, Alan L. 1981. "Hasidism and Moonism: Charisma in the Counterculture." *Sociological Analysis* 41 (4): 375–90.

Berk, Fred. 1975. *The Hassidic Dance.* New York: n.p.

Berman, Saul J. 1980. "Kol Isha." In *Rabbi Joseph H. Lookstein Memorial Volume.* Ed. Leo Handman. 45–66. New York: Ktav Publishing.

Blacking, John. 1973. *How Musical Is Man?* Seattle: University of Washington Press.

Bohlman, Philip V. 1989. *The Land Where Two Streams Flow: Music in the German-Jewish Community of Israel.* Urbana: University of Illinois Press.

———. 1993. "Musical Life in the Central European Jewish Village." In *Modern Jews and Their Musical Agendas.* Ed. Ezra Mendelsohn. 17–39. Oxford: Oxford University Press.

Buber, Martin. 1948. *Hasidism.* New York: Philosophical Library.

———. 1966. *The Origin and Meaning of Hasidism.* New York: Horizon Press.

Butler, Judith. 1990. *Gender Trouble: Feminism and the Subversion of Identity.* New York: Routledge.

Chabad Nigunim. 1977. New York: Kehot Publication Society.

Cherney, Ben. 1985. "Kol Isha." *Journal of Halacha and Contemporary Society* 10 (Fall): 57–75.

Clifford, James, and George E. Marcus. 1986. *Writing Culture: The Poetics and Politics of Ethnography.* Berkeley: University of California Press.

Cohen, M. Steven. 1983. *American Modernity and Jewish Identity.* New York: Tavistock Publications.

D'Andrade, Roy G., and Claudia Strauss, eds. 1992. *Human Motives and Cultural Models.* New York: Oxford University Press.

Danzger, M. H. 1989. *Returning to Tradition: The Contemporary Revival of Orthodox Judaism.* New Haven, Conn.: Yale University Press.

Davidman, Lynne. 1991. *Tradition in a Rootless World: Women Turn to Orthodox Judaism.* Berkeley: University of California Press.

Dawidowicz, Lucy S. 1967. *The Golden Tradition: Jewish Life and Thought in Eastern Europe.* New York: Holt, Rinehart and Winston.

Doubleday, Veronica. 1990. *Three Women of Herat.* Austin: University of Texas Press.

Douglas, Mary. 1969. *Purity and Danger.* London: Routledge and Kegan Paul.

Encyclopedia Judaica. 1971. Ed. Cecil Roth. Jerusalem: Ktav Publishing.

Feld, Steven. 1990. *Sound and Sentiment: Birds, Weeping, Poetics and Song in Kaluli Expression.* 2d ed. Philadelphia: University of Pennsylvania Press.

Freilich, M. 1962. "The Modern *Shtetl:* A Study of Cultural Persistence." *Anthropos* 57:45–54.

Friedan, Betty. 1963. *The Feminine Mystique.* New York: W. W. Norton.

Friedfertig, R. S., and F. Schapiro, eds. 1981. *The Modern Jewish Woman: A Unique Perspective.* New York: Lubavitch Educational Foundation for Jewish Marriage Enrichment.

Friedman, Mannis. 1990. *Doesn't Anyone Blush Anymore?* San Francisco: HarperCollins.

Gellerman, Jill. 1977. "The *Mayim* Pattern as an Indicator of Cultural Attitudes in Three American Hasidic Communities: A Comparative Approach Based on Labananalysis." Working Papers in Yiddish and East European Studies. New York: YIVO.

Geshuri, Meier S. 1952 [1936]. *Music and Hassidism in the House of Kuzmir/Mazimierz and Its Affiliation: Modzitz.* Jerusalem: n.p.

Goodman, Lenn E. 1992. *Neoplatonism and Jewish Thought.* Albany: SUNY Press.

Greenberg, Blu. 1981. *On Women and Judaism.* Philadelphia: Jewish Publication Society of America.

Hajdu, Andre, and Jaacov Mazor. 1971. "Hassidism: The Place of Music in Hassidic Thought." In *Encyclopedia Judaica.* Ed. Cecil Roth. 1422–23. Jerusalem: Ktav Publishing.

Harris, Lis. 1985. *Holy Days: The World of a Hasidic Family.* New York: Summit Books.

Heilman, S. C. 1992. *Defenders of the Faith: Inside Ultra-Orthodox Jewry.* New York: Schocken Books.

Herndon, Marcia. 1975. *Symposium on Form in Performance.* Austin: University of Texas Press.

Heschel, Susannah. 1983. *On Being a Jewish Feminist.* New York: Schocken Books.

Heskes, Irene, comp. 1985. *The Resource Book of Jewish Music: A Bibliographic and Topical Guide to the Book and Journal Literature and Program Materials.* Westport, Conn.: Greenwood Press.

Hundert, Gershon David, ed. 1991. *Essential Papers on Hasidism: Origins to the Present.* New York: New York University Press.

Idelsohn, Abraham Z. 1973. *Thesaurus of Hebrew Oriental Melodies.* 10 vols. New York: Ktav Publishing.

Jewish Publication Society of America. 1955. *The Holy Scripture.* Philadelphia: Jewish Publication Society of America.

Jones, Alexander. 1966. *The Jerusalem Bible.* Garden City, N.Y.: Doubleday and Co.

Kaufman, Debra R. 1991. *Rachel's Daughters: Newly Orthodox Jewish Women.* New Brunswick, N.J.: Rutgers University Press.

———. 1995. "Engendering Orthodoxy: Newly Orthodox Women and Hasidism." In *New World Hasidim: Ethnographic Studies of Hasidic Jews in America.* Ed. Janet Belcove-Shalin. 135–60. Albany: SUNY Press.

Kaye-Kantrowitz, M., and I. Klepfisz, eds. 1986. *The Tribe of Dina.* Montpelier, Vt.: Sinister Wisdom.

Kepel, Giles. 1994. *The Revenge of God: The Resurgence of Islam, Christianity, and Judaism in the Modern World*. University Park: Pennsylvania State University Press.

Kirschenblatt-Gimblet, Barbara. 1987. "The Folk Culture of Jewish Immigrant Communities: Research Paradigms and Directions." In *Jews of North America*. Ed. Moses Rischin. 79–94. Detroit: Wayne State University Press.

Kisliuk, Michelle. 1997. "(Un)doing Fieldwork: Sharing Songs, Sharing Lives." In *Shadows in the Field*. Ed. Gregory Barz and Timothy Cooley. 23–44. New York: Oxford University Press.

Koskoff, Ellen. 1976. "The Concept of Nigun among Lubavitcher Hasidim in the United States." Ph.D. dissertation, University of Pittsburgh.

———. 1978. "Musical Composition in an American Hasidic Community." In *Selected Reports in Ethnomusicology*. Ed. James Porter. 153–74. Los Angeles: Department of Ethnomusicology, University of California.

———. 1989. "The Sound of a Woman's Voice: Gender and Music in a New York Hasidic Community." In *Women and Music in Cross-Cultural Perspective*. Ed. Ellen Koskoff. 213–33. Urbana: University of Illinois Press.

———. 1993. "Miriam Sings Her Song: The Self and Other in Anthropological Discourse." In *Musicology and Difference*. Ed. Ruth Solie. Berkeley: University of California Press.

———. 1995. "The Language of the Heart: Men, Women, and Music in Lubavitcher Life." In *New World Hasidism: Ethnographic Studies of Hasidic Jews in America*. Ed. Janet Belcove-Shalin. 87–106. Albany: SUNY Press.

Kranzler, George. 1961. *Williamsburg: A Jewish Community in Transition*. New York: Philipp Feldheim.

Krinsky, Rabbi Yehuda. 1973. *Chabad Nigunim*. NC 101.

Kristeva, Julia, ed. 1980. *Desire in Language: A Semiotic Approach to Literature and Art*. Trans. Leon S. Roudiez. New York: Columbia University Press.

Kugelmass, Jack, ed. 1988. *Between Two Worlds: Ethnographic Essays on American Jewry*. Ithaca, N.Y.: Cornell University Press.

Landau, David. 1993. *Piety and Power: The World of Jewish Fundamentalism*. New York: Hill and Wang.

Levin, S. 1990. "King of Chasidic Music." *L'Chaim*, August 17.

Levy, S. 1973. *Ethnic Boundedness and the Institutionalization of Charisma: A Study of the Lubavitcher Hassidim*. Ann Arbor, Mich.: University Microfilms.

Lubavitch Educational Foundation for Jewish Marriage Enrichment. 1981. *The Modern Jewish Woman*. Brooklyn, N.Y.: Lubavitch Educational Foundation for Jewish Marriage Enrichment.

Lubavitch Foundation of Great Britain. 1970. *Challenge: An Encounter with Lubavitch-Chabad*. London: Lubavitch Foundation of Great Britain.

Lubavitch Women's Organization. 1984. *Aura: A Reader on Jewish Womanhood*. New York: Kehot.

MacCormack, Carol P. 1980. "Nature, Culture, and Gender: A Critique." In *Nature, Culture, and Gender*. Ed. Carol P. MacCormack and Marilyn Strathern. 1–24. Cambridge: Cambridge University Press.

Mahler, Raphael. 1985. *Hasidism and the Jewish Enlightenment*. Trans. Eugene Orenstein. Philadelphia: Jewish Publication Society of America.

Maimonides, Moses ben. 1941. *Maimonides on Listening to Music.* Ed. Henry George Farmer. Medieval Tracts on Music 1. New York: Hinrichsen.

———. 1965. *Code.* Book 5: *The Book of Holiness.* Chap. 21, Sec. 2. Trans. Louis I. Rabinowitz and Philip Grossman. New Haven, Conn.: Yale University Press.

Mayer, Egon. 1979. *From Suburb to Shtetl: The Jews of Boro Park.* Philadelphia: Temple University Press.

Mazor, Jaacov, and Andre Hajdu. 1971. "The Musical Tradition of Hasidism." In *Encyclopedia Judaica.* Ed. Cecil Roth. 1421–22. Jerusalem: Ktav Publishing.

Mazor, Jaacov, Andre Hajdu, and Bathja Bayer. 1974. "The Hassidic Dance-Niggun: A Study Collection and Its Classificatory Analysis." *YUVAL: Studies of the Jewish Music Research Council* 3:3–51.

Meiselman, Moshe. 1978. *Jewish Woman in Jewish Law.* New York: Ktav Publishing.

Merriam, Alan. 1964. *The Anthropology of Music.* Evanston, Ill.: Northwestern University Press.

Mindel, Nissan. 1973. *Rabbi Schneur Zalman.* 2 vols. New York: Kehot Publication Society.

Minerbrook, Scott, and Miriam Horn. 1991. "Side by Side, Apart: the Difficult Search for Racial Peace in Brooklyn." *U.S. News and World Report,* November 4, 44.

Mintz, Jerome. 1992. *Hasidic People: A Place in the New World.* Cambridge, Mass.: Harvard University Press.

Morris, Bonnie J. 1990. "Women of Valor: Female Religious Activism and Identity in the Lubavitcher Community of Brooklyn, 1955–1987." Ph.D. dissertation. State University of New York at Binghamton.

———. 1995. "Agents or Victims of Religious Ideology? Approaches to Locating Hasidic Women in Feminist Studies." In *New World Hasidim: Ethnographic Studies of Hasidic Jews in America.* Ed. Janet Belcove-Shalin. 161–80. Albany: SUNY Press.

———. 1998. *Lubavitcher Women in America: Identity and Activism in the Postwar Era.* Albany: SUNY Press.

Myerhoff, Barbara. 1980. *Number Our Days.* New York: Simon and Schuster.

Navon, Ruthi. 1988. *Lead Me to Your Way.* 7/70 Productions. New York.

Newman, Louis I. 1963. *Hasidic Anthology.* New York: Schocken Books.

Nigal, Gedalyah. 1994. *Magic Mysticism and Hasidism: The Supernatural in Jewish Thought.* Northvale, N.J.: Jason Aronson.

Powdermaker, Hortense. 1966. *Stranger and Friend: The Way of an Anthropologist.* New York: W. W. Norton.

Poll, Solomon. 1962. *The Hasidic Community of Williamsburg.* New York: Free Press of Glencoe.

Powers, Harold S. 1980. "Mode." In *The New Grove Dictionary of Music and Musicians.* Ed. Stanley Sadie. 376–450. London: Macmillan.

Quinn, Naomi, and Dorothy Holland, eds. 1987. *Culture Models in Language and Thought.* Cambridge: Cambridge University Press.

"Rabbi Using Modern Medium in Call for Traditional Values." 1983. *New York Times,* January 23.

Reiter, Rayna Rapp, ed. 1975. *Toward an Anthropology of Women.* New York: Monthly Review Press.

Rice, Timothy. 1994. *May It Fill Your Soul: Experiencing Bulgarian Music.* Chicago: University of Chicago Press.

Robertson, Carol E. 1989. "Power and Gender in the Musical Experiences of Women." In *Women and Music in Cross-Cultural Perspective.* Ed. Ellen Koskoff. 225–44. Urbana: University of Illinois Press.

Rosaldo, Michelle. 1974. "Woman, Culture, and Society: A Theoretical Overview." In *Woman, Culture, and Society.* Ed. Michelle Rosaldo and Louise Lamphere. 3–19. Stanford, Calif.: Stanford University Press.

Roseman, Marina. 1991. *Healing Sounds from the Malaysian Rainforest: Temiar Music and Medicine.* Berkeley: University of California Press.

Ruby, Jay, ed. 1982. *A Crack in the Mirror: Reflexive Perspectives in Anthropology.* Philadelphia: University of Pennsylvania Press.

Sawa, Suzanne Meyers. 1987. "The Role of Women in Musical Life: The Medieval Arabo-Islamic Courts." *Canadian Women's Studies* 8:93–95.

Schneider, Susan Weidman. 1984. *Jewish and Female: Choices and Changes in Our Lives Today.* New York: Simon and Schuster.

Schneur Zalman of Liady. 1968. *Liqqutei Amarim (Tanya).* Trans. N. Mindel. New York: Kehot Publication Society.

Scholem, Gershom. 1961. *Modern Trends in Jewish Mysticism.* New York: Schocken Books.

Schultz, Ray. 1974. "The Call of the Ghetto." *New York Times,* November 10, 34.

Severo, Richard. 1984. "Reagan Grants Hasidim 'Disadvantaged Status.'" *New York Times,* June 29, B5.

Shaffir, William. 1974. *Life in a Religious Community: The Lubavitcher Chassidim in Montreal.* Toronto: Holt, Rinehart and Winston.

———. 1995. "Boundaries and Self-Presentation among the Hasidim: A Study in Identity Maintenance." In *New World Hasidim: Ethnographic Studies of Hasidic Jews in America.* Ed. Janet Belcove-Shalin. 31–68. Albany: SUNY Press.

Sharitonow, Rabbi Samson. 1973. *Nigunei Sholom: Songs of Chabad from the Renowned Chosid and Composer, Rabbi Sholom Charitonow.* J.S.S.A. Productions, SN422.

Shelemay, Kay Kaufman. 1998. *Let Jasmine Rain Down: Song and Remembrance among Syrian Jews.* Chicago: University of Chicago Press.

Shostak, Marjorie. 1983. *Nisa: The Life and Words of a !Kung Woman.* New York: Vintage Books.

Signell, Karl L. 1986. *Makam: Modal Practice in Turkish Music.* New York: Da Capo Press.

Sklare, Marshall. 1972 [1955]. *Conservative Judaism.* New York: Schocken Books.

Slobin, Mark. 1980. "The Evolution of a Music Symbol in Yiddish Culture." In *Studies in Jewish Folklore.* Ed. Frank Talmage and Dov Noy. 313–33. Cambridge, Mass.: Association for Jewish Studies.

———. 1982. *Tenement Songs: The Popular Music of the Jewish Immigrants.* Urbana: University of Illinois Press.

———. 1989. *Chosen Voices: The Story of the American Cantorate.* Urbana: University of Illinois Press.

Staiman, Mordechai. 1994. *Niggun: Stories behind the Chasidic Songs That Inspire Jews.* Northvale, N.J.: Jason Aronson.

Stambler, B. and H. Stambler. 1962. *Lubavitch Wedding.* Living Jewish Music. CGL 624.

Sugarman, Jane. 1997. *Engendering Song: Singing and Subjectivity at Prespa Albanian Weddings.* Chicago: University of Chicago Press.

Turner, Victor. 1969. *The Ritual Process: Structure and Anti-Structure.* Chicago: Aldine.

"'We'll Bring Moshiach Now!': Eli Lipsker Releases New Chassidic Record." 1981. *Crown Heights Chronicle,* December. 2–4.

Werner, Eric. 1961. *Hebrew Music.* Cologne: Arno Volk/Oxford University Press.

———. 1976. *A Voice Still Heard: The Sacred Song of the Jews.* University Park: Pennsylvania State University Press.

Wiesel, Elie. 1972. *Souls on Fire: Portraits and Legends of the Hasidic Masters.* New York: Random House.

Wohlberger, Lionel. 1992. "Music of the Holy Argument." Ph.D. dissertation, Wesleyan University.

Zalmanoff, Rabbi Samuel. *Chabad Nigunim.* Vol. 2. Nichoach N-5721. New York.

Zalmanoff, Rabbi Samuel, ed. 1948a. *Chabad Melodies.* Vol. 1. Collector's Guild CG l615. New York.

———, ed. 1948b. *Sefer Ha-Nigunim.* Vol. 1. New York: Nichoach Publishers.

———, ed. 1957. *Sefer Ha-Nigunim.* Vol. 2. New York: Nichoach Publishers.

———. c. 1965. *Sefer Ha-Nigunim.* Vol. 3. New York: Nichoach Publishers.

———. 1966. *Chabad Nigunim.* Vol. 6. Nichoach N-5725. New York.

Zborowski, Mark, and Elizabeth Herzog. 1952. *Life Is with People: The Culture of the Shtetl.* New York: Schocken Books.

Zenner, Walter P., and Janet S. Belcove-Shalin. 1988. "The Cultural Anthropology of American Jewry." In *Persistence and Flexibility: Anthropological Perspectives on the American Jewish Experience.* Ed. Walter P. Zenner. 3–38. Albany: SUNY Press.

Index

ELLEN KOSKOFF is an associate professor of ethnomusicology at the University of Rochester's Eastman School of Music, where she teaches courses in world music and special topics courses in ethnomusicology and directs the Balinese *gamelan angklung (Lila Muni)* and the *gamelan joged bumbung (Kambang Salju)*. She is the editor of *Women and Music in Cross-Cultural Perspective*, the general editor of volume 3 (the United States and Canada) of *Garland Encyclopedia of World Music*, the author of articles in a number of publications, including *New Grove Dictionary of Music and Musicians, Journal of the Society for Ethnomusicology*, and *American Women Composers' Forum*, and the host of the WXXI (Rochester, N.Y.) radio program "What in the World Is Music."

Music in American Life

"Happy in the Service of the Lord": Afro-American Gospel Quartets in Memphis
   Kip Lornell
Paul Hindemith in the United States   *Luther Noss*
"My Song Is My Weapon": People's Songs, American Communism, and the Politics
   of Culture, 1930–50   *Robbie Lieberman*
Chosen Voices: The Story of the American Cantorate   *Mark Slobin*
Theodore Thomas: America's Conductor and Builder of Orchestras, 1835–1905
   Ezra Schabas
"The Whorehouse Bells Were Ringing" and Other Songs Cowboys Sing   *Guy Logsdon*
Crazeology: The Autobiography of a Chicago Jazzman   *Bud Freeman, as Told to
   Robert Wolf*
Discoursing Sweet Music: Brass Bands and Community Life in Turn-of-the-Century
   Pennsylvania   *Kenneth Kreitner*
Mormonism and Music: A History   *Michael Hicks*
Voices of the Jazz Age: Profiles of Eight Vintage Jazzmen   *Chip Deffaa*
Pickin' on Peachtree: A History of Country Music in Atlanta, Georgia
   Wayne W. Daniel
Bitter Music: Collected Journals, Essays, Introductions, and Librettos   *Harry Partch;
   edited by Thomas McGeary*
Ethnic Music on Records: A Discography of Ethnic Recordings Produced in the
   United States, 1893 to 1942   *Richard K. Spottswood*
Downhome Blues Lyrics: An Anthology from the Post–World War II Era
   Jeff Todd Titon
Ellington: The Early Years   *Mark Tucker*
Chicago Soul   *Robert Pruter*
That Half-Barbaric Twang: The Banjo in American Popular Culture   *Karen Linn*
Hot Man: The Life of Art Hodes   *Art Hodes and Chadwick Hansen*
The Erotic Muse: American Bawdy Songs (2d ed.)   *Ed Cray*
Barrio Rhythm: Mexican American Music in Los Angeles   *Steven Loza*
The Creation of Jazz: Music, Race, and Culture in Urban America   *Burton W. Peretti*
Charles Martin Loeffler: A Life Apart in Music   *Ellen Knight*
Club Date Musicians: Playing the New York Party Circuit   *Bruce A. MacLeod*
Opera on the Road: Traveling Opera Troupes in the United States, 1825–60
   Katherine K. Preston
The Stonemans: An Appalachian Family and the Music That Shaped Their Lives
   Ivan M. Tribe
Transforming Tradition: Folk Music Revivals Examined   *Edited by Neil V. Rosenberg*
The Crooked Stovepipe: Athapaskan Fiddle Music and Square Dancing in Northeast
   Alaska and Northwest Canada   *Craig Mishler*
Traveling the High Way Home: Ralph Stanley and the World of Traditional
   Bluegrass Music   *John Wright*
Carl Ruggles: Composer, Painter, and Storyteller   *Marilyn Ziffrin*
Never without a Song: The Years and Songs of Jennie Devlin, 1865–1952
   Katharine D. Newman
The Hank Snow Story   *Hank Snow, with Jack Ownbey and Bob Burris*

Milton Brown and the Founding of Western Swing   *Cary Ginell, with special assistance from Roy Lee Brown*

Santiago de Murcia's "Códice Saldívar No. 4": A Treasury of Secular Guitar Music from Baroque Mexico   *Craig H. Russell*

The Sound of the Dove: Singing in Appalachian Primitive Baptist Churches   *Beverly Bush Patterson*

Heartland Excursions: Ethnomusicological Reflections on Schools of Music   *Bruno Nettl*

Doowop: The Chicago Scene   *Robert Pruter*

Blue Rhythms: Six Lives in Rhythm and Blues   *Chip Deffaa*

Shoshone Ghost Dance Religion: Poetry Songs and Great Basin Context   *Judith Vander*

Go Cat Go! Rockabilly Music and Its Makers   *Craig Morrison*

'Twas Only an Irishman's Dream: The Image of Ireland and the Irish in American Popular Song Lyrics, 1800–1920   *William H. A. Williams*

Democracy at the Opera: Music, Theater, and Culture in New York City, 1815–60   *Karen Ahlquist*

Fred Waring and the Pennsylvanians   *Virginia Waring*

Woody, Cisco, and Me: Seamen Three in the Merchant Marine   *Jim Longhi*

Behind the Burnt Cork Mask: Early Blackface Minstrelsy and Antebellum American Popular Culture   *William J. Mahar*

Going to Cincinnati: A History of the Blues in the Queen City   *Steven C. Tracy*

Pistol Packin' Mama: Aunt Molly Jackson and the Politics of Folksong   *Shelly Romalis*

Sixties Rock: Garage, Psychedelic, and Other Satisfactions   *Michael Hicks*

The Late Great Johnny Ace and the Transition from R&B to Rock 'n' Roll   *James M. Salem*

Tito Puente and the Making of Latin Music   *Steven Loza*

Juilliard: A History   *Andrea Olmstead*

Understanding Charles Seeger, Pioneer in American Musicology   *Edited by Bell Yung and Helen Rees*

Mountains of Music: West Virginia Traditional Music from Goldenseal   *Edited by John Lilly*

Alice Tully: An Intimate Portrait   *Albert Fuller*

Long Steel Rail: The Railroad in American Folksong (2d ed.)   *Norm Cohen*

The Golden Age of Gospel   *Text by Horace Clarence Boyer; photography by Lloyd Yearwood*

Aaron Copland: The Life and Work of an Uncommon Man   *Howard Pollack*

Louis Moreau Gottschalk   *S. Frederick Starr*

Race, Rock, and Elvis   *Michael T. Bertrand*

Theremin: Ether Music and Espionage   *Albert Glinsky*

Poetry and Violence: The Ballad Tradition of Mexico's Costa Chica   *John H. McDowell*

The Bill Monroe Reader   *Edited by Tom Ewing*

Music in Lubavitcher Life   *Ellen Koskoff*

Typeset in 10.5/13 Minion
with Agfa Nadianne display
Designed by Paula Newcomb
Composed by Jim Proefrock
at the University of Illinois Press
Manufactured by Thomson-Shore, Inc.

University of Illinois Press
1325 South Oak Street
Champaign, IL 61820-6903
www.press.uillinois.edu